THE TEST

Nicholas Daventry pulled Caro toward him and brought his mouth down on her soft, full lips. His hands slid down her shoulders to her waist. Caro felt their caress through the thin material of her gown and her breath caught in her throat.

So this was what it was like. And with a clarity that she would not have thought possible, Caro envisioned a certain look she had seen in the eyes of women as they had drifted slowly over the marquess.

No! A warning voice sounded in her head. I will *not* be like those others! And with a supreme effort, Caro tore herself away.

But even as she did so, she realized that in this test of her resolve, she had been found wanting . . . wanting so very much. . . .

D1453100

EVELYN RICHARDSON decided she would have preferred to live between 1775 and 1830 even before studying eighteenth century literature in graduate school. Now living in Boston, she enjoys access to the primary sources that allow her to explore the specific details of the period and immerse herself in the same journals that her heroines enjoy.

THE BLUESTOCKING'S DILEMMA

by

Evelyn Richardson

A SIGNET BOOK

To B., my romantic hero

SIGNET
Published by the Penguin Group
Penguin Books USA Inc., 375 Hudson Street,
New York, New York 10014, U.S.A.
Penguin Books Ltd, 27 Wrights Lane,
London W8 5TZ, England
Penguin Books Australia Ltd, Ringwood,
Victoria, Australia
Penguin Books Canada Ltd, 10 Alcorn Avenue,
Toronto, Ontario, Canada M4V 3B2
Penguin Books (N.Z.) Ltd, 182–190 Wairau Road,
Auckland 10, New Zealand

Penguin Books Ltd, Registered Offices:
Harmondsworth, Middlesex, England

First published by Signet, an imprint of New American Library,
a division of Penguin Books USA Inc.

First Printing, November, 1992
10 9 8 7 6 5 4 3 2 1

1

THE STRAINS OF MUSIC and laughter, mingled with the sharp scent of evergreens, floated upstairs as Caro, perched inconspicuously in the shadows on the top step, pulled her skirts closer around her and craned her neck to get a better view of the brilliant assemblage gathered below for the annual Christmas masquerade at Mandeville Park. Despite her uncle's best efforts and the enormous sums spent on the introduction of every modern comfort, the ancient house still remained, as her cousin Lavvy scornfully referred to it, "a drafty old pile." It was against these frigid currents that Caro hugged her mother's old cashmere shawl tightly around her. Regardless of her uncomfortable position, she would not have missed the ball that had been the sole thought of the entire household for the past month. From her maid, Alice, who had been commandeered to lend a hand in the creation of Miss Lavvy's costume, to Lavinia herself, who was the darling of the household and queen of the event, Mandeville Park had been a bustle of frantic preparation. Accustomed as Lavvy was to the unqualified admiration of those who surrounded her, with the possible exception of her brother Tony, Viscount Blessington, who remained unmoved by any creature possessed of only two legs, Lavinia Mandeville had been annoyed by the intrusion of her young cousin into a household that revolved around her. However, it had not taken the beauty long to realize that it behooved her to win the support of Lady Caroline Waverly. Caro, gifted with a keen understanding and a helpful nature, carried out her wishes far more discreetly and with far more alacrity than the maids who were more accustomed to Lavvy's demanding ways, or her mother, who, though properly adoring of her beautiful daughter, did draw the line at some things and could certainly not be entrusted with the delivery of the billets doux which continuously arrived from a variety of directions. Shy and observant, and model of discretion that she was, Lavvy's young cousin was the ideal messenger in these delicate affairs and her usefulness soon outweighed any disarrangement she might have caused the ravishing Lavinia.

Though well aware of the self-centered nature of her cousin, Caro, in her loneliness, had been more than happy to run every tiresome errand. The only child of the renowned diplomat Lord Hugo Waverly, Lady Caroline had been accustomed to accompanying her peripatetic parent to all his diplomatic posts where she had been the most important member of the widowed statesman's household. From the time she could talk, and for as long as she could remember, Caro had been surrounded by guests ranging from petty potentates to rulers of international importance. But this year, the talents of Lord Waverly were being called upon in some delicate negotiations in St. Petersburg. Even Lord Waverly, intrepid traveler that he was, had some qualms about taking a motherless child of twelve to such a distant and foreign land. Caro had offered a token protest, but seeing the determined set of her ordinarily unconcerned father's jaw, she had quickly resigned herself to the kindly but dull hospitality of Mandeville Park, merely admonishing her parent to dress warmly and take care to avoid the wiles of Russian ladies.

She had journeyed with him to Dover and saw him off, managing to keep a cheerful smile on her face until the vessel was out of sight. Even then she only gave way to tears of loneliness for the briefest of moments until William—butler, forager, and general factotum of the Waverly menage—had comforted her. "There, there, Miss Caro. You'll be right as rain in no time, you'll see. You'll go to visit your cousins, and though they don't hold a candle to his lordship, they're a sight better than being surrounded by a pack of Roosians."

Caro had summoned up a watery smile and resolved to do her best so that William and her father would be proud of her. And if her best meant catering to the whims of a young lady more spoiled than the most spoiled of beauties who had ever cast admiring eyes at her handsome father, well, so be it. Still, she missed him most dreadfully. Particularly in this merry holiday season. Caro would have given a good deal to see the twinkle in his bright blue eyes and hear the laughter in his voice as he swung her in his arms declaring, "There's my girl. And how goes it with the most precious lady in all of Europe, the Indies, and Araby?"

Caro sighed and blinked back the lonely tears that began to prick her eyes. Just then, a particularly violent blast of cold air made her gasp and hug herself more tightly as the ballroom door was opened wide and then immediately closed. A laughing couple made quickly for the privacy of the little alcove under the stair landing just beneath Caro's perch. Candlelight gleamed on fair curls and Caro just had time to identify her cousin before Lavinia's teasing voice scolded, "Well, Sirrah, now that you have dragged me from my guests in this unseemly and precipitate manner, state the reason for this importunate behavior."

"Ah, Lavvy, what man would not do his utmost to steal a precious minute alone with the belle of the ball," a deep voice replied. There was a silence during which the unwilling observer, acutely uncomfortable, held her breath and wished most desperately they would go away.

A rustle of clothing and the scent of her cousin's perfume wafted up the staircase. "Nicky Daventry, you naughty thing!" Despite the words, her cousin's voice, though slightly breathless, sounded rather more pleased than angry.

"I don't beg your pardon, Lavvy. What else could a man do when he is so close to such intoxicating beauty and after being treated so cruelly all evening. Lavvy, we can't go on like this. I must have you. Say you'll marry me."

There was more silence, more rustling, and then a tinkling, slightly nervous laugh, "Marry you? Why, Nicholas, what an absurd notion!"

"But I love you and you love me," the deep voice protested.

"Well, of course, but what has that got to do with marriage? Now don't poker-up at me, Nicky. You can't expect me to tie myself to a younger son with no expectations and who is a soldier, besides. With that dreadful Napoleon on the loose, you could be killed at any moment and then where would I be?"

There was an ominous pause before she continued brightly, "Now stop looking like a thundercloud and escort me back to the ballroom. I mustn't be gone too long or our guests will miss me."

"And it would never do for the beauteous Lavinia Mandeville to miss a single opportunity to be the cynosure of all eyes." A distinctly cynical note had replaced the pleading one.

Lavinia appeared to hesitate. "Now, Nicky, don't be so out-of-reason cross. You know it was impossible. Come along. I shall let you have the next waltz." She offered this with all the appearance of someone making a magnanimous concession. However, it appeared to have no effect.

"You go. A man don't feel like dancing when he discovers his affections have been trifled with."

"Oh, do stop being so gothic, Nicky." She was exasperated now and not making the least effort to hide it. "Very well, then." And Lavinia marched off towards the ballroom, head held high and her back as stiff as a ramrod.

There followed a deep sigh and Caro, acutely uncomfortable over her inadvertent eavesdropping, tried to squeeze back farther into the shadows. Unfortunately, she pulled back into a garland of greens draped over the banister, which tickled her nose. Struggle though she did with the sneeze that threatened to overcome her, in the end she could not prevent it and a loud "aachoo" resounded across the landing where she was ensconced.

The disastrous effects of this lack of control were immediate. Quick steps approached up the stairs and a dark furious face peered down at her. "Who the devil are you and what are you doing here?" the deep voice she had heard begging her cousin moments before demanded angrily.

"If you please, sir, I'm Caro." This appeared to do nothing to assuage his wrath and as the face remained truly alarming she continued hurriedly, "I'm Lavvy's cousin. Please don't be upset. I didn't mean to overhear only—only I was watching the dancers and then you came and I couldn't escape without calling attention to myself, which would have been most inopportune." There was a pause while this sank in. "Besides, Lavvy said I might watch," she added defensively.

He seemed satisfied. The angry light faded from the dark-blue eyes to be replaced by a somber look. "Then you know my life is ruined by that jade, your cousin. The only woman I have ever loved enough to propose to and she tells me I'm not good enough and then returns to the dancing without so much as a by-your-leave. Hah! Women! They make me ill.

If they aren't nagging you, they are using you to feed their own petty vanity. Well that tears it. I'm off. I shall never put my heart forward to be trampled on again. I shall return to the Peninsula and cover myself with glory. At least I *know* Boney's my enemy, and glory is far more enduring than love it appears.'' He gave a cynical snort.

"I am most dreadfully sorry. I am sure Lavvy didn't intend to be quite so mean-spirited, but she's so very pretty you know, and everyone pets her so much that she is rather selfish." Caro, though she felt bound to defend her cousin, could not help acknowledging the truth. She paused for a moment, reflecting. "Besides, are you so very sure you were in love with her?"

"What a question," he began explosively. "Who could not be in love with her? She is enchanting—so graceful, so vivacious, so delicate—she is every man's dream. How can you ask such a thing?"

Privately Caro thought that if her cousin were every man's dream, then the male sex was in a worse state than she had previously supposed, but she refrained from comment. "Well," she began slowly and thoughtfully, "you seem more angry than sad. If you were truly in love with her, you would be so very sorry you could not be mad. Besides, though you greatly admire her beauty, you don't sound as though you like her very much." Caro paused, before adding triumphantly, "If you want to know what I think, I think your pride is more hurt than your heart is."

He was at first thunderstruck and then furious. "Why, of course I love her! And what would a mere chit of a schoolgirl know about love? Why, I have been dreaming of her ever since I saw her. Every man who sees her must be in love with her—and they are. They are drawn to her like moths to a flame and . . ." Here he paused as the import of his words sank in. "And she adores it, the hussy. She didn't care about me except that I admired her, and having just come from the miserable campaign in the Peninsula, I was more exciting than the rest." He grimaced ruefully and looked down into the wide gray eyes regarding him sympathetically. "Perhaps you're in the right of it, young Caro, and I shall recover sooner than I thought."

She smiled shyly. "I hope so. And I am persuaded that being a soldier must be far more amusing than being tied to Lavvy. She can be a trifle *exigeante* you know."

A tiny sigh escaped her. With her knees hugged up against her, swathed in the enormous shawl and masses of glossy dark hair tumbling down her back, she looked like a small child, though her attire and her presence proclaimed her to be not much less than five or six years younger than Lavinia. At the same time, there was such a wisdom and understanding in the dark-fringed eyes and the apologetic smile tugging at the corners of her generous mouth that she projected the world-weary air of one far older and more sophisticated. Truly, she was an odd little thing, but he found himself liking her. She had completed the destruction of his worshipful vision, a process that Lavvy herself had started. But Caro had done it with such sympathy and concern that somehow he felt he had gained rather than lost a friend out of the whole affair.

Her voice interrupted this train of thought and he realized that she was still speaking. Nicholas came to with a start. "I beg your pardon, I was not attending."

Caro nodded, a twinkle of amusement in her eyes. "I asked you what it was like in the Peninsula. Have you seen Wellington? Do you think we make any progress there? Of course one reads the dispatches, but they say so little." Her questions tumbled out one after another. What sort of foe were the French? Were they such fierce fighters as it was rumored? How did they eat in such a war-torn land? Were the Spanish grateful for their presence?

Decidedly, he thought, an absurd little creature, but a refreshing one and a blessed change from all the others who barely even pretended the most desultory interest in the events taking place. Even Lavinia, who had taken such delight in announcing to envious friends and jealous beaux, "Captain Daventry has just come from the Peninsula, you know, where he covered himself with distinction." This was always accompanied with a melting look in Nicholas's direction, but in truth she did not wish to know anything about the action which had resulted in his being invalided home. A wounded officer was a romantic addition to her entourage and his convalescence at his family's nearby estate had allowed him to devote more time and attention to her than anyone of perfect health could have. In all their talks, Lavinia had never evinced the least curiosity over the battle raging in Europe and after having exclaimed over his arm in its sling and the dashing scar on his temple, she did not care to hear more. She had reproached him, in fact. ''Really, Nicholas, you shouldn't talk of such things, you know. People find them quite upsetting.''

His quiet reply, ''Well they are upsetting'', had drawn a brief look of reproof.

''Yes, I daresay, very likely. But tell me, what do you think of my new bonnet? Is it not divine? I would not have thought to procure such a thing outside of London, but Mama has discovered the most talented milliner right here in Haslemere.'' And indeed, she had looked so enchanting dimpling up him that it had driven thoughts of anything else clean out of his head.

Perhaps it was the very contrast she provided to the grim scenes of war that had made Nicholas long to make her his. After the discomfort of camp life and the rough companionship of his fellow soldiers, Lavinia had seemed like an angel—all grace, beauty, gaiety, and elegance—and he had worshipped her blindly. More for what she was than who she was, he now supposed. But it had taken this infant with her serious gray eyes to show this to him. The vision of peace and beauty faded to be replaced by a picture of Lavinia as she truly was: lovely and amusing, yes, but not a little self-centered, and definitely with her heart set on capturing a more glamorous prize than Captain Nicholas Daventry. He smiled ironically. No doubt she would catch one and he could count himself lucky to have escaped. It was all owing to Caro that he would be able to gather himself together and make his way toward the ballroom in a relatively cheerful frame of mind. Nicholas, who had been staring fixedly into space while mulling over these thoughts, turned to thank her, but she had vanished into the darkness at the top of the stairs.

2

CARO, FEELING ALL THE awkwardness of an interloper in a tender scene, had taken advantage of the first opportunity to escape. At first she had felt only the greatest scorn for yet another of the poor fools who had fallen victim to her cousin's charms. But after hearing the sincerity in his voice, she realized that he was not like Lavinia's other admirers, who were only interested in attracting the attention of the reigning belle and cared no more for her than she did for them. Recognizing that her self-centered cousin truly meant something to Nicholas Daventry, Caro felt a great anger rising up in her. She had ignored the promptings of her overactive conscience and had stooped to the level of a vulgar gossip to share her own brutally honest view of the beauty with Captain Daventry. There was something about the handsome soldier that captured the interest of the lonely girl. After so many weeks of running errands for her cousin, she felt the greatest satisfaction in freeing someone else from Lavvy's fascinating sway. Looking up into his dark blue eyes, so alert and so reminiscent of her father's, Caro had resolved that at least one man would not spend his life in thrall to Lavinia.

Seeing that her words had had their desired effect, she had been assailed by so many doubts and such a sense of disloyalty to a relative whose family had so generously provided her with a home that she immediately felt an impulse to escape. However, Caro would not have been Caro or Hugo Waverly's daughter had she been able to resist the chance to find out firsthand what was happening in the world. Giving in to this urge, and resisting the impulse to flee, she had questioned Captain Daventry closely, listening eagerly to the vivid descriptions of camp life and reveling in the opportunity for intelligent conversation. It wasn't until the handsome soldier, struck anew by the revelations about his lady love, had fallen into a fit of abstraction that Caro had suddenly become aware of the delicacy of the situation. Covered with embarrassment, she had cast about for a way to extricate herself. When she saw that Nicholas, his gaze fixed on the space occupied by an enormous chandelier, was in the grip of his own disturbing thoughts, and quite unaware of her presence, she beat a hasty retreat to her bedroom. There she scolded herself soundly for not having returned to it the moment she had first heard voices. "You're a dreadful snoop, Caro Waverly," she admonished herself severely, pulling off her chemise. "And what's more, you did it on purpose. You might have fled unseen, but you could not resist the chance to learn what fatally attracts every man to Lavvy. Once again you have let your curiosity get the best of you and plunge you into another scrape." She flung on her nightdress and buried her head in the pillows, but she could not erase the mental image she had of her cousin locked in Captain Daventry's powerful arms, her lovely face tilted up towards his. Nor could she forget the passionate sighs and the frantic rustlings she had heard.

Caro had never given much thought to love and romance. Her mother had died when she was so very young that she had never seen her parents together. To be sure, there had been many women who had cast their lures at her dashing papa, but they had all seemed more interested in being flattered and admired than they were in love. At school in Bath, she had always refrained from the giggling discussions concerning the dancing master, a handsome French emigre, and had thought her schoolmates' interest in the opposite sex inordinately silly. They would smile slyly as they taunted, "Just you wait, Caro Waverly, you'll see." To be sure, Lavinia was no different from these schoolgirls who devoured the novels smuggled in from the circulating library in Milsom Street or from the women who had flirted with her father. But there was something about Captain Daventry—perhaps it was the intensity in his blue eyes as they had followed her cousin or the look that had come over his face when he had spoken of her that had caught Caro's attention and made her see romance in quite another light.

She wasn't at all sure that she liked the idea of wanting so desperately to be with someone or of caring so passionately for another person. Therein lay the road to unhappiness, she felt quite sure. Far better to rely on oneself for happiness than to have it inextricably bound to someone else. Why, only tonight, she had seen the misery that could come of it. Knowing her shallow cousin as she did, Caro felt certain that a man who appeared to care so deeply about things as Nicholas Daventry was well out of it. He could never bear being tied to someone whose mind and attention flitted as easily as a butterfly from one thing to the next, never alighting long enough to understand or appreciate it, always looking for the next object of interest. Still, she had felt sorry for the very real hurt she had read in his eyes. Somehow Caro found all this most upsetting, both the revelations and her furtive role in the episode, and she devoutly hoped there would be nothing more to make her recall the evening's events.

She was not to be so lucky, for as she descended to the breakfast room the next day, she heard her uncle's voice booming out across the hall. "What? Are you mad, girl? You sent Nicholas Daventry whistling down the wind? You'll not find another such as he, mark my words. He's twice the man of any of these town beaux you have fawning over you. You've made a rare mistake, Lavinia, and I'm sorry for it."

"Oh, do hush, Papa. You know I couldn't marry Nicholas. He's nothing but a poor soldier. Would you have me an army wife dragged from one camp to another?" A stubborn note had crept into her voice and Caro could picture the mutinous set to her cousin's jaw. She was just about to flee to the safety of her own room when the butler appeared beside her bearing another tray of coffee and toast and she was caught.

Trying not to attract any attention, Caro slipped into her place just as Lady Mandeville was saying in a soothing voice, "Now, George, you know Lavinia has better prospects than that. Why no one could have asked for a more brilliant Season. The Marquess of Edgecombe and the Earl of Welham were most particular in their attentions. Why even the Duke of Hatherill seemed much taken with her. You would not have her waste her life with Nicholas, though I am sure he must be a very dear boy. After all, I have known Abigail Daventry since we were at school together, and certainly the family is an excellent one, as well as being our neighbors, but one must acknowledge, when all is said and done, that he is the younger son. It would be the height of absurdity for Lavinia to consider him when she could be the Marchioness of Edgecombe or the Countess of Welham.''

"Humph. The girl's a fool if she chooses either one of those court cards over Nicholas, but I wash my hands of the affair.''

"Oh, Papa, do not be so out of reason critical. The Earl of Welham and the Marquess of Edgecombe are leaders of the *ton* and highly sought after.'' Lavvy's patience, never in great supply, was beginning to wear thin.

Lady Mandeville defended her daughter. "Indeed, George, either one would be a brilliant catch. Why I am sure Sally Jersey told me she had given up on the Marquess this age until she saw the particular attention he paid Lavvy. And everyone knows the earl is one of the *ton's* most eligible bachelors.''

Here the Lord Anthony Mandeville, having just strolled in and helped himself to an enormous plate of eggs and bacon, came to his beleaguered father's aid. "What's all this? Why, I made sure that Lavvy would marry Nicholas. He's a great gun. The stories he tells of the army would make your hair curl. He was mentioned in the dispatches, you know. Ponsonby told me so. They say that even Wellington called him a hero. You must be all about in the head to turn down a fellow like that,'' he remarked, dropping into his chair and eyeing the eggs with satisfaction.

"I know it is difficult for you to fathom, Anthony, but I wish to be a wife, not a companion-at-arms,'' Lavinia sniffed.

Anthony grinned and took another forkful of egg. "It's a fortunate thing. You'd be dreadful at it. Can't imagine why a bang-up fellow like Nicky would want you as a life's companion. Terrible shame though, it would be nice to have him in the family. Would almost make a fellow glad to have a sister.'' Tony's eyes danced at the murderous look on Lavvy's face.

"You beast!'' she hissed, descending from the lofty heights of disdain to sisterly fury. "You have not the least sensibility! Papa, make him be quiet.''

Caro watched in an agony of indecision. She hated to see such dissension in a family she had grown to love—even Lavvy, as much as it was possible to care about someone as self-absorbed as her cousin—and she cast about frantically for a way to soothe troubled waters without intruding into what was really none of her affair.

"Oh, I'll be quiet. I have nothing to say to such a nod-cock." Tony turned to his cousin, "At least Caro has more sense than to set her cap at some wealthy caper merchant with a title, don't you Caro?"

Caro was about to reply, but her angry cousin burst in. "Oh, this is beyond enough! Both the Earl of Welham and the Marquess of Edgecombe are extraordinarily well thought of by everyone." She cast a darkling look at her brother. "They're both in the Four-in-Hand Club."

"So's Nicky Daventry who can drive circles around each one of them and doesn't have to add buckram wadding to his shoulders either. But you were going to say something, Caro?"

"Merely that as I don't believe I ever shall marry, I do not have a very helpful opinion to offer." And that, she thought to herself as three pairs of astonished eyes swiveled on her, has stopped the arguing.

"There's the spirit," the earl and his son chimed in together while Lavvy and her mother sat silent, transfixed with horror.

Lavvy was the first to recover. "Not marry!" Whatever will you do? Whatever will become of you? Why that is the most absurd notion . . ."

"I expect I shall be tolerably well amused. After all, I am now," her cousin replied equably. "And I would as liefer have that than endure a Season of nothing but smiling and dressing up."

"Not have a Season?" Lavinia could not begin to comprehend such a heretical notion. "Whatever shall you do?"

Caro chuckled at the patent amazement in her cousin's voice. "I could never be a diamond like you, Lavvy, and it's only the diamonds who enjoy such display. I leave it to you to be the incomparable in the family."

Lady Mandeville finally gathered her wits together. "Not even my brother Hugo could be so ramshackle as to deny his daughter a Season. Why, I never heard such a nonsensical notion. What can he be thinking of not to insure his daughter's future?"

"But he has, Aunt. He has left me Waverly Park when I attain my majority. Papa says it's a millstone around his neck. And besides, I am a much better manager than he is,'' Caro defended her parent.

This further proof of her brother's madness completely silenced Lady Mandeville who, left with nothing to say, stared uncomprehendingly at her niece.

3

WHETHER OR NOT Lord Hugo Waverly's ramshackle ways would have included allowing his daughter to dispense with a Season had never become an issue as he died of a mysterious and fatal illness while in Russia. Before his death, he had become Castlereagh's unofficial ear at that duplicitous court, and he left his daughter alone in the world with the estate in Hertfordshire and twenty thousand a year.

But Caro's predictions for Lavvy and herself had all come true. After a second Season, even more brilliant than the first, Lavinia had become Countess Welham and one of the most dashing matrons in the Upper Ten Thousand. Even the birth of two lively boys in close succession had not dimmed her elegance or style. Relegating her darlings to a vast army of underlings, she continued to grace every possible social event where, now that she was married, she was sought out by more admirers than she had been before. Nothing it seemed, not even the death of her husband a mere five years after her brilliant match, stopped the ascent of her social star, though it did make things slightly more complicated. Undaunted, and never one to be kept from her admiring audience for long, she immediately perceived how dear Cousin Caro, although barely acknowledged by Lavvy in the intervening years, could be of use to her. The briefest mourning period acceptable to the *ton* completed, the countess penned a letter to her cousin begging her to come to London as her companion, to lend the young widow a respectable countenance and to allow her to remain in her own establishment without having to turn to parents on either side.

It was this letter that Caro read one dreary day in January, sitting in front of the library fire at her own establishment. Caro's other prediction had also come true and the winter of 1817 found her free and the mistress of an estate near Berkhamstead, Hertfordshire.

Closer to her father than most children after their years of travel together, Caro missed him desperately. Being her father's daughter, she would have buried her grief and soldiered on stoically, had the mourning period not provided her with a perfect opportunity to live precisely the reclusive and scholarly life she had dreamed of for herself. "For you know, I consider the custom of a Season to be a barbaric ritual designed for the purest show," she confided to Helena Gray, leading light among the instructresses at Miss Chillingford's Select Seminary for Genteel Young Ladies. Miss Gray had readily agreed with her favorite pupil.

She had agreed even more readily when Lady Caroline had proposed that she leave the education of genteel young ladies to lesser talents and accompany her to Hertfordshire as her companion. "Not that I consider you need a companion to lend you countenance, but I know the world and how censorious it will be of a young lady who not only refuses to subject herself to the doubtful bliss of matrimony, but who proposes to set up her own establishment," Miss Gray had replied to Caro's generous offer. Then, a humorous gleam in her hazel eyes, Helena continued, "But chiefly, I come because I would miss you and the eagerness to learn which, in the years you have been here, has transformed my occupation from one of drudgery to one of challenge, and I cannot say that I relish the prospect of it being drudgery again."

Caro, touched by this last admission, had acted quickly and, bidding the briefest of adieux to the proprietress and her envious schoolmates, had quitted without a backward glance the establishment that had been her home for five years.

She had thrown herself into the improvement of Waverly Court which had been under the nominal care of two aged retainers during her father's peregrinations. They were only too happy to accept the offer of a small cottage and the prospect of spending their declining years in comfort on the estate, thus giving Caro free rein to employ whomever she wished. She had delegated this task to the enterprising William having sketched for him a general idea of her plans for the place. "As it is a smallish estate, I intend to employ the methods of Mr. Tull and Mr. Townshend to ensure the highest degree of productivity. In short, I wish Waverly to become a model of progressive agriculture, and I do not care to have my efforts subverted by some old rustic who thinks I am acting in defiance of the laws of God and nature.''

Seeing the determined set to his mistress's jaw, William's weather-beaten face broke into one of his rare grins. ''Now don't you fret yourself, Miss Caro. I shall find people as will help you out, nor will they worrit you over your being a single young lady alone in the world.''

He had been as good as his word, even managing to unearth a highly respectable housekeeper, Mrs. Crawford, and Susan, a forthcoming young woman, as a maid for Caro. On her side, Caro had been extraordinarily grateful at having such a genial and competent household assembled for her. Accustomed to William's resourcefulness in the most trying of situations—uncovering accommodations or palatable meals in barren surroundings and foreign climes—Caro was nonetheless surprised at his ability to procure such respectable help for a female establishment. William, however, had dismissed her heartfelt appreciation. ''I told them as there was households grander than this, but they would never find a kinder nor more understanding mistress.''

And indeed, he had proved correct. Miss Caroline was different, to be sure, and there was much talk around the kitchen table as to her unusual ideas, but as Mrs. Crawford maintained and the others concurred, ''She's a funny little thing. Her head is stuffed full of strange ideas and odd notions, but she knows what she's about. Why even Farmer Tring allows as how she has a good head on her shoulders and knows what price to pay for fodder and seed. And if she prefers to bury her head in books and improve the estate instead of going to assemblies and parties, I say let her.'' They all nodded solemnly, though, privately, Susan wished that her mistress were a little more interested in the social affairs of the surrounding neighborhood because that would have given the little maid an excuse to give her talents free rein. For Susan had aspirations. Born with the soul of an artist to the burgeoning family of a local farmer, she had vowed she would become more than a village dairymaid and had seized every opportunity to learn the dress and coiffures of grand folk. She had practiced long winter evenings on her sisters' hair in an effort to replicate those she had seen on the local gentry at church. Her previous position, as under housemaid at the Hall, had been more valuable to her for the peeps she had taken at Ackermann's *Repository* and *La Belle Assemblée* while dusting the morning room, than for the small remuneration she took home to her parents.

Her mother's difficult pregnancy had forced Susan to leave her post to look after the little ones and she had been in despair at this setback to her hopes for advancement. Then, as if by magic, William had appeared with his undreamt of offer. To be a lady's maid so soon! Even if Lady Caroline Waverly had been the most pettish and demanding of mistresses, Susan would have been ecstatic at the sudden realization of all her hopes. However, Caro was the merriest, kindest, and most interested of employers and Susan had been her devoted slave from the moment she had looked into the smiling gray eyes and heard, "I am so glad that William was able to convince you to come and help me. I fear I am a sad case, but I count on you to take me in hand."

Susan had taken this charge to heart with the fervor of a zealot. She was bound and determined that whenever Lady Caroline Waverly set foot in public, even if it were to inspect some promising ewes at Farmer Tring's or to purchase some ribbons for the refurbishment of a bonnet, she would outshine all the females within twenty miles who had any pretensions to fashion.

To do her justice, Caro always did look elegant, but she favored the most quiet and severe of styles. "Why ever would I wish to look like some gaudy butterfly?" she would laugh when her maid tried gently to steer her towards brighter colors, more frivolous designs, and less serviceable materials. "I leave such matters to those who wish to catch a husband. Let them spend their days worrying over such matters. There is so much else I would rather do with my time."

Still, Susan did not despair, for when she could persuade her mistress to let her do her hair or add a frill or some lace, Caro was always appreciative. "You do have an eye, there's no mistake. A deft touch here, a twist there and you trick me out so I even make Lady Belham and her daughters look to their laurels and no one could spend more time on their toilettes than they. Thank you, Susan. I only hope that some day you have a mistress who does more justice to your talents."

"Never, Miss," the maid had declared stoutly. "It's just a crying shame there's no one to appreciate how pretty you are."

"I, pretty?" Caro had been amazed. "I don't suppose I ever thought of such a thing."

"And I don't believe she ever has, poor thing," Susan had later confided to Mrs. Crawford. "It's that rackety life she led with no mother to teach her how to go on and now she lives like a hermit, only paying the necessary social calls. I know she thinks she's happy, but it would do her ever so much good to go to balls and have an admirer or two." The little maid sighed gustily.

The housekeeper nodded sagely. "Perhaps she will. William says that a letter arrived from her cousin in London the other day. It's only natural that someone in her family should wish to give her a Season. I do believe she used to spend her school holidays with her father's sister and her family."

"Oh, I do hope so," Susan breathed, hardly daring to wish for such a thing when she had already been showered with such good fortune.

Her mistress, however, was rather inclined to view the invitation as a nuisance than an opportunity. "Bother! I shall just have to write and tell her I am unable to come," she exclaimed to Helena when, having read through the list of Lavvy's many and brilliant invitations, the boredom of having to remain at home, and the naughtiness of her two boys, Caro finally divined the true import of the missive.

Her companion looked up from the latest issue of *Blackwood's Edinburgh Magazine*. "But why shouldn't you? You might enjoy yourself."

"What, with all that needs to be done here and planting to be looked after? Why I wouldn't dream of it!"

But Caro had reckoned without her cousin. Never one to be thwarted in her pursuit of pleasure and admiration, Lavinia was not about to take no for an answer. An indifferent correspondent at best, she nevertheless took umbrage by return post. "My dear Caro, I am persuaded you cannot actually prefer the dubious charms of the country to those of London. No doubt those who have cultivated the land there far longer than you are entirely capable of doing so for another year. In the meantime, I am in most desperate need of your company now. Do not forget, dear Cousin, that the Mandevilles were prepared to stand by you in your need. Do not, I beg of you, desert me in mine. After all, I have never asked much of you and now I beseech you, please come.''

Suspicious of Lavvy's motives though she might be, Caro could not repay the many kindnesses of the beauty's family by forsaking their eldest daughter. Nor could she ignore the real note of pleading in Lavvy's letter. Cocking a rueful eyebrow at her friend, she apologized, "Helena, I fear that her objections are unanswerable. They did offer me a home for so many years and she truly is desperate. I feel that we must go.''

"Of course you must, but are you certain you wish me to accompany you? After all, I could remain here and carry out your wishes.''

"What and leave me to face the *ton* alone without any hope of intelligent conversation for the entire Season? Never, Helena. If I go, you must definitely accompany me,'' Caro responded firmly.

"Very well then, I shall be delighted to go with you and shall take it as my duty to ensure you attend as many museums, concerts, and exhibitions as you do balls and ridottos.''

Caro smiled gratefully at her. "Thank you, Helena. You truly are the best of friends.'' She sighed. "I hate to leave just at this particular moment, but William can carry out all my instructions and I feel certain that he would be far more amused running things in my absence than he would be as an extraneous servant in a fully staffed household. I shall, however, take Dimmock to look after the coach and horses. No doubt Lavvy remains as indifferent and unenthusiastic a rider as ever, but I do not intend to allow her dislike of strenuous exercise to curtail ours. Perhaps Tim can come to help Dimmock.'' And with this last remark, Caro jumped up to go apprise the household of her plans, leaving Helena to thank Providence once again for having brought Lady Caroline Waverly into her life.

Helena, the only daughter of a clergyman who had rejected the fat livings that his illustrious family and connections could have procured him in favor of providing true spiritual guidance to a poverty-stricken parish in Yorkshire, had been left nearly destitute when her well-intentioned but improvident parent had died. Her grand relations, who had cut off all contact with such an undutiful son who had felt he must serve the church instead of allowing it to advance him, were obviously not going to be forthcoming with any offers of assistance. Aside from a very fine library of clas-

sics and an education that would have put many an Oxoni-
an's to shame, she had no means of support. In desperation,
Helena had written to her father's most constant correspondent, the Reverend Titus Chillingford. Knowing him to be
as immersed in works of the early church fathers as her own
father had been, Helena had not held out much hope from
that corner and was therefore most surprised and pleased to
learn that the Reverend Chillingford's sister was proprietress
of a school in Bath and dreadfully in need of someone to
replace a wayward instructress who had run off with the
dancing master.

Having consigned her precious books to the care of Titus,
Helena arrived in Bath exhausted after the long journey and
demoralized by the loss of both her family and her home.
Miss Chillingford had been all that was kind, but to Helena,
accustomed as she was to intimate conversations with a first-
rate scholar, the task of teaching geography and French to
a bevy of silly schoolgirls was dull in the extreme. That was
until Lady Caroline had appeared on the scene.

Helena had immediately recognized a spirit as independent and intellectually curious as her own and the more she
came to know of the serious girl with the intelligent gray
eyes, the more she came to care for her. After Lord Waverly's death, Helena, aching for the distress she had read in
her favorite student's face and knowing full well the feelings
that must accompany such a loss, had been the only one
able to offer some degree of solace to the girl.

Her appreciation of Caro had only increased since that
young lady had set herself up as mistress of Waverly. Helena
admired her former pupil's grasp of the theories of modern
agriculture and applauded her resolve to run an estate that
would be a model of productivity. As a companion, she
thoroughly enjoyed the impish humor, the energy, and
the genuine care and concern that Caro lavished on those
she allowed close to her. Quiet and reserved with strangers,
Caro was vivacious, warm, and loving with her intimates—
a delightful friend for those with the wit to understand and
appreciate her. Helena did sometimes wish for a wider social circle for Caro, but she was the first to admit that the
society of such a hamlet as Berkhamstead had little to offer
as far as peers for Lady Caroline.

Squire Althorpe and Sir George Belham were the kindest
of men—upright, responsible landlords who kept a protec-

tive eye on their newest neighbor—but they were bluff country gentlemen whose interests extended no further than
hunting. Even Caro's grasp of land management exceeded
theirs and they had never encountered a copy of *Blackwood's Edinburgh Magazine* or *The Edinburgh Review* in
their lives, much less read one. Both of these hearty land-
owners had been all that was helpful in aiding Caro to establish herself, and while they were genuinely supportive of
their unusual neighbor, they were slightly baffled by her.
Nevertheless, she so excelled at all those skills they could
appreciate—superb horsemanship, command of her tenants—that they were ready to give her the benefit of the
doubt in areas where they were less knowledgeable. In fact,
their wives and daughters who shared no common interest
with Berkhamstead's newest inhabitant were more inclined
to be critical. But they followed the men's lead and included
Caro in all their invitations, most of which she gracefully
declined on the pretext of still being in mourning. To Helena, however, she confided, ''Frankly I do not know what
I shall do when I can no longer use that as a reasonable
excuse. They are so very dull and their conversation, even
if it rises above fashion to the more enlightening topic of
the condition of the local poor, is decidedly flat.''

Thus Helena, as well as Susan, rejoiced in the invitation
to London. While she sympathized with her friend's distaste
for the empty rounds of the *ton,* she nevertheless was dis-
mayed by the prospect of such a warm and vital creature
spending the rest of her days as a country recluse. Though
it would put an end to her idyllic situation, Helena hoped
as desperately as did Susan that Caro would find someone
in town who could appreciate her, challenge her, love her,
and give her the opportunity to grow and blossom in a way
that Helena, despite her skill as a teacher, could not.

Helena was well enough acquainted with the world to
realize that she expected a great deal of society in this regard and she was sanguine enough to admit that, though
Caro did not have a loving helpmeet to share her life, she
did have a richer existence and exerted far more control over
it than did most women. Still, Helena sighed as she closed
her review and returned it to the pile on the table, she did
wish Caro could find someone worthy of her. And the sooner
they got to London, the more likely Caro was to encounter
such a person.

4

ALWAYS ORGANIZED AND EFFICIENT and blessed with a staff who shared these capabilities, Caro, once fixed upon the project of removing to London, made her preparations with dispatch. Within a week the household was set to function smoothly without their mistress's immediate guidance and support and there was little for Caro to do except pack her few possessions and be off. It was to this end that Caro was in the library one morning deciding which volumes of her father's well-stocked library were essential to her existence and which were not. She had just regretfully returned Plutarch's *Lives* to the shelf when she was interrupted by William announcing, "There be a Marquess of Everleigh to see you, my lady."

"Drat!" she exclaimed, climbing down from the ladder and picking her way through the pile of volumes on the floor. "I suppose I must see him," she sighed, knowing that William, who remained entirely unimpressed by such worldly accoutrements as titles, must consider the visitor to be someone of importance if he so audibly addressed Caro as "my lady." It also meant that whoever it was, was within earshot. Frantically she tried to straighten her hair which had escaped its pins during her exertions and she just had time to wipe the smudge of dust off her cheek as her caller entered.

William had been entirely correct. The Marquess of Everleigh was an impressive figure of a man. Over six feet, he looked forbidding in the extreme as he entered, riding crop in hand. The severe lines of the dark green riding coat emphasized the thick dark hair, high cheekbones, and brilliant blue eyes set deep under dark brows, while the exquisite tailoring revealed powerful shoulders and a narrow waist. The set of his jaw and the compressed line of finely shaped lips betrayed that this was not a social call and Caro, coming forward to greet this oddly familiar visitor, approached him warily as she cast madly about in her mind for some clue as to their connection.

"My name cannot be unknown to you, ma'am, as you responded with the curtest of refusals to my exceedingly generous offer to purchase several acres of virtually useless farmland." There was more than a hint of annoyance in the deep voice.

Now she remembered—the letter! And yet, the letter on heavy paper embossed with the marquess's coat of arms lying on her desk where she had tossed it in fury on reading the proposal could not fully account for the strange feeling that she had encountered him somewhere before. However, Lady Caroline Waverly was not one to resist a challenge from the Marquess of Everleigh or anyone else. "It is not 'useless farmland,' or at least it won't be when I am through with it." Chin up, she stared so directly in her visitor's eye that he, too, experienced the sudden sensation that he had met this spirited lady somewhere before.

"And how do you propose, ma'am, to make it more valuable than I can by digging a canal through it?" he challenged.

"I am sorry to disappoint you, my lord, but the methods I envision for the cultivation of my fields will yield them far more productive than any canal could. Furthermore, the profits from my success will be kept right here in Berkhamstead instead of lining the pocket of some grasping manufacturer who will no doubt waste them indulging himself in the fleshpots of London or expend them in some vulgar display of wealth in the north."

If the Marquess had appeared imposing before, he was positively threatening now as he pulled himself to his full height and glowered down at her. "*I* am that despicable person you so scornfully describe, ma'am. And I will have you know I do it to provide work and to lower the prices of necessary goods for all those soldiers so blithely cast aside by the society they offered their lives to preserve in the miserable campaign in the Peninsula and the slaughter that was Waterloo."

Something about the way he pronounced the words "miserable campaign in the Peninsula" struck a chord in Caro's memory and carried her back to a winter's night long ago. She could smell the pungent scent of pine boughs as a young

soldier described to her the hardships he and his fellow
companions-at-arms were enduring in Spain. Of course! The
face was a little less bronzed and he had filled out since
recovering from his wounds. The crinkly wrinkles at the
corners of his eyes were more noticeable and the strong
features more pronounced now that the softening effects of
youth had disappeared, but it was most definitely the dashing Captain Daventry who stood before her.

"But . . . but I thought you were only a younger son!"
she blurted out, forgetting entirely that her visitor was not
privy to the memories recalled by his words.

"What!" The marquess was nonplussed.

"I beg your pardon," Caro apologized. The man was
looking at her as if she had run mad, and indeed, it must
appear that way. "I mean, I thought that is why Lavvy refused you, because you were a younger son with no expectations." Really, Caro, you are babbling like an idiot, she
scolded herself.

But comprehension had dawned on the Marquess. "And
you're the Christmas Waif."

"The Christmas Waif?" It was Caro's turn to look blank.

"Yes. You were sitting up there on the top step swathed
in that enormous shawl, your eyes as big as saucers and you
looked so tiny and forlorn that I was sure you were some
poor lost thing the Mandevilles had given shelter."

"I was." She was amused. "But I am also Lavvy's
cousin, Caro Waverly. My papa and her mama were brother
and sister. Papa was in the diplomatic service and ordinarily
I lived with him at whatever post he served, but that time
he had gone to Russia and did not wish to take a child to
such an inhospitable climate. So I was dispatched to school
and the Mandevilles gave me a home at holidays."

"Don't tell me your father was Hugo Waverly?"

Her eyes sparkled. "You know him?" she asked eagerly.

"Yes. I had occasion to come across him in Vienna while
he was attached to Castlereagh at the Congress. I expect it
was that trip to Russia and his knowledge of their political
aspirations that made him invaluable to the Foreign Secretary. For my part, I found him a brilliant conversationalist
and an original thinker."

"Yes, he was and he always shared his life and thoughts
with me for as long as I can remember. I miss him dreadfully. After being with him, society seems quite dull." Caro

gave herself a mental shake lest he think her wallowing in self-pity. "But I keep myself tolerably amused with Waverly Park. It was a relief to leave Miss Chillingford's and all those silly girls to come here."

"And become a ferocious bluestocking," the marquess continued.

"I am not a bluestocking!" She was indignant. "I don't stuff my head with facts merely to parade my erudition. I just prefer books to people. One can pick them up and lay them down whenever one wishes. They give one companionship and stimulation without demanding that one be charming or beautiful or up on the latest *on-dit*. Besides, I like to learn new things and I like to be useful."

"And yet you think that you are being useful in opposing my canal scheme." He cocked an eyebrow at her.

"Yes, I do," she defended herself stoutly. "Mine is a superior scheme to yours because it will continue to employ people and to produce food cheaply for them, while yours will only be good while the canal is being built. In the end the only people who will benefit from the cheaper prices afforded by water transport will be those in the cities far away from Berkhamstead. At least I shall be able to see whether my efforts are effective."

The marquess shook his head, but the gleam in his eyes was now one of interest rather than anger. He so rarely encountered people who held strong opinions or beliefs that he found her a refreshing change—even though her plans were directly opposed to his, and misguided at that.

Caro tilted her head, trying to read the expression on the marquess's face. He was so quiet that she felt certain she had made some sort of an impression, but she was not altogether certain just exactly what sort of an impression it was. "Besides, this land is all I have of my family. It *is* my family. Surely, now that you are Marquess of Everleigh, you must be rich as the Golden Ball and able to purchase any land you wish." She raised a speculative eyebrow.

"One might be pardoned for harboring such a belief, but one would have reckoned without such stiff-rumps as you and Colonel Folliot-Smythe."

"Oh, the colonel. He is opposed to any scheme that isn't of his own devising. Now that he is no longer in the army he takes out all his combative instincts on his neighbors. I daresay that if I were to complain to him about you and tell him how pleased I am that he did not accept your offer, he would turn around and snap it up in an instant.''

A reluctant grin tugged at the corners of his mouth. ''While you, of course, are not the least bit combative. As I recall, your reply to my modest proposal fairly bristled with indignation. Why I am amazed that I had the temerity to seek you out after receiving it.''

''Perhaps I was a bit strong, but I had good reason to oppose you. *He* is merely being contrary,'' Caro defended herself spiritedly.

''And now you propose machinations by which to deliver him to me all unwitting. You are a devious person, Lady Caroline Waverly, but if it will accomplish my purpose and allow both of us to bring prosperity to those we wish to help, then by all means, do what you must. I shall not give you away.'' The grin was wider now and there was a distinct twinkle in the blue eyes.

Caro was not to be mollified. ''Very well then. I see him every morning on my ride. I shall do what I can, In the meantime, you must give your word to stop pestering me for I warn you, I shan't give in.''

''Very well, young stiff-neck, then we are agreed.'' The marquess held out a shapely hand.

Caro hesitated a moment before taking it. ''Very well. Thank you. William will see you out.'' And with that, Caro rang the bell, hoping that for once in his life, William would answer with dispatch. She was not disappointed, as William, with the confidence of a privileged retainer, had been hovering close to the door from the moment he had closed it behind the marquess.

''Now, there is a woman who was glad to see the back of me,'' Nicholas remarked as he mounted his horse. Caesar's ears twitched and he rolled an eye at his master. ''No, truly, she did not care for my offer in the least, but I believe she liked me better at the end than she did at the outset.'' Caesar snorted, fretful at his rider's loquacity and impatient to be gone. ''A bluestocking of the worst sort, she won't rest until she's worn out the parish with her good deeds. Not that she isn't something of an original.'' A reminiscent gleam lit his eyes as he remembered her indignant rejection at his relegation of her to the ranks of female pedagogy. Yes, decidedly an original, the marquess concluded. He hoped that she wouldn't immure herself in the country becoming more and more circumscribed in her existence and narrower and narrower in her views. She did have a certain spark and he would hate to see it quenched in the well-meaning but arid existence of an ape-leader.

For her part, Caro had not dismissed the marquess from her thoughts as quickly as she had from her library. So, *that* was what had become of the dashing Captain Nicholas Daventry. Instead of covering himself with more glory on the battlefield, he appeared to have inherited the title which had been so noticeably lacking in Cousin Lavinia's eyes. How ironic. Did he suffer from the unfairness of it all or had he truly retained his perspective on his former love as he seemed to have done that Christmas so long ago? Caro was more curious than she cared to admit, even to herself. Well, he was the Marquess of Everleigh now and undoubtedly the darling of the *ton*. Even someone as unfamiliar with the world of fashion as Caro Waverly could recognize in Nicholas Daventry a man who would capture the interest and acclaim of the Upper Ten Thousand. Unlike so many of society's members, he was possessed of a physical presence as imposing as his title.

Caro sighed and shook her head. In truth, she had preferred Captain Daventry. This new marquess verged on being autocratic. It had taken her some time to recognize in him the kindly soldier who had sat on the stairs regaling her with stories of life in the Peninsula and answering her questions with as much consideration as if she were a grown-up. She sniffed. Helena had always maintained that money and position often had a deleterious effect on human nature and in this case she appeared to be entirely correct. Where Captain Daventry had been all consideration, the Marquess of Everleigh expected to get his way immediately and without interference of any sort. It was a great shame and it made Caro even less eager to visit her cousin than she had been before. But there was nothing for it. She owed a debt of gratitude to the Mandevilles even if she did not owe it to Lavinia and she would do her best to repay their many kindnesses by providing companionship for their adored daughter.

Taking a last quick glance around to make sure she had not left any special friends behind her on the shelves, Caro tied up the last package and headed off to change into her riding habit. After a morning spent in the library and then this annoying interruption, she most definitely felt in need of a gallop across the park to clear the cobwebs from her brain.

5

SEVERAL DAYS LATER saw their arrival at the Countess of Welham's imposing mansion in Grosvenor Square. Until his marriage, the Earl of Welham had lived happily enough in the family townhouse in Berkeley Square where there had been a Welham since it had been built. His bride, however, after several delicate hints as to the difficulty of holding any truly brilliant affairs in such a modest residence, had convinced him to move to the very impressive edifice which dominated one end of Grosvenor Square.

It was before the wide stone steps of this particular establishment that Caro and her entourage arrived late one mild afternoon, having made good time from Berkhamstead. The countess, who had been resting, sent word that she would be with the two ladies as soon as she had refurbished her toilette. "As though we were fresh as daisies after all this time in the carriage," Caro could not refrain from remarking in an acid undertone.

"I believe that these beauties take a great deal of maintenance," her companion replied, eyes atwinkle.

"Oh well, it will only put her in a better humor to see how dusty and creased we are. Besides . . ." Caro began, but the rest of her observation was drowned by a commotion seeming to come from the back hall. Caro and Helena looked around in surprise. Such a brouhaha was not in keeping with the picture that either one of them had of the countess's elegant household.

They did not have to wait long to discover the cause as two small boys, followed by what appeared to be a bundle of rubbish, erupted into their view. Catching sight of the two ladies, they came to a screeching halt. The ball of dirt slammed into their legs, yelped, and shook itself, revealing two bright dark eyes, and a shiny black nose.

Caro, finding herself the object of some scrutiny by two

pairs of very blue eyes, took the situation well in hand. "Why, hello." She smiled her infectious smile. "I am your Cousin Caro. This is my friend Miss Helena Gray and you must be Cedric and Clarence, but I do not know who this is." She bent over to pat the mess of dirt, and then shook the somewhat grimy hands of its companions.

"How do you do. Mama told us you were coming. I am Clarence, ma'am," the elder of the two spoke.

"How do you do, Clarence. But you must call me Cousin Caro, you know."

"And I'm Cedric and are those your horses that John was putting in the stables? They are bang-up pieces of horseflesh if you ask me." Cedric's face was alight with enthusiasm. Shorter than his brother by half a head, he was a good deal grimier and appeared to be the more adventurous of the two—an impression enhanced by the fact that he had lost his two upper front teeth.

Clarence tried to quell his junior with a frown, but to no effect.

"And your carriage is a splendid piece of work. Mama's is silly. It's all painted beautifully, but it lurches dreadfully and is not at all well sprung. I always get sick when we go down to Mandeville."

Caro chuckled. "Well, I do hope you will ride in mine without feeling queasy. Dimmock is the best of coachmen and we always journey most comfortably. But who is this?" She pointed to the mop of fur at their feet which, encouraged by her tone, began to lick her hand.

"Oh well, that's . . ." Cedric broke off looking to his brother for guidance.

"You see, we were out in the stable looking at your horses when we heard some yelping and shouting. Along came Argos with a fresh chop in his mouth and Lord Berwick's stable boys chasing after him. He must have stolen it from the kitchen. But, poor fellow, you can see he is starving," Clarence spoke in defense of their new friend.

"So Clarence told them to leave Argos to him in his most grown-up voice and that he would take care of the poor creature." Cedric imitated his brother's commanding tones and stance to perfection, much to the ladies' amusement. "But now we aren't 'zactly sure what to do with him. He's a clever thing. He came when we called him and he looks ever so intelligent, but Mama will never let us have a dog.

She doesn't even wish us to have ponies." Cedric sighed and his blue eyes grew wistful.

"Argos?" Caroline looked quizzically at the disreputable pile that regarded her hopefully through soulful brown eyes.

"Yes. Argos was Ulysses' dog, you know," Cedric replied proudly.

"I realize that. I was just searching for some resemblance." Caro could hardly repress the laughter in her voice.

"Argos was noted for his faithfulness and this dog followed us home and waited for us ever so long outside the door until Cook said he could come in, so that's where he got his name," Cedric elaborated.

"We were hoping we could get John Coachman to say he is his so that Cook will take care of him. Then maybe we could visit him sometimes." Though less mournful sounding that his brother, Clarence could not keep a certain hopeful tone from his voice and it wrung Caro's heart.

Observing the two blond heads bent over the little dog and listening to them both as they reassured it that they would find it a good home, she resolved to ensure that they kept it. Knowing her cousin, Caro felt she could hazard a reasonably accurate guess as to the nature of the boys' existence. Lavvy would welcome her two fine-looking sons as long as they were clean, quiet, and adoring towards their mother. But let them deviate from this or demand any sort of interest or attention from her, she would send them away. Remembering back to her own childhood, Caro knew precisely how long it was possible for an active, intelligent child to remain clean, docile, and out of scrapes and knew that the times the boys were in accord with their mother's view of correct behavior must be few and far between. A childhood without any sort of pet seemed to Caro a monstrous situation and she immediately cast about for some scheme to remedy it.

Thus when Lavvy finally appeared, floating down the staircase in a cloud of rosewater to greet her cousin, she found Caro with a most determined look on her face and the light of battle in her eyes. "You have come just in time, Caro, for we have been invited to the Countess of Mortmain's rout. It is the first event of any real note this Season and is sure to be brilliant, though undoubtedly a dreadful squeeze. I count upon you to lend me support in my first venture out of mourning. I am sure I have lived a recluse so long I look positively dowdy.'' In fact, the Countess of Welham was looking extremely charming in a round dress of jaconet muslin over a peach-colored sarsnet slip. The color of the ensemble enhanced her delicate complexion and fair hair, while the tightly cut bodice revealed a figure that had blossomed into ripe maturity.

Caro sighed. It all seemed so unfair that her cousin was more beautiful than ever. Formerly possessed of an ethereal, childlike quality, she now radiated all the assurance of womanly beauty. The slight, boyish lines had matured into voluptuous curves and the soft round cheeks and chin had firmed into a more classical silhouette. However, if her features had blossomed, her character had not undergone a similar transformation. After casting a quick glance at her cousin, which left Caro acutely aware of all the deficiencies of her outmoded and travel-stained toilette, Lavvy turned on her sons. ''Clarence, Cedric, whatever are you doing here? Where is Mr. Welbeck and what ever is that dreadful thing there?'' Lavvy's voice rose in annoyance as she angrily twitched a flounce away from the general direction of the dirty mop that offended her.

''We've come to have tea with you, Mama, as you directed when you allowed Mr. Welbeck the afternoon off to consult with Sir Evelyn on the manuscript he just purchased,'' Clarence replied timidly.

''When Sir Evelyn was here the other day, they went on for ages. Mr. Welbeck does seem to know heaps and heaps about old books,'' Cedric chimed in eagerly, exhibiting a winning smile that he hoped would make his mother forget the rest of her question.

But Lavvy, proof against the wiles of her youngest, was not to be put off. Directing a quelling look at Cedric, she turned to his brother. ''I hope *you* have some explanation for this, this . . . creature,'' she demanded.

Clarence gulped as two pairs of eyes, his mother's icily demanding and his brother's entreating, fastened on him. ''Well, well, you see . . .'' he was seeking desperately for an answer when help came from an unexpected quarter.

''Lavvy, can't you see that your son has rescued a Transylvanian Long Hair? Poor thing, it must have been lost for quite some time, judging from its condition. Its owner must be quite desperate at losing such a valuable creature.'' Caro sighed and shook her head sadly.

"Desperate?" Lavvy's rigid calm dissolved into a blank stare.

"Oh, yes. They are extremely rare as they are bred only on the Rackoczy estates and given as a mark of favor to their especial friends. I saw a few when Papa and I were in Vienna and I recall Princess Esterhazy confiding in me that she was quite wild to own one, only her family had once so offended the Rackoczys that she was destined never to have one," she continued, refusing to look at her companion who was struggling to maintain her composure.

"I am sure that your boys, growing up as they have with parents in the first stare of fashion, instinctively recognized the pure blood under its filthy exterior." At this point, Caro was beginning to wonder how long she would be able to keep her own countenance under control. Really, the succession of emotions flitting across her cousin's face was as humorous as it was transparent, not only to Caro, but to her sons as well.

The boys' spirits rose as they watched disgust replaced by surprise and finally by a calculating look in their mother's eyes. Clarence stole a brief, questioning glance at this curious person who seemed to have transformed the stuffy house the moment she had entered it. A broad wink from a twinkling gray eye confirmed his suspicions that this Lady Caroline was a "right 'un" and he poked his younger brother sharply in the ribs just as that young man was about to burst forth with a string of awkward questions.

Lavinia, having entirely missed the interchange, looked thoughtful. "Perhaps I should inquire as to whom it might belong. I daresay we shall have to keep it until it can be restored to its proper owner. Clarence, Cedric, take it out to the stables so that John can feed it and make it more presentable. We must take care that we restore it in excellent condition. But I won't have it in the house, mind you."

Caro, seeing the disappointment in the little boys' eyes, swiftly intervened, "Oh, no, Lavvy, these animals are bred especially for human companionship. I have seen them as lapdogs in some of the finest drawing rooms in Vienna. I expect this one is more accustomed to sleeping on damask than it is on straw. After all, it won't be long. I shall ask Princess Esterhazy if she knows who has sustained such a loss, for I am persuaded that she, if anyone, would know."

Lavinia was torn. She had never cared for animals of any

sort—nasty smelly things—but the idea of rendering a service to someone like the princess had definite appeal. Furthermore, it was too provoking that her little cousin, who had
no use for such things, should be on such friendly terms with
any of the *ton's* most influential members. "Very well then,
but if it so much as looks at the new draperies in the drawing room, it will be sent to the kitchen. Now, off with you."

"Yes, Mama. Thank you, Mama," Clarence breathed.
Then, hardly daring to believe their good fortune, the boys
headed obediently for the door with Argos sticking close to
their heels, but not before they had bestowed their benefac-
tress with exultant and grateful smiles.

Seeing the happiness in their eyes, Caro began to feel that
perhaps life in London would not be so very empty and dull
after all. As she followed a gaily chattering Lavvy into the
drawing room, she was able to listen with unaccustomed
equanimity to the fashionable entertainments in store for
them.

Further assurance that the ladies were among congenial
company appeared not many minutes later in the form of
the Lord Anthony Mandeville whose energetic pull on the
bell reverberated throughout the mansion, penetrating even
the satin-covered sanctuary where the ladies had just seated
themselves. Within moments, they could hear him taking the
steps two at a time, barely allowing Wigmore time to open
the door and announce him before he burst in like a blast
of fresh air upon the ladies.

"Caro! Famous to see you!" The viscount strode across
the room to give his cousin a hearty buffet. His sister's polite cough recalled his attention to the other occupants in
the room and with a sheepish grin he continued, "Hello,
Lavvy. You're looking fine as fivepence. Welham's death
has done you good. Gave you a rest from all that racketing
about."

He threw his cousin a conspiratorial wink as Lavvy, rigid
with indignation, burst out, "Really, Anthony, how can you
say such a thing! Have you no sensibility? I am sure I was
excessively grieved to lose Welham and life without him has
been extraordinarily dull."

"But now you have called upon Cousin Caro and . . ."
he raised an eyebrow and smiled encouragingly in Helena's
direction.

"Oh, I do beg your pardon, my wits have gone begging,"

Caro apologized. "Helena, this is my cousin Anthony Mandeville and Tony, this is Helena Gray, who allowed herself to be lured away from a brilliant career at Miss Chillingford's Select Seminary for Genteel Young Ladies to immure herself at Waverly lending me countenance and providing me with intelligent companionship."

"And now you have consented to do the same for Lavvy. I only wish I knew what she put forward as inducement to bring you here. Knowing you, I feel that only some extraordinary bribe or threat was offered to force you to leave your country retreat for the frantic rounds of the *ton* which, no doubt, Lavvy intends to plunge you into immediately."

A clock chiming on the mantel brought him to with a start. "Lord, I must be off. Promised to meet Ponsonby at Tattersall's twenty minutes ago and if I don't get there soon, he'll likely have chosen some showy piece of horseflesh with no wind and riddled with spavins." Grabbing his walking stick, he started for the door, only to turn at the threshold. "I wish that you could join us, Caro, as I am sure you could do with a good mount to make your life here bearable, but I shall be happy to select something for your approval if you like."

Caro thanked him kindly for his concern, reassuring him that all had been arranged on that score. "I should have known you would not have left the country without some provision. I look forward to riding with you in the park." Tony turned to go, but this time it was his sister who called him back.

"Anthony," she fixed him with a meaningful stare, "we are counting on your escort to the Countess of Mortmain's rout this evening."

"Oh lord, I had forgot, I . . ."

"Tony . . ." There was no brooking the tone in Lavvy's voice.

A rueful grimace spread over her brother's cheery countenance. "I shall be there, but only if you bring Caro to keep me company and protect me from all the town tabbies and their eager protegées." And with that parting shot, he was gone, leaving his sister seething with frustration.

"Really, you would think he would grow up someday and Papa refuses to make him find a wife. I can see it will be left up to me to find someone to be a steadying influence, but how I am to convince such a woman to put up with a madcap like Tony, I am sure I cannot tell.'' Lavvy gave an exasperated sigh.

''Don't refine upon it too much. Tony's a good sort. He's just young. He'll find someone who adores him and looks to him for guidance and in no time at all, he will be the most solid country gentleman you could hope for,'' Caro soothed.

''Tony? Why his life is nothing but one long scrape. He is always tumbling into some sort of trouble or other. How Papa and Mama can bear it is more than I can say.'' Lavvy gave a resigned little shrug.

''But, knowing Tony, I feel sure he always manages to extricate himself without anyone's help. And Uncle George was never one to be alarmed by high spirits. It is a pity Tony could not have served in the Peninsula, army-mad as he is, but that truly would have worried Aunt and Uncle Mandeville.''

''I suppose you are right,'' Lavvy agreed cautiously, ''but still I wish he would be a little more the thing. He is rather like a firework and one can never be quite sure what direction he will go off in next. However, I expect now that you are here, he will be around more often. Certainly we can count on his presence this evening, unenthusiastic though it might be. You must keep him amused by talking to him of horses while I cast about for suitable partners.''

Caro nodded. Privately, she could not imagine the viscount liking anyone that his sister chose. But if it would keep Lavinia from finding partners for Caro, then it was worth it.

6

IN FACT, the Countess of Welham was the only one in several households looking forward to the Countess of Mortmain's rout with any sort of pleasurable anticipation. Tony, Caro, and Helena, resigned to attending, were all searching for some way to extract even the slightest amount of amusement from an evening that promised to be nothing so much as a crush of people jealously observing one another and stepping on each other's toes in a stuffy ballroom. The music would be audible only to those directly in front of the players and refreshments would be impossible to obtain without fighting one's way through the mass of guests. Yet, they all derived some solace from the thought that they could rely on each other for conversation on some topic other than the latest *on-dits*. Tony knew that he could count on Caro to acknowledge a promised dance when his sister became importunate in her demands that he partner Lord So-and-So's whey-faced daughter or some gawky heiress that Lavinia favored.

Meanwhile, in an equally imposing residence in Berkeley Square, another prospective guest was deciding that, unwilling though he might be, he too could not avoid attendance at the opening event of the Season. Frowning at the gilt-edged invitation on the mantelpiece, Nicholas turned to address the two ladies sipping tea in front of the drawing room fire.

"I should be more than happy to escort both of you to the Countess of Mortmain's, Mama, though it is like to be a sad crush. I collect that Clary is still adamant in her refusal to have a Season?" He cocked an eyebrow at one of the room's occupants, a slight girl with her brother's dark hair and blue eyes. She looked to be no more than eighteen except for the fine lines around the eyes which were those of someone much older and more accustomed to life's painful experiences.

Lady Clarissa Daventry, last of the children born to a mature woman, had appeared in the world after much travail on her mother's part and, as a result of this difficult labor, had a twisted spine. This deformity, though not immediately visible when the young lady was seated, caused her to walk with a decided limp and had kept her from being involved in any physical activities. Consequently, she had thrown her energies into painting and the pianoforte and was an accomplished artist in both these areas. Though blessed with a pleasing face and a quick mind, she had early on recognized that most other children were inclined to look askance at one who enjoyed such quiet pursuits as she did, and thus Clary had led a contented but solitary existence at Everleigh with her governess and her music master.

Of late, her ailment had become painful as well as inconvenient and at long last she had allowed her adored brother to convince her to come to London to seek advice from the finest medical men the country had to offer.

Personally, Clary did not hold out much hope for such a cure, but Nicholas had been so optimistic that she could not find it in her heart to resist in the face of such concern. Furthermore, she could see that the Marchioness of Everleigh would never again move amongst her friends in the *ton* unless her daughter were to accompany her to the metropolis. So, after some demur, Clary had allowed herself to be persuaded. However, she had been adamant in her continued refusal to have a Season or attend any of the countless fashionable affairs to which they had been invited.

Nicholas had scoffed at the notion that she would appear nothing but a poor awkward cripple to the members of the *ton*. Though she loved her brother for his belief that her sweetness and charm, coupled with her considerable talents would make those around her forget her deformity, Clary could not help thinking that in this instance Nicholas was wrong. Wishing to avoid hurting the brother who had been her idol for so many years, she had not flatly refused to appear in society, but thus far she had successfully escaped all contact with the outside world.

For his part, Nicholas had been remarkably circumspect in promoting his plans, of which the medical consultation formed only the smallest part. He was determined to enlarge his sister's circle of friends and help her grow accustomed to moving about more in society. He did not expect to overcome her resistance with ease, but there was no harm in trying. In time, Clary might become so accustomed to being invited to join him that she might actually do so. Thus he was not at all put out when she said, "Thank you, Nicky. I would infinitely prefer to stay here, but Mama must go."

The marquess merely smiled and shook his head at her before turning to his mother. "You will attend with me, will you not, Mama?"

The dowager hesitated. She hated leaving her daughter home alone, but it had been so long since she had been a participant in a world where she had once been one of the brightest stars. Her husband's death, followed by her eldest son's unexpected and tragic hunting accident had kept her immured in the countryside and it was not until Nicky, home at long last from the wars, had taken charge and offered his escort that she had gotten out at all. The dowager's conflicting thoughts, writ large on her countenance, were immediately visible to her two children who made light of her reservations.

"Don't be a nodcock, Mama. You *know* you are longing to go, if only to see if Lady Blandford's daughter is the incomparable she claims her to be. Letters are one thing when you have very little expectation that the recipient will find out for herself. But if Araminta were as her mother insists she is, Nicky would surely know of her and he did not so much as blink when you read the letter to us." Clarissa threw a challenging look at her brother.

Nicky grinned, "Now, Clary, how can you say such things when I have been leading a most circumscribed and respectable existence as responsible landlord, attentive son, and, I might add, devoted brother to a sister who refuses to go out and observe for herself."

Clary's eyes danced with amusement. "Don't fly up into the boughs, brother dear. I may have been playing the pianoforte the evening Sir William and his family came to dine, but I saw how both Susannah and Jane were casting sheep's eyes at you. Though I do not move in society, I am neither blind nor stupid. Besides, when Colonel McIntyre came to tell us how you were going on after returning to the Continent, he was full of stories about Spanish beauties and Belgian ladies who fairly swooned over the handsome Captain Daventry."

"Oh, Neill. You cannot believe a word that man utters. He is full of Banbury tales," her brother scoffed.

Clary looked smug. "That's as it may be, but I know what I know." Then, changing the subject, "Do go, Mama. I shall be most content here by myself. I had rather be alone this evening because I wish to try some of the new music we procured from Chappell the other day. Besides, now that Nicky is the head of the family, every matchmaking mama will be forcing her daughter on him. You must not leave him unprotected."

Nicholas grimaced. "She's in the right of it, Mama. My life is no longer my own. I cannot look at a woman but I see myself reflected in her eyes as the husband of her dreams."

"Poor Nicky," Clary teased, but her mother, smiling at her son with maternal pride merely replied, "Well, you are."

"What? Nicky? Why they'd be bored within a fortnight. He would bury himself in *Blackwood's* and *The Edinburgh Review,* go off to attend his political meetings without a thought for them, or bury himself at Everleigh and spend his time riding about the countryside at breakneck speed. No, I suspect Nicky would make a far better flirt than a husband."

"Clarissa! How can you say such things about your brother?" The countess was shocked. "Especially when he has been all that is kind and attentive to us."

"I was only funning, Mama. You know I consider him the best of brothers, spending far too much time at Everleigh with only us for companionship." Clary's eyes were lit with a special warmth as she regarded her brother's handsome profile and she sighed inwardly. She truly did wish he could find someone to love, but after Lavinia Mandeville there had never appeared to be anyone.

Of course, he had not confided in his sister, but close as she was to her favorite, Clary could guess. She had seen the light in his eyes and heard the reverence in his voice whenever he spoke of Lavinia. And then, after the Christmas ball at Mandeville Park, he had never mentioned her again. There had been a certain grimness about his mouth and an unhappiness in his expression for weeks afterward, and he began to chafe to get back to his regiment. Clarissa barely knew Lavinia, but she had conceived a fierce dislike for the woman who had spurned someone as magnificent and true as her brother, Nicholas. Giving herself a mental shake, Clary turned her thoughts to the issue at hand. "Truly, you must go, Mama. You know how much you will enjoy it."

"Very well, then, if you are certain you will be comfortable here alone."

"I shall be more than comfortable. I shall look forward to an uninterrupted evening at the pianoforte. So you see, I should be very poor company indeed, even if you were here," the marchioness's daughter assured her.

Thus, not many hours later, the Marquess of Everleigh escorted his mother up the broad marble staircase of the countess's impressive mansion in Park Lane. True to prediction, it was dreadfully crowded and they were forced to wait for an age as the press of guests moved slowly up the stairs to be greeted by their hostess, resplendent in a diamond parure and a turban of truly terrifying proportions.

At long last they entered the ballroom, ablaze with light and already stiflingly hot from the number of guests. The dowager looked eagerly around for old acquaintances, her eyes bright with excitement at being back among the *ton,* while her son, steering her to the relative calm of a marble pillar, sighed. It was like so many other affairs with women, beautifully attired in gowns and jewels of all descriptions and hues, scrutinizing each other, comparing, and commenting to their friends, all the while casting not entirely covert glances at the male members of the assemblage. The men, less conspicuously than the women, were doing precisely the same thing. Nicholas could picture the *on-dits* being passed along as he intercepted the exchanges of a sly glance here, a raised eyebrow there. He almost wished himself back on the Peninsula, for after all this was no less a battlefield, but the enemy remained hidden and one could never confront it.

A silvery voice at his side broke into the marquess's reverie. "Why Nicholas, how charming to see you."

He turned to see Lavinia smiling up at him. Like Caro, he too could not help thinking how much more beautiful she had grown. The Lavinia Mandeville who had spurned him so completely had been a mere girl while this was a woman, secure in herself and her charms. The flirtatious look had gone to be replaced by a smile that was a thousand times more seductive.

As he bent over the dainty hand, he observed that the figure underneath the blue satin slip had also matured into voluptuousness. The corsage, which was cut very low, revealed enticingly rounded shoulders and bosom, while the magnificent sapphire necklace called attention to the creamy softness of her skin. "Lavinia." He tore his eyes away from this distracting vision to find her looking up at him, a tiny smile of amusement curving her delicate lips and a knowing sparkle in the blue eyes.

Her voice, however, when she finally spoke, was plaintive. "I am delighted to be recognized. After all this time in seclusion, I began to fear that no one would know me. Widowhood is a most lonely state, I assure you," she sighed.

Nicholas raised a dark eyebrow. Even for Lavinia, this was doing it much too brown. "I hardly think so. Society does not forget an incomparable so quickly."

"Why thank you, Nicky." Her voice still held a wistful note. "But I know how fickle it can be. And there is always a new crop of hopeful young beauties to catch the interest of the *ton*. I vow I have been away from it all so long I have even forgot how to dance." She dimpled up at him.

As the musicians had just struck up and sets were forming for the quadrille, his mother urged him, "Do go on, Nicholas, I see Amanda St. Clair heading this way and I have not seen her for ten years at least." There was nothing for it but to offer Lavinia his arm and beg her to do the honor of accompanying him, but all through the dance his thoughts were in a turmoil.

Here was the woman he had dreamed of for so long, someone who had chosen a brilliant marriage over love, or whatever it was that she had felt for him. Nicholas had tried to hate her, or at least her misplaced values, but he had not been able to stop himself over the years from picturing her as he had last seen her at the Christmas ball so long ago.

As time had passed, the image had faded from his mind and he had relegated Lavinia Mandeville to the ranks of those members of the *ton* for whom position was everything. Nicholas regretted that she was that way, but he had accepted it and gone on to other, more important things. Now, here he was, the Marquess of Everleigh, wealthy in his own right and head of the family as well, and it seemed that Lavinia was more than ready to recapture their former intimacy.

He should have scorned her for a heartless beauty. But somehow he could not help being intrigued—as much by her unabashed pursuit of him as by her loveliness. Nicholas couldn't understand himself. Half of him was enjoying being with her and the other half was saying, Nicholas, you fool. To her you are merely the most eligible bachelor in the room. Unbidden, another face from the past stole into his consciousness and he wondered what the Christmas Waif would say now. She had offered him words of wisdom then. Undoubtedly she would shrug her shoulders, curl a scornful lip, and dismiss him as an idiot beneath her consideration, as someone who had learned nothing from the lessons of time.

7

IN POINT OF FACT, Caro was doing very nearly that, though her disgust was directed more at her cousin and her predatory ways than at any folly on Nicholas's part. Watching them perform the graceful figures of the quadrille, she was forced to admit that they did make a handsome couple. The black coat so beautifully molded to his broad shoulders and the snowy cravat merely emphasized the marquess's dark good looks, while his powerful frame, nearly a head taller than any other man in the room, made Lavinia appear even more delicate and ethereal.

Caroline snorted to herself. The fragility was the merest illusion, for no one of Caro's acquaintance could be more single-minded than her cousin. No sooner had Nicholas appeared in the ballroom than Lavvy had decided to make him hers. Caro had seen her cousin stiffen the moment her eyes caught sight of his commanding figure, but she had continued a running commentary on the room's occupants before adding in an offhand manner, "Why there is Nicholas Daventry. He is come into the title now. Such a tragic set of coincidences, both his father and his brother. They say he made a tremendous fortune in his own right—something to do with the consols and Waterloo. Until now he's kept himself buried at Everleigh. I must go and talk with him and his mother. Mama would be most annoyed with me if I were to ignore one of our neighbors." And with that she was off, her eyes fastened tenaciously on the marquess and his mother as they made their way through the crowd.

Caro turned to see Helena's hazel eyes twinkling at her obvious disgust. "That man has no more chance than a trout on a line and Lavinia will be the new Countess of Everleigh before the year is out," Caro muttered darkly.

Her companion laughed. "You are quite in the right of it, but most men would be pleased at the prospect. After all, Lavinia was born to the part and would fill the role most gracefully.''

"Yes," Caro was forced into unwilling admission. "But she doesn't care for him in the least, you know. I don't believe that she cares for anyone but herself.''

"Very likely true, but that does not mean she would not make him a good wife. After all, very few marriages in the *ton* are based on more than the barest civility,'' Helena replied. "Besides, she shall have some competition for the marquess's attention for I see Sally Jersey has just joined them.''

Caro glanced over but remained lost in thought. Annoyed though she had been by his arrogant ways, somehow she did not wish for the marquess to fall into her cousin's clutches. She could not help remembering the companionable way he had sat down on the cold stairs at Mandeville Park so many Christmases ago and conversed with her so intelligently, as though she were of an equal age and experience. Even though marriage to her cousin was precisely what that young soldier had once aspired to, Caro felt now, as she had then, that he deserved something more than Lavinia with her unceasing appetite for attention and admiration and her demanding ways.

She sighed and gazed around the ballroom. Caro had guessed how it would be—hot, crowded, and dull—but she had promised Susan that she would take careful note of what everyone was wearing and how their hair was arranged in order to report back to that aspiring young person. In fact, with the exception of Lavinia, the little maid was the only one in the Grosvenor Square household who had looked forward to the event. Even Helena, loyal though she was, had demurred. The Countess of Welham obviously did not expect a mere companion to accompany them, but Caro had been adamant that her companion lend her moral support. Susan had been in her element, selecting Caro's dress of Urling's net over a white satin slip. Though her mistress insisted that she was not a young miss making a come out and could therefore dispense with the obligatory white muslin, the maid had been equally obstinate that she at least wear white.

"But, Susan, I am not making any appearance in society nor am I here to find a husband, and furthermore, I do not wish to be confused with anyone who is,'' Caro protested.

"That's as may be, my lady," the maid responded firmly, "but you don't wish to be thought of as an ape-leader either. There." She finished placing a rose in her mistress's glossy dark hair and stood back to survey the effect.

Catching a glimpse of herself in the looking glass. Caro had been forced to admit that Susan knew whereof she spoke. The effect of her costume and coiffure were perfect— young, but not youthful, and sophisticated enough in their simplicity to declare the wearer above the follies of a young miss in her first Season. "Of course you are right, as always." She smiled at her Susan who turned pink with pleasure. "And I shall take great pains to remember what everyone is wearing, though I mistrust my ability to describe them to you, not being at all familiar myself with *La Belle Assemblée* and Ackermann's *Repository*. I have not the least notion what to call everything." She paused as a thought struck her. "What a nodcock I am! I shall subscribe to both of these arbiters of taste and give them to you. Then if I am fortunate enough to avoid attending any more balls, you will not be deprived of any reporting on the fashions there."

Susan was so overcome by this that she could only stammer her thanks, which her mistress brushed quickly aside. "Think nothing of it. You obviously have the interest and the skill. We must help you develop them. I am only sorry you have such a poor advertisement for them in me, but I shall try to do better. In the meantime, perhaps I shall be able to recall clearly enough to sketch things when I return." And Caro was off, leaving Susan breathless with excitement and longing for the warm kitchen back at Waverly Court so she could share her good fortune with Mrs. Crawford.

Thrilled as she was to be in London, the little maid did miss the sympathetic housekeeper and her own sisters who would have been able to share in her excitement. To be sure, London and a mansion in Grosvenor Square were the height of her aspirations. Certainly there were few households in town as elegant as the Countess of Welham's, but the servants were as supercilious as the mistress and would not lower themselves to sharing a cozy chat with a country bumpkin. But they shall do, Susan resolved to herself. In the meantime, she would throw all her energies into improving her skills and insuring that each time her mistress appeared in public she would be exquisitely turned out.

Her resolve was not entirely selfish. For, despite Caro's claims to the contrary, Susan firmly believed that her mistress would be happier were she to find a suitable partner—not just anyone, mind you, but someone as clever and kind and energetic as Lady Caroline herself. Susan had seen enough of marriage and childbearing not to believe that a woman of independent means might be a good deal happier free of such encumbrances as a husband and children. But Lady Caroline was so warm and so loving with her intimates that it would be the greatest of pities were she to spend the rest of her life as a solitary soul instead of being surrounded by the loving family she deserved. And if Susan could be instrumental in procuring this blessed state for her mistress, well then, she meant to spare no effort in doing so. Besides, little though she had seen of the Countess of Welham, Susan had taken an immediate dislike to the lady along with her hoity-toity abigail, and she had become possessed of a burning desire to outshine both of these self-satisfied and arrogant women. It was a challenge, to be sure, but one which she was more than eager to tackle. She made a vow that no matter what it took, she would look after her mistress so skillfully that both of these ladies would be forced to sit up and take notice.

Meanwhile, Susan's mistress was so intent on observing and remembering every detail of attire on every lady of fashion she saw, that she was not the least aware of the viscount until a genial voice boomed in her ear, ''Why I've seen men purchase a coach and pair with less scrutiny than you are subjecting this room to. Whatever are you looking at?''

Caro jumped. ''I'm sorry Tony, I didn't see you,'' she squeaked.

''That's as plain as the nose on your face. Now, if you were my sister, I should say that you were thinking that Lady So-and-So is looking hagged or the Marchioness-of-Whatever appears quite dowdy in that outmoded gown, and that nobody in the room can hold a candle to the Countess of Welham, but I feel reasonably sure that none of those thoughts has crossed your mind.''

''Well, no, I . . .'' Caro blushed. ''It's my maid, Susan, you see.''

The viscount looked blank.

"She dreams of becoming a dresser of the first rank and though I am little enough proof of her ability, I believe her to have some talent. Such aspirations should be encouraged, so I am trying to remember every detail to relate to her," Caro explained.

"Beside which, you would be bored to tears with all this frivolity if you did not have some higher thoughts to occupy your mind." A teasing smile lit up the viscount's amiable countenance.

"Well, yes," she admitted slowly.

"Now that you have fulfilled your duty, perhaps you will help me fulfill mine and dance with me." Seeing that she was about to refuse, he pleaded, "Come, be a good fellow, Caro. If you won't be my partner, Lavvy will see that I am not dancing and she will cast about for one of the many eligible young ladies she is forever throwing at my head and make me ask one of them—most likely Mary Throckmorton who is the most platter-faced thing you could ever hope to meet. Squints, as well. But Lavvy says that such things are of no account. The Throckmortons go back to the Conqueror and they also hang on to their blunt—not like poor Fotheringay whose good name doesn't seem to be impressing the duns." A gusty sigh escaped the viscount. "Why does life have to be so difficult? All a fellow wants to do is keep a good stable, set a good table, and take in a mill or two with his friends, but people won't let one alone," he complained with such a darkling look in his sister's direction that Caro burst out laughing.

"Very well then, Tony, I shall be happy to have this dance with you. You can tell me all about the sweet goers you saw at Tattersall's the other day." She sighed enviously.

"You should have been there, Caro. I'm not in the market for a hunter just now, but Farnham is selling up and you should have seen his bay—most powerful shoulders and chest I ever remember having come across. If you dance with me, I shall tell you more." And excusing himself to Helena, the viscount led Caro onto the floor where he continued to regale her with descriptions of this thoroughbred and that hunter until Caro's mind was reeling.

"How lucky you are to be a man and go wherever you wish." Caro could not hide the wistful note in her voice.

The viscount was much struck. He had never thought a

great deal about it because his sister seemed to enjoy the hours she spent dressing and parading before the *ton* at balls, routs, and other fashionable locales. It had always seemed a dead bore to Tony, but he had assumed that females enjoyed that sort of thing. Now, hearing his cousin's tone, he began to realize how flat such an existence must be for women who were not like his sister. Lord, what if he had been born a woman and had been forced to have a come-out instead of being allowed to attend prizefights and race meetings? He shuddered at the thought and resolved to do more to make Caro's stay in London more interesting.

Not being precisely nimble-witted, the viscount had taken quite some time to arrive at these conclusions and the look of concentration on his face was so excruciating that Caro had not dared interrupt him until the dance had ended and they were in danger of being left the only couple on the floor. She coughed delicately to no effect. ''Tony!'' she hissed.

''Eh, oh.'' he came to with a start. ''What?''

''I am not accustomed to the fashionable world, but I can't think it is very good *ton* to stand like blockheads after the dance is over,'' she responded confidingly.

''Oh, sorry. No, of course not. Thinking, you see,'' he apologized.

''I know,'' she responded sympathetically, ''but perhaps you had better do it somewhere else.'' And they headed back to the alcove where Helena was seated with an amused expression on her face.

''Well, what I mean to say is that I had thought all females were alike,'' Tony replied, looking sheepish. Then, seeing the confusion on his partner's face, he tried again. ''Well, I mean, Lavvy likes these sorts of affairs, so naturally, I thought every woman did.''

Comprehension dawned. ''So you thought that I would of course find the same amusement in the *ton* as she did.''

''Yes. You see, well, I'm sorry for it. Should have known you were too much a right 'un not to be bored to tears. Stands to reason. Well, what I mean to say is, if I find it a dead bore, so must you and though I can't take you to a mill or to Tatt's, I could take you to something more exciting than this.'' The viscount dismissed the countess's brilliant assemblage with a derogatory wave of the hand.

Caro was hard put to it to stifle the spurt of laughter that rose up inside of her.

His brow, wrinkled for a moment in intense concentration, suddenly cleared. "I have it, the very thing! We'll go to Astley's!"

"Astley's? Famous! Papa took me there once years ago and ever since I have been dying to go back. I should love it."

"That's done then," Tony replied, thinking as he looked down into her shining eyes that she looked like the little girl years ago who had clapped her hands when he had let her ride his pony. He felt so pleased with himself that he was even able to greet his sister upon her return with some enthusiasm and lead her onto the floor.

8

IN FACT, everyone who attended the rout returned from it having enjoyed more than they had anticipated. Between Tony's irreverent attitude and his insouciant remarks, Helena and Caro had been tolerably amused while Lavvy, expecting to be welcomed back after her enforced absence from the most fashionable haunts of the *ton,* had not been disappointed. Her encounter with Nicholas had been most gratifying. Really, his succession to the title appeared to have made a man out of him. It lent an air of distinction to his already dashing good looks. And he had seemed to recognize a change for the better in her, if the admiration she had read in his eyes was anything to go by. Truly, this promised to be a most interesting Season.

In fact, Lavvy had not been a little put out when her only cicisbeo during her seclusion, Sir Evelyn Willoughby, arriving at the Countess of Mortmain's had immediately hurried over to beg her hand in the waltz and thank her profusely for allowing her sons' tutor to lend him assistance. Mr. Welbeck was a brilliant young man—so clever of the countess to have acquired his services. Since this was precisely the reason Lavvy had hired the bibliomaniac tutor, she should have been highly gratified at the success of her stratagem. But all of a sudden, Sir Evelyn, his effusive thanks, and his undying appreciation were far less important now that the Marquess of Everleigh had appeared on the scene. After all, Sir Evelyn was taking up a dance she could have shared with Nicholas. Still, it would not do to appear too interested in the marquess, so she had bestowed a brilliant smile on the enraptured Sir Evelyn and allowed him to lead her to the floor.

For his part, Nicholas had remained in a pleasant state of abstraction the rest of the evening. While he labored under no illusions as to Lavinia's character, he had been unable to erase entirely the thoughts of his lost love. To discover her again, even more beautiful than he had remembered all those years he had spent abroad fighting Boney, had been something of a shock. Especially since she was so delighted to see him. She seemed so much more approachable now, so much warmer and more welcoming than ever before. Perhaps marriage and motherhood had softened her. It most certainly appeared so. A cynical voice in his head warned the marquess that spoiled beauties were likely to remain just that, but he silenced it by vowing to keep an open mind while letting his curiosity get the better of him.

It was in the interests of furthering this inquiry that the marquess appeared the next day on the countess's imposing doorstep, bearing an exquisite bouquet of hothouse blooms, ruthlessly plucked from the conservatory at Daventry House.

Wigmore, finding himself in a quandary, hesitated when the handsome gentleman asked for his mistress. On the one hand, the countess never appeared before one o'clock. On the other, she never turned away an admirer of such obvious attractions as the marquess. The butler decided that it was better to err in favor of the gentleman and went off in search of Miss Crimmins who could share some of their mistress's wrath with him should he have made the wrong decision. Before doing so, however, Wigmore led the marquess to the drawing room at a stately pace, bidding him wait while he went to alert the countess.

It was some time before Nicholas, adjusting his eyes to the light streaming into the room, realized that he was not the only occupant.

Her chair pulled up to a boulle table that more nearly resembled a sphinx than an article of furniture, Caro, with her chin propped in her hands, was absorbed in the latest issue of *The Edinburgh Review*. So engrossed was she that she was oblivious to the slight chunk of the doors as Wigmore closed them behind him, nor did she look up as the marquess quietly crossed the carpet to stand next to her.

For his part, Nicholas was somewhat startled to discover his antagonist of the previous week so firmly ensconced in Grosvenor Square. Then considering Lavvy's widowed state and her recent emergence from mourning, he supposed Caro's presence there made perfect sense. Judging from what he had divined of the lady's character and interests, the marquess felt quite certain that her appearance involved some duress. Hoping to confirm for himself the measure he had taken of her mind, Nicholas stole closer, trying to get a look at the article which was the object of such intense concentration. It was "Minutes of the Evidence taken before the Committee appointed by the House of Commons, to inquire into the State of Mendicity and Vagrancy in the Metropolis and its Neighborhood." The marquess's lip curled. He should have known that such a devoted bluestocking would not be reading anything less than a treatise on the causes of pauperism. However, in spite of his scornful attitude, he bent closer to read the opening sentence. Still Caro did not look up until he unwittingly leaned across the stream of light coming through the window. His shadow obscured the page. Caro jumped. "Good heavens! How you startled me! Do you always sneak up on a person like that?" she demanded crossly.

Nicholas was indignant in turn. "I didn't sneak up. I was conducted here in a perfectly respectable manner by Lavinia's butler. It was *you* who took *me* by surprise.

"Well, of all the unjust . . ." Caro began. Then her eye fell on the enormous bouquet. It was her turn to look scornful. Really, men were dreadfully stupid. Here was the person who had been so obviously and callously rejected by her cousin six years ago, yet one dance with Lavinia and he was back on her doorstep like a hopeful puppy. Caro was glad she had never been in love, nor did she intend to be. It made ordinarily intelligent people behave in the most ridiculous fashion.

Something of her train of thought revealed itself in her expressive face and Nicholas, feeling greatly at a disadvantage, was just about to embark on a long and tangled speech of self-defense when there was a commotion outside and the doors were flung open to reveal two mildly grubby little boys and Argos who, after his bath and some tender care, now more closely resembled the rest of the canine species.

"Cousin Caro, Cousin Caro," Cedric burst out. "Wigmore told us we would find you here." He stopped, surveying the pile of books and magazines with distaste. "But whatever are you doing with those things when it is such a glorious day outside?"

Caro laughed. "I was reading. Surprising as it may seem, sometimes the printed word can be very interesting."

A snort behind her brought to everyone's attention the

presence of a visitor. Clarence was the first to recover. "Excuse me, sir. If we had known Cousin Caro had a caller, we should not have interrupted," he apologized while his younger sibling looked the marquess up and down.

Unaccustomed to the bold scrutiny of a six-year-old, Nicholas was amused. He could see that his height and bearing were points in his favor, but the bouquet in his hands was definitely not."

"Are those for Cousin Caro?" Cedric asked suspiciously.

"No, they most certainly are not," the marquess and Caro snapped in unison and then stopped, each one looking slightly conscious at the surprise on the boys' faces.

Anxious to retrieve the situation before it deteriorated further, Caro continued, "But you were looking for me, were you not?"

"Well yes, but it is not all that important if you are busy," Clarence demurred.

"Yes it is," Cedric insisted. Then, seeing his brother's hesitation, he plunged in. "Well, it's about your horses. We were wondering if we might go visit them—that is, if Dimmock doesn't mind." Then, thinking that perhaps his new cousin might wonder that they were not on good terms with their own coachman, he added, "Of course, John is a very good fellow, but Mama's horses . . ." He rolled his eyes.

"That bad are they?" Caro was barely able to conceal her grin.

"Couple of bone-setters—showy, though," Ceddie acknowledged.

"Well, in that case, I suggest we not only visit my horses, but that we try them out and see if they meet with your approval."

The boys' eyes shone. "Thank you ever so much, Cousin Caro. It's most kind of you." Clarence smiled at her shyly. "Mama never lets us come with her when she goes out in her carriage."

He sounded so wistful that Caro felt an urge to march upstairs, grasp her cousin's beautiful shoulders, and give her a good shake. But she suppressed it, contenting herself with, "What a pity. If only you could ride with me so you could get some exercise as well as some fresh air. But I had to send Tim back to Waverly for Xerxes." The instant she uttered these words, Caro was sorry, remembering Cedric's reference to Lavinia's strictures concerning ponies. Hastily covering up this faux pas, she continued, "Come along then. I must fetch my bonnet and send word to have the carriage brought 'round. I am sure the marquess will excuse us."

And with that, she quitted the room with such dispatch that she left Nicholas wondering if there was something wrong with him that she always dismissed him so precipitately or if it was just her manner with everyone. Whatever it was, he admitted reluctantly that he found it just the tiniest bit disconcerting.

"I do wish that Cousin Caro would talk to Mama, maybe she could convince Mama it is alright for us to have ponies," Cedric's voice broke into the marquess's thoughts.

"Do you not ride then?" Nicholas was incredulous.

"She thinks that we are too young. We might hurt ourselves," Clarence explained. "Mama is extremely solicitous of our welfare because she says that now we are all she has left," he defended his parent, but there was an undercurrent of weariness in his voice that left the marquess with the impression that this last was an oft repeated phrase trotted out when there was any difference of opinion between the countess and her sons.

"Oh, I see. Well, yes, that explains it," Nicholas replied, though, having been hoisted on his first pony at the tender age of two and never having suffered any ill effects, he most certainly did not see. And where was the boys' uncle in all this? Surely the horse-mad Tony Mandeville could not be aware of the true state of affairs as he would never have allowed it to continue for so long. Then, considering more carefully Anthony's carefree bachelor existence and Lavinia's frequent complaints about her brother's ramshackle ways, Nicholas could understand Tony's playing least-in-sight around Grosvenor Square. He sighed. It was a great pity though, and something should be done about it.

"Now that Cousin Caro is here," Ceddie began confidently, "and she knows how much we want ponies, she'll convince Mama to let us have them. After all, she made her allow us to have Argos here and he has been no trouble. Well," he amended carefully, "almost no trouble. Luckily Cousin Caro found the tassels he chewed off the draperies in the morning room and gave them to Susan to sew on before Mama noticed."

"Argos?" Nicholas surveyed the dog with new appreciation. He remembered Lavinia's aversion to his own beloved spaniel, Prince, all too well.

"Yes. Cousin Caro says he's a rare Transylvanian Long Hair." Clarence rose quickly to the defense of their new companion. "Cousin Caro also says that her friend Princess Esterhazy is most desperate to acquire one and that Argos' owner must be quite frantic at his loss so Mama said we must keep him until the owner can be found." Observing the gleam of amusement in the marquess's blue eyes, he hesitated, "Is there such a thing as a Transylvanian Long Hair, sir?"

"Of course n . . ." Nicholas paused, unwilling to ruin such a piece of strategy and one so kindly meant. "Of course. I don't know whether it is a hound or a terrier, but I do believe I have heard of such a breed." He struggled to keep his tone as serious as possible, "But then, it is so rare, that it is entirely possible that no one is very familiar with it."

"There! You see, Clarence? I told you so!" Cedric exclaimed triumphantly.

Clarence remained unconvinced. "Yes, I see what you mean, sir," he concluded doubtfully, cocking his head to look speculatively at the marquess. He was rewarded with a significant wink, confirming his initial impression that the marquess was a right one just like Cousin Caro. In fact, he reflected, judging from his encounters of the past week, perhaps grown-ups weren't half bad after all. Before he could explore this revelation further, he heard his cousin's brisk step in the hall and Wigmore's sepulchral voice informing her that the carriage awaited them. "Come, Ceddie. We mustn't keep the horses or Cousin Caro waiting," Clarence admonished his brother. Turning to the marquess, he held out his hand, "It was a pleasure to meet you, sir and . . . thank you."

Nicholas shook it gravely. "The pleasure was mine, I assure you." He smiled, thinking as he did so that he had made a far more favorable impression in the few brief moments with these two children than he had in either of his encounters with their cousin. They were charming boys, he concluded as he watched them run downstairs. Their mother would have made sure of that, but he wondered what sort of boyhood they had living the hothouse existence that they did. Unconsciously following the example set by Caro, he resolved to do what he could to make their lives more exciting.

9

THIS PLAN WAS FOREMOST in his mind when Lavinia appeared in the drawing room some ten minutes later. "Why Nicholas," she exclaimed floating gracefully toward him, one delicate white hand extended. "How perfectly charming to see you. When Wigmore told me who was below I positively rushed Crimmins through my toilette. I am sure I must look a dreadful fright," she sighed, knowing full well that every curl was in place under the dainty Parisian mobcap and that the pelerine collar of her pink jaconet morning dress framed her face to perfection, its delicate tint making her appear as youthful as when Nicholas had first met her.

The marquess's eyes swept appreciatively over the countess, well aware that the charming disarray of curls peeking out from under the cap owed far more to art than haste. Well enough versed in the ways of females, he felt reasonably certain that she had changed her costume the moment a visitor was announced.

In fact she had. The instant Wigmore had disappeared, she had rounded on Crimmins who was struggling with the buttons of a shaded yellow jaconet with stripes, "Crimmins, not *that* old thing! Why it makes me look positively hagridden!"

"But madam selected this one," the abigail responded firmly. Devoted though she might be to her lady, Crimmins was not about to assume blame that was not hers.

"That's as may be, but you should know better than to let me choose it," Lavinia snapped.

The maid smiled grimly to herself as she went in search of a replacement. So, this Marquess of Everleigh was a personage of some importance to her ladyship. It was not a name Crimmins had heard before. This would bear some watching. Perhaps she would even unbend enough to share a cup of tea with Mr. Wigmore in the interests of gaining more information.

It was a great pity, that it was, that his lordship had died so unexpectedly leaving her mistress widowed like that, and her so gay and full of life. Not that his lordship could hold a candle to his wife. Oh, he had been as kind as could be, lavishing both mistress and maid with every conceivable luxury, but he had not had much in the brain box, poor man. It had taken all his mental faculties, not to mention an extremely knowledgeable valet to turn him out as exquisitely as he always appeared. But beyond that, he had not had much thought for anything else. It had been Lavinia who had created the brilliant gatherings and filled his amiable silences with gay chatter. It was the Countess of Welham who had made the couple into the leading lights of the fashionable world. Well, Crimmins hoped this new gentleman was someone who was more worthy of her mistress and one who would give her the gaiety she needed so much, poor lamb. And tucking one ringlet under the cap, Crimmins had sent her mistress on her way with no less excitement and hope than her devoted servant harbored in her desiccated breast.

For all her angular frame and dour expression, Miss Crimmins possessed the soul of a romantic. She had taken one look at the Countess of Welham's melting blue eyes and delicate figure and had become her devoted slave—not that she would ever have admitted to such a thing. In spite of the warnings from the other servants about my lady's selfishness and her uncertain temper, Crimmins had taken the position with alacrity. If her mistress were demanding, why so she should be. Anyone as beautiful and petted as Lavinia could not help herself. And if she seemed oblivious to the needs of others, how could she help it, beset as she was on all sides by eager admirers who demanded her attention.

All the small displays of temperament, the heedlessness to others' comfort were invariably forgiven when Lavinia, exhausted from some ball, would allow Crimmins, who had waited until all hours for her return, to brush her hair, massage her forehead, and dab her temples with lavender water, remarking as she gave herself up to these tender ministrations, "It is not easy being an incomparable, Crimmins. People are forever wanting your attention and they are always ready to notice a wrinkle or a spot, or when you are not looking quite the thing.'' And Crimmins would murmur soothingly, knowing that her mistress would be restored by the inevitable barrage of floral tributes that would appear in Grosvenor Square the following morning. She hoped that this time around, the countess would find someone strong enough to take care of her and keep her from tiring herself out as she always did in an effort to respond to her constant court of admirers.

In the meantime, much the same thoughts were going through her mistress's head as she peeped provocatively up at Nicholas over the fragrant bouquet he offered. ''How lovely they are, Nicky,'' Lavinia sighed dreamily. ''I do love beautiful things, and it's been so long since anyone has brought me flowers.'' She allowed just a hint of tears to sparkle in the big blue eyes. Then, with a brave attempt at gaiety, she laughed, ''Though I vow, you must have stripped the conservatory bare. Foolish man, you always were so extravagant.'' She dimpled up at him, treating him to the full and devastating effect of her rosebud mouth, pearly teeth, and sweeping lashes.

Nicholas smiled down at her appreciatively. ''I find that hard to believe, Lavvy. You always had an admiring entourage around you, lavishing you with tributes, and now you are more beautiful than ever.''

She looked up at him wide-eyed, ''Really?''

''Truly. You may depend upon it. You know that I am not like one of your town beaux. I do not offer Spanish coin.''

''No, you never did.'' A tiny smile hovered at the corner of her mouth. ''But there are no beaux now. Widows are not very amusing, you know, and no one wants to call on one.'' Her voice quavered pathetically. ''You know me, Nicky. I must have gaiety, music, and laughter, and I have been immured in this house with no one, positively no one to keep me amused.''

In spite of himself, Nicholas was touched. He knew, and had known since the disastrous evening she had rejected him, that Lavinia was a vain and frivolous creature. And he knew how miserable she must have been when cut off from the admiration and excitement to which she was accustomed.

Having been the center of attention all her life, she would have had no resources to fall back on for amusement. She must have been amazingly bored and lonely. Imagining her in this state brought to mind someone else who would have reveled in it. He could picture Lady Caroline Waverly delighted with the excuse to keep the world at bay and plunge into her projects and her books and he could not help remarking to himself on the irony of it all.

"Nicky," a silvery voice interrupted his fit of abstraction.

He started. "Beg your pardon, Lavvy. I was just thinking how flat your life must have been. We shall have to do something about it." And before he knew it, the marquess found himself extending an invitation to the countess and her companions for an evening at the opera.

Lavinia was all grateful delight. "Oh, Nicky, I knew you would understand. I knew I could count on you to rescue me." She clung to one muscular arm. "You always were kinder than my other admirers.

"Just not as brilliant a catch," he could not help replying sardonically.

"Oh no, Nicky!" Lavvy was scandalized at such plain speaking. "It was never that! You were always my favorite, but Papa and Mama would never have countenanced my marriage to a younger son."

Nicholas's vision of the bluff Earl of Mandeville did not precisely coincide with this interpretation, but he let it pass. However, some doubt must have revealed itself in his face for Lavvy continued hastily, "Of course, I was excessively fond of Herbert, but I felt none of the passionate attachment toward him that I did toward you."

She looked so earnest, her big blue eyes pleading, and the hand on his sleeve trembling slightly, that Nicholas almost believed her, but somehow he could not entirely wipe from his mind the way she used to pull away during his most ardent lovemaking with a light laugh and some excuse—he was pulling her dress, disarranging her coiffure, or stepping on her slipper. Still, he supposed that in her own way, she was speaking the truth.

It was difficult to picture anyone being passionately attracted to the foppish Earl of Welham, no matter how convivial he was. So whatever Lavinia had felt towards the dashing Captain Daventry had been bound to be more intense than the emotions she experienced toward her husband.

Nicholas smiled reassuringly at her, "You flatter me,

Lavinia, but I thank you for the compliment, just the same. And now I am afraid I must go. I promised Mama and Clarissa that I would drive them in the park. I look forward to escorting you to the opera.''

She glanced coyly up at him, ''I shall count upon it, but I depend upon you to tell me how to go on. I vow I am tremendously rusty after this period of isolation and I no longer have the least notion how to conduct myself.''

''Nonsense! I saw you at the Countess of Mortmain's rout. As always, you were the cynosure of all eyes. You have not lost your power to charm even the coldest of men.''

She laughed gaily. ''Naughty man! Does nothing escape your eagle eye? You always were too observant by half. Now be off with you, for I have a dressmaker coming. I must refurbish my wardrobe. I have not a single thing to wear that is not black or gray and I am extremely *ennuyée* with looking so hag-ridden. Black is not my best color and I find myself heartily sick of it.'' She glided over to ring for Wigmore.

''Lavvy, you know there is not a color in the world in which you do not look perfectly charming, but I can see how you might be looking forward to a wider selection for your new wardrobe, which, I have no doubt, will be as exquisite as always,'' he responded gallantly, bowing over her hand.

''And now who is the flatterer, my lord?'' Lavvy teased, but she could not hide the satisfaction in her voice. ''Do not be a stranger, Nicholas,'' she admonished as he followed the silent butler to the door. Really, Lavinia thought to herself in annoyance, must Wigmore always be so prompt?

Driving through the park sometime later with his mother and sister, Nicholas was reflecting on the latest encounter with his lost love. There was no denying that her beauty continued to exert its heady power over him despite his acknowledgment of her vanity. Lavinia was still the creature of the fashionable world that she had always been, but her widowhood seemed to have softened her in some indescribable way, and he found himself feeling sorry for her.

For her part, Lavvy was well satisfied with the outcome of the marquess's visit. Secure in her own power to attract, she had felt confident of his favorable response at such a public place as the Countess of Mortmain's rout. But given the churlish way he had gone off and left her after she had pointed out the impossibility of their marrying, then going all through the war without so much as a word, she had not been at all sure if he would pursue her beyond their encounter at the rout.

His subsequent call had been promising, but it could have been merely the result of good manners. Certainly he had not singled out anyone else for his attention the rest of the evening at the countess's. Lavvy had made sure of that. But there had been a look in his eyes today, as though he were assessing her, passing some sort of judgement on her, and Lavinia had not been altogether certain how to act. Deciding to play the part of the lonely widow had been just the right touch. The moment her eyes had filled with tears, his face had softened and she could see traces of her own former adoring Nicholas. Yes, she sighed with satisfaction as the dressmaker pinned and draped, events were proceeding very well indeed.

Not that the Countess of Welham had been entirely bereft of cicisbeos since her seclusion, but she had not been able to continue with the retinue of admirers she had formerly attracted, nor had she been able to flaunt them in public. To be sure, Sir Evelyn Willoughby had been extremely devoted, but having someone visit you ostensibly to discuss old books with your sons' tutor or because he was interested in the education of your boys was not the same as having a devoted gallant. Well, all that was changed now and Lavinia looked forward to making the most of it.

Meanwhile, the object of the countess's congratulatory musings was being boisterously hailed by her brother. "Nicky!" Tony exclaimed joyously, easing an enormous and fidgety bay through the press of riders in the direction of the marquess's carriage. "Glad to see you in town, old fellow." He ran an experienced eye over the marquess's cattle. "Those Wilmington's grays? Lucky dog! I've had my eye on them for months. Didn't know he was selling up."

Nicholas grinned. "That's because you move with too rackety a crowd. We serious older fellows stick together. He wouldn't part with his precious pair to a mere whipster like you who has more bottom than sense. He wanted nothing less than the head of an ancient titled family for these. But here, say hello to Mama and Clary."

"Delighted to see you here," Tony extended a huge paw

to the marchioness before turning to her daughter. "By Jove, but you've turned into a taking little thing," he exclaimed.

Clary laughed and blushed. The viscount's astonishment was too patent to be anything but absolutely genuine and it did more for her spirits than she realized. "Now Tony, I thought you only reserved such flattery for horses. If you stay on the town much longer, you will be in danger of becoming a ladies' man."

He pulled a face of mock horror. "Never say so!" Then, catching sight of another elegant equipage pulled by an equally stunning pair, he boomed, "Cousin Caro," and waved her over towards the group.

Dimmock, displaying a skill equal to the viscount's maneuvered between a lumbering barouche and a precariously balanced phaeton to reach them.

"Well, now I am cast totally in the shade and my reputation with Clarence and Cedric is ripped to shreds," Caro declared, running an eye over the marquess's team. "Where did you find such a stunning pair?"

"Don't be a nodcock, Caro." Tony was disgusted. "Don't you see they're Wilmington's grays? Even the merest whipster would recognize them."

"You forget, Tony, that I have been leading an exemplary life deep in the country, not frivoling it away in the metropolis where *some* people seem to have nothing better to do than ogle other people's cattle," she teased.

"Now, Caro, you know that ain't so. Why I've been down at Mandeville this age. I've only come up to London because Mama and Lavvy would worry me to death if I weren't here to escort Lavvy around. And what's a fellow to do for amusement, I ask?" Tony was aggrieved.

"And certainly the latest crop of fillies on display at Tattersall's is far more interesting than that being paraded around at Almack's, not to mention a good deal less threatening." Caro fixed the viscount with a wicked smile.

With some effort, Clarissa was able to maintain her composure, but Nicholas laughed outright. Tony grinned good-naturedly. "Touché, Coz. But Wilmington's grays are more than just any matched pair. And he wouldn't sell them to just any well-breeched swell. Nicky may talk head of the family, but I'll wager it's his hands more than his lineage that convinced Wilmington. I've seen him handling them—most sensitive mouths and most responsive pair I've seen in a long time. It takes the lightest of touches to guide them and a strong arm to hold 'em once they're sprung.''

For a man of as few words as the viscount, this was praise indeed. Impressed by this encomium, Caro and her companions looked at the marquess with new respect. ''You are very daring to ride behind such a high-spirited team,'' she remarked to Clarissa.

''Oh, no,'' Clary responded, smiling shyly at Caro. ''I trust him implicitly.'' But at Caro's skeptically raised eyebrow, she chuckled and added a hurried disclaimer, ''Well, by that I mean that I trust I shall either be dead or survive unscathed. In either case, I shall not be subjected to a physically painful experience.''

''Clarissa!'' Her mother was shocked. ''How can you say such a thing when Nicky was so kind as to volunteer to take us for a drive in the park?''

''I do not disagree, Mama. Nicky is solicitude itself where we are concerned.'' Clarissa's eyes softened as they rested on her brother. ''But that does not blind me to the risks he takes once he has the ribbons in his hands.''

''Now Clary, must you be so brutally honest? You alarm Mama and she will not let you ride with me. Then where will you be when you wish to take the air?'' For all his bantering tone, there was an expression of concern that Nicholas was unable to hide as he glanced at his fragile sister swathed in shawls. Despite her wrappings, she had a becoming flush on her cheeks, inspired by the fineness of the day and the bustle around her which she could enjoy from the safety of the carriage without having to participate.

A casual but not entirely uninterested observer, Caro was surprised and just the slightest bit intrigued by this interchange. It certainly revealed a hitherto unexpected side of the marquess's character. Somehow Caro had not expected that the dashing soldier, the romantic lover, or the arrogant lord would be such a devoted brother and it gave her pause. Perhaps she had been a trifle harsh in her critical attitude toward him. Caro resolved to be more open-minded in the future.

10

HOWEVER, THIS NEW perspective on the marquess disappeared some evenings later as he arrived to escort the countess, her cousin, and her cousin's companion to the opera. Another huge floral tribute had arrived that day for Lavinia, who had left Caro no doubt as to its origin. "It's from Nicky," she declared, not bothering to conceal the triumphant note in her voice. "I vow, that man is the most importunate suitor. One would have thought that all those years in the army and now his assumption of the responsibilities entailed in being head of the family might have sobered him, but he is as impetuous as ever, dear boy—and so handsome," Lavinia concluded dreamily.

Heartily sick of listening to the catalogue of the marquess's obvious attractions, Caro was about to inquire as to the nature of the performance they were about to attend. To be sure, Lavinia had said it was the opera, but whose and which one? Who was to perform? Having scorned the empty pleasure-seeking life of the *ton*, Caro had never given the slightest thought to the other amusements the capital might offer, merely being thankful she was free to avoid it. Now, all of a sudden, it occurred to her that there were many delightful things she might have missed in her dogged avoidance of the *ton* and its haunts. "Cousin . . ." she began, only to be interrupted by Lavvy as she continued.

"Truly, he is far more masterful than the Duke of Hatherill or Lord Edgecombe," the countess dismissed with a pretty shrug of her shoulders the two gentlemen to whom Nicholas had once compared so unfavorably, and then she bent down to absorb the heady scent of the bouquet, congratulating herself on the success of her campaign thus far.

"Lavvy," Caro began again.

Reluctantly, Lavvy abandoned her daydream of a love-smitten Marquess of Everleigh on bended knee pleading with

her to do him the honor of becoming his Marchioness.
"What?"

"I was just wondering what opera we are to see?"

"Lord, I don't know. What does it signify? If Nicholas
has chosen to escort us, we are certain of enjoying ourselves," she responded sharply.

To Caro, the presence of the Marquess of Everleigh was
not necessarily a guarantee of the success of an evening,
but seeing she would get nowhere with her cousin, she gave
up.

"I believe that the *Times* was advertising *Le Nozze di
Figaro*, but it did not list the performers," a quiet voice
added from the corner of the drawing room.

"Thank you, Helena. That will be wonderful. I could
look forward to anything, but I had liefer it were Mozart
than Handel." Caro's eyes lit up with anticipation. She had
heard arias performed at musicales, but never an entire opera
and suddenly an evening at which she had dreaded being an
uncomfortable but necessary accessory to Nicholas's and
Lavvy's flirtations actually seemed accessory to Nicholas's
and Lavvy's flirtations actually seemed to hold promise of
enjoyment.

"If it is not Catalani singing then it does not matter, for
one cannot truly claim to have been to the opera with any
hope of impressing the *ton* unless one can say they have
heard the Catalani. But enough of this. I must be going.
Madame Henriette promised to make a few alterations on
the gown I am to wear this evening."

Indeed, as Lavinia, clinging to the marquess's arm, made
her way to the box that evening, she looked as exquisite as
ever in a white lace dress over a white satin slip with a low,
tight corsage of rose-colored satin that revealed a creamy
expanse of bosom and emphasized the faint flush in the
countess's cheeks. Following in her cousin's wake, Caro felt
extremely plain indeed in a serviceable white crape over
white sarcenet. Until now, if she had thought about it at all,
she had been perfectly satisfied with its simple lines; but
next to Lavinia's gown, it appeared positively dowdy.

Stop it, Caro Waverly, she admonished herself. You
should be above such things. You know you wouldn't wish
to spare half the time for your toilette that Lavvy does, so
don't repine now. But somehow this salutary scolding could

not stop the most unwelcome pang of envy that struck her
when she observed the look in the marquess's eyes as they
rested appreciatively on her cousin. Nor was the marquess
the only one enjoying the picture Lavvy presented. Caro
could see quizzing glasses raised in several boxes as the
Countess of Welham took her seat and acknowledged these
admiring glances with a small satisfied smile.

Caro sighed. She had thought she was above such mean-
spirited thoughts. *And you are,* she resolved, giving herself
a mental shake and forcing herself to turn her attention to
the stage. In a short while, her conscious attempt to fix her
thoughts elsewhere was rewarded and she became engrossed in the opera with no thought in her head but the
beauty of the music and the exquisite voices. Her spirits
soared. Not since her arrival in London had she been so
absorbed in something and she felt like the old Caro, free
to follow her own interests without having to be forever
conscious of the observations and strictures of the fashionable world around her.

Her total preoccupation with the spectacle before her was
tangible. Glancing in the direction of Lavinia's companions
to assure himself of their comfort, Nicholas was struck by
the thought that he had never seen Lady Caroline Waverly
so relaxed and happy. This was succeeded by an even more
surprising revelation which was that her pleasure in the entire scene made her appear quite pretty—beautiful in fact.
The marquess had never really stopped to consider Caroline
as a female before. She had always been Lavinia's younger
cousin and as such had paled in comparison to the older,
more sophisticated woman. In their initial encounter this
year she had figured as an adversary, though an adversary
worth reckoning with, at that. Since then, the evidence of
her erudition and her pedagogical bent had caused him to
write her off as a bluestocking, one of those charmless females who preferred to overwhelm their fellows with ped-
antry rather than relate to them as human beings. Now,
however, observing the sparkle in the gray eyes and the full
red lips which were parted in breathless anticipation, he
began to revise his opinion.

Just as the marquess was digesting these new and slightly
unsettling perceptions, the door to the box opened and a
tall, exquisitely attired gentleman entered. The lights glinting off silvered locks, and the magnificent ruby buried in a

snowy cravat contrasted with the severity of a dark coat tailored to perfection.

"My dear Countess, I am enchanted to see that you were so encouraged by your reception at the Countess of Mortmain's that you are once again gracing society. May I be the first to inform you that the world has been an extremely dull place without you?" he murmured bending low over Lavinia's hand.

"You are too kind, Sir Evelyn. I have not been out of society so long that I do not recognize the most blatant flattery," Lavinia responded modestly. However, her triumphant expression belied the gracious disclaimer. "And what brings you here? I thought, purist that you are, you avoided the theatrics of opera in favor of the more restrained pleasures of the Academy of Ancient Music."

The exquisite gentleman sighed, "How true, but one will sacrifice a great deal for the pleasure of convivial company and Fortescue absolutely insisted we come to *Figaro.*" Then, recollecting his surroundings, he smiled apologetically and continued, "But do introduce me to your companions. Nicholas I am well-acquainted with. I am reasonably certain that, barbarian that he is, he can have only one aesthetic reason for attending such an evening." He smiled meaningfully at Lavinia who summoned up a conscious blush as she laid a possessive hand on her escort's arm.

"Of course you know the Marquess of Everleigh. This is my cousin, Lady Caroline Waverly and her companion, Miss Helena Gray."

The newcomer looked at Lavinia's companions with some interest for he had been one of the crowd surveying the theater through his quizzing glass. He had remarked upon these two unusual ladies who, oblivious to the critical observations, the malicious comments, and the general drama of gossip enacted all around them, were actually concentrating upon the action on stage. Furthermore, they were, to all intents and purposes, enjoying it immensely. Intrigued by such a novelty, Sir Evelyn could not help inquiring, "And pray tell me, ladies, how do you find the entertainment at hand?"

Caro turned a glowing face toward him. "Oh, I am enjoying it immensely, thank you. The characters do remind one of those in a Shakespearean comedy. Of course, part of the success of this is owing to the librettist, but what I find most fascinating is that somehow through his music Mozart manages to imbue his characters with a unique personality. Helena and I were just remarking at the extraordinary individuality his musical passages confer upon them. Personally, I prefer *Don Giovanni* for the power of the music, but this is an extremely accomplished piece of work. I had not fully appreciated it before.''

His curiosity piqued, Sir Evelyn pulled up a chair and sat down next to the two women. ''I find it highly unusual that you should feel this way, for most people, if they stop to consider it all prefer his *Abduction from the Seraglio* which is indeed a most attractive piece of music.''

''Yes,'' Caro tilted her head considering this carefully, ''but I believe that its chief recommendation is that it has an aria here or there which demands a great deal of skill from the performers, while in this opera it is the musical whole which captures the attention. Most people seek the sensational performance over the subtly accomplished which is what this calls for.''

Sir Evelyn appeared much struck by this interpretation. ''I do believe you may be in the right of it, Lady Caroline— a sad commentary on the taste of the general public, but nonetheless true.'' He shook his head.

''Well, I don't repine,'' Caro declared stoutly. ''I find that I am forever at odds with the *ton* so I have become accustomed to it.''

Sir Evelyn laughed gently before turning his attention to the countess, who was becoming annoyed that the general conversation appeared to be turning to such a boring topic. Overhearing Caro's last remark, the marquess could not help but concur. He had been listening—at first, most unwillingly but critically to the dialogue. It was just the pedantic sort of conversation he had come to expect from Lady Caroline, but the more it continued, the more intrigued he became. Certainly the discussion was far more enlightening than his companion's animadversions on the quiz of a gown that Abigail Beauleigh had seen fit to appear in or how hagridden Sally Jersey was looking. The more he considered it, the more Nicholas remarked upon the contrast Caro's conversation offered to her cousin's. It was true that unlike Lavvy, she did not manage to look absolutely enchanting with every utterance. But on the other hand, she had no need to. What she had to say was interesting enough in and of itself to capture attention. Unable to refrain from commenting, the marquess turned to Caro, "So you are not an admirer of the Singspiel tradition, then, Lady Caroline?"

"In general, no," she replied cautiously, well aware of the challenging gleam in his blue eyes. "Of course it is all very pretty and the *Magic Flute* a more uplifting work than the rest, but ordinarily I prefer the richness and complexity of Mozart's other operas. And you, my lord?" It was Caro's turn to raise one interrogative dark brow.

The marquess found himself at the *point non plus*. On the one hand, he was congratulating himself with a certain grim satisfaction for having known that Lady Caroline would naturally be drawn to the more intellectual and challenging aspects of Mozart's compositions. After all, no bluestocking worthy of the name would admit to enjoying those works that incorporated the songs and tales of popular culture. On the other, he was forced to admit that he himself found the particular school of Singspiel to be trivial and, at times, even dull. "I," he began, groping frantically for an answer that would show him to be a man of taste and intelligence while at the same time depressing her own intellectual pretensions, "Well, actually . . ." Unfortunately for him, Nicholas looked up for an instant while he grappled with this problem only to discover Lady Caroline regarding him with a twinkle of amusement in her big gray eyes and a sympathetic smile quirking the corners of her generous mouth.

"Never fear, my lord. I shan't tell a soul, especially Lavvy, that you happen to find yourself in agreement with a bluestocking," she whispered confidentially.

Nicholas was taken aback. Accustomed as he was to being far more perceptive than his fellow man, he was unused to having his cynical observations interpreted so accurately. Even less was he accustomed to being confronted with them. Ordinarily an articulate man, he found himself at a momentary loss for words.

"Yes, I expect it is a trifle disconcerting to have one's negative opinion thrown in one's face, but I believe it is always a salutary experience," Caro teased.

A reluctant grin tugged at his lips. "Salutary perhaps, but lowering, nonetheless. However I do not apologize for thinking you a bluestocking when you try so very hard to ensure that one thinks of you as nothing else,'' he responded with a chuckle.

Caro laughed. ''You are quite in the right of it, but far from being insulted that you are forced to view me in such a dreary light, I am made most comfortable by it.''

''Comfortable?'' Nicholas was again nonplussed.

''Yes, comfortable. Most women do not wish to be thought bluestockings for fear of being considered too serious to be attractive when the *ton* demands that they be an ornament to society rather than a critic of it. And for most women who must make marriage their goal, the risk of being thought unattractive is to be avoided at any cost. Nor can they afford to offend any male. Therefore, every man is fair game and subject to their stratagems to win acclaim and possibly a husband. Thus, a man must be constantly on the alert to preserve his freedom. However, a man conversing with a woman who is not consumed with the idea of such pursuit may relax and pay attention to the matter at hand rather than worrying about being caught in the parson's mousetrap.''

Nicholas was silent for a moment, struck by the novelty of this opinion. ''You make it sound like some deadly game,'' he protested.

''It is, for the stakes are very high, are they not?''

''But very enticing, for all that matter, and it can be most exciting, depending on the players.'' A wicked grin spread over his features.

''I would not know,'' Caro responded stiffly.

''No, you would not, but you might try playing it before you condemn it out of hand. After all, experimentation is the best way to proceed if one wishes to establish the truth of one's theories. You might find it more pleasurable than you expect,'' he teased, a disturbing gleam in his eye.

''I . . .'' It was Caro's turn to be bereft of speech, but fortunately for her, Lavinia had decided that attention had been diverted from herself for long enough.

''Nicholas, the next act is beginning. You are distracting Caroline and she particularly wished to hear this opera. Come, tell me how your dear Mama goes on. I was charmed to see her the other night.'' Lavvy leaned forward to place a hand on his arm, allowing him a tantalizing view of a beautifully rounded bosom, but not before she had bestowed a brilliant smile on Sir Evelyn who, hearing the opening strains, took his leave.

Privy to her cousin's ploy to draw all eyes, or at least the male eyes, back to herself, Caro could not suppress her amusement. She quickly turned her head so that only Helena would see the cynical smile that rose to her lips.

However, it was not before the marquess, ever observant, had detected it. He frowned. That chit! How could she act so smug and superior to Lavinia when she had never put her mind to anything except her books. Books were all very well, but they were not so tricky to deal with or as unpredictable as human beings, particularly the male sex.

Out of the corner of her eye, Caro saw Nicholas's expression and a conscious look spread over her face. She ducked her head, smiling at him apologetically. She looked so guilty, and her gesture was at once so candid and so disarming, that the marquess had to fight back the crack of laughter that welled up inside him. To give Caro her due, the very transparency of Lavinia's stratagem was humorous. Heretofore, Nicholas had often reacted to Lavvy's unabashed self-centeredness in much the same way that Caro had, finding a certain ironic amusement in it all. What the marquess was finding difficult to bear was the thought of what Caro's impression must be of him. Though he had indulged Lavinia in her blatant pursuit of him and though it diverted him for the moment to cater to her whims, he was not the least taken in, nor was he the putty in her hands that it might seem. The marquess was very well aware that any wealthy, well-looking man would have fulfilled the countess's needs, particularly if he were a peer of such exalted rank as the Marquess of Everleigh. He was not a little intrigued by Lavvy's attempts to wipe out the past and recapture his interest, all of which took a certain amount of courage—a courage the marquess was inclined to admire. Dalliance with such an accomplished beauty was undeniably a pleasurable pursuit. Nonetheless, Nicholas did not wish to be regarded as a complete dupe, particularly by a mere slip of a girl. Though he could not explain exactly why Caro's opinion was of the least importance to him, it was.

Perhaps it was because of the remarkably clear-eyed way she seemed to view things, unhampered by the prejudices and preconceptions of the *ton*. It was a way of seeing that was so different from that of anyone else he knew, yet so

similar to his own perceptions of the world. Her judgment
was hers alone and perhaps that was why it meant so much
to him to have her look favorably upon him. At any rate, he
had found her last expression unusually appealing. It had
been self-deprecating, confiding, and, yes, almost intimate,
as though the two of them were the only participants in
some secret agreement.

Though beloved of his friends and the men he had commanded in the field, Nicholas Daventry had never had anyone to whom he had felt at all close or with whom he had
shared anything. He realized that this special moment of
rapport with Caro, though entirely novel, was rather pleasant and somehow reassuring. He had never sought out companionship before, primarily because no one had ever
seemed to understand how he thought or felt. Enjoying his
own ideas in private was infinitely preferable to attempting
an explanation of them to an uncomprehending and unap-
preciative companion.

Considering this, he realized that this was not the first
time he had sensed a peculiar understanding between himself and Lady Caroline Waverly. He smiled as he conjured
up the picture of the Christmas Waif sitting on the stairs,
with her glossy dark hair tumbled down her back, hugging
her knees as she commiserated with him over her cousin.
Suddenly, Nicholas felt an overwhelming urge to reassure
Caro that he didn't care in the slightest about Lavinia, that
he had been responding, as any gentleman would, to a lady
in obvious need of an escort, and that he was perfectly well
aware of the countess's machinations. But the opera ended
and he drove the ladies home, Lavvy chattering all the way,
without ever being able to say this. Frustrated, the marquess
determined to clear up this misconception at the earliest
possible moment.

11

HOWEVER, THE NEXT DAY when the marquess appeared at Grosvenor Square, it was to utter confusion. Wigmore cast a disparaging eye toward the drawing room from which emanated a babble of excited voices. "It's Master Tony, sir," he murmured apologetically as he led Nicholas upstairs and opened the doors upon the viscount, his two young nephews, and Lady Caroline Waverly.

"When are we going, Uncle Tony? Soon, soon?" Ceddie demanded eagerly.

"Why tonight, I expect, lad. That is, if you wish to see the Steel Castle with Uranda the Enchanter and the pantomime called *The Golden Age.*"

"Oh, yes please, sir," the little boy breathed, scarcely able to believe the treat that was in store for them.

"Will we see Mr. Astley himself?" Clarence wondered.

"No, he has long since passed away, but you will see Mr. Ducrow, the most bang-up rider you could hope to see," his uncle reassured him.

"Even in the deepest country I have heard of Mr. Ducrow," Caro added. "It is said that he is the greatest trick equestrian the world has ever produced. I should like to know how he does it, how he manages his horses and convinces them to let him perform the feats one is always hearing of."

"Well, of course you must come with us and see for yourself. You did say the other evening that you wished to go," Tony declared stoutly. "And bring Miss Gray if she wishes," he continued.

"Oh yes, do please join us, Cousin Caro," the boys joined in enthusiastically.

Caro blushed with pleasure, never having been able to remember the time when her presence had really been of importance to anyone. It was true that her father, who had loved her dearly, had taken her everywhere with him, but that had been different. And though she had always been most aware of his affection, she had never felt that she contributed much to any situation because she was far too young to have anything to offer. Later on, at school, the girls had been forever saying, "Oh, Caro, don't be such a high stickler" or "Don't be so serious," and though they had sought her out when they needed help with their lessons, they rarely included her in any of their schoolgirl pranks. Even Lavinia, though in desperate need of Caro's presence, had made it abundantly clear that she considered Caro herself something of a necessary bore.

But now, three faces were turned expectantly toward her, each one eager that she share the evening with them. "Why, thank you. I must first check with Lavinia to see if she needs me. If you are indeed certain you wish to include a lady in this particular outing, I should be delighted to come. I must say that when I read the description in the *Times* announcing the performance with the clowns, the pantomimes, and the scenery, not to mention Mr. Ducrow, I found myself quite longing to go."

"Good, it's settled then. Now I must be off because I told Coggeshall I would meet him at Manton's half an hour ago. I shall be back to collect you all later." The viscount grabbed his hat, nodded to Nicholas, and tore down the stairs at his usual breakneck speed.

"Hooray!" Ceddie exclaimed. "I'm glad you're going, Cousin Caro. Now we shall be merry as grigs."

A chuckle from the corner reminded them that they were not alone.

"I do beg your pardon, my lord, I was so intrigued by the prospect of the evening's entertainment that I had quite forgot you were here," Caro apologized.

She looked so stricken that Nicholas laughed outright. "Never mind. I recognize that a visitor such as I am quite cast in the shade by the delights of Astley's Amphitheater. You are always riding roughshod over my sense of consequence, are you not, Lady Caroline? No doubt it is good for my soul. However, I . . . ."

Whatever the marquess was feeling was lost in a whish of skirts, the scent of perfume, and the countess's silvery tones. "Nicholas, how delightful! Wigmore just informed me that you had arrived." Catching sight of the room's other occupants, Lavvy looked to be not best pleased and she continued more sedately, "But I see you are already being entertained. Clarence, Cedric, did you make yourselves properly known to the Marquess of Everleigh?"

"Yes, Mama," Clarence responded dutifully, wilting under his parent's minatory eye.

His younger brother, however, was made of sterner stuff. "Mama, Uncle Tony was here and he is taking us to Astley's Amphitheater this evening and we're going to see the Steel Castle and a pantomime and clowns and horses, and all sorts of wonderful things. And Cousin Caro is coming too," Ceddie burst out.

"That is, of course, unless you need me, Lavvy, but I could not recall that there was anything of importance we were to do this evening," Caro apologized.

"Oh no, nothing of importance," Lavvy began angrily, then warned by the wary look in Caro's and Nicholas's eyes that it behooved her to tread carefully, she laughed brittlely, "If that isn't just like Anthony, going off on one of his queer starts without consulting me. Why he doesn't even know what time Clarence and Cedric go to bed."

Seeing the boys' faces fall, Nicholas interjected hurriedly, "But I am certain the performance will not be that late and, after all, what can one late bedtime signify in the face of an opportunity such as this?" The marquess was unprepared for the rush of feelings that enveloped him as three pairs of grateful eyes turned in his direction. He had merely intended to be helpful, but when he saw how much the simple gesture meant to the boys, he was immensely touched. As for Caro, the smile that lighted up her face as one gray eye closed in a conspiratorial wink, again made him experience that special sense of intimacy and he found himself wishing he could join the merry little group at Astley's and share in their pleasure.

Nicholas felt certain that Caro's enjoyment of it all would be as intense as her appreciation of the opera had been the other evening. He suddenly realized what a pleasure it was to be with someone who was unsophisticated enough to participate unselfconsciously in the amusements London had to offer.

A delicate cough interrupted these reflections and recalled the marquess to the original purpose of his visit. "I can see that I have come, at least for one of you ladies, on

a fruitless errand. Mama is giving a small musicale this
evening—nothing formal, you understand—just a few friends
to hear Signor Clementi. We are fortunate enough to have
engaged him as Clary's pianoforte teacher and he has quite
kindly consented to give us an evening of music. I believe
he is even to play one piece with Clary. At any rate, Mama
has invited her friends and, without wishing to alarm Clary
who avoids social gatherings if at all possible, I was hoping
to include people more near her own age. However, an evening of the pianoforte, no matter how well performed, quite
pales in comparison to the delights of Astley's. But I would
take it as a special favor if you were to come, Lavinia.''
The marquess directed a devastating smile in the countess's
direction, knowing full well that she would prefer such tame
entertainment to an evening at home, especially if it would
put him in her debt.

The countess had not been the reigning toast of London
for nothing. "Well, I had rather planned . . ." She paused
as if weighing this invitation against a host of others, then
appeared to come to some decision. "Thank you, Nicky. It
will be lovely to see your dear Mama and sister again and
hear the news from home." She moved closer to the marquess, laying a possessive hand on his arm. "You really
must hear Nicholas's sister Clarissa play sometime, Caro.
She is truly a most accomplished performer and such a
charming young person. I vow I quite dote on her. We shall
have to introduce you to each other so that you can have a
friend closer to your age here in town. It is a pity that she
can not join the little party at Astley's.''

For all the world, as though I were the veriest schoolgirl,
Caro muttered furiously to herself. *Well, I shan't be put out.*
"Yes, I quite agree with you, Lavvy, and I look forward to
renewing our acquaintance which, though brief, was most
enjoyable,'' she responded sweetly, knowing full well how
her having made such a connection without Lavvy's help
would put her cousin's nose out of joint.

The significance of the interchange was not lost on the
marquess. He grinned appreciatively. So the little cousin
had claws did she? Lady Caroline Waverly might not aspire
to a place in the *ton*, but she did not appreciate being relegated to the ranks of green girls fresh from the schoolroom.
And Lavinia, though accustomed to dominating every scene,
did not relish any competition, even if it was from a mere

cousin who, as she had attempted to make abundantly clear, was young and inexperienced to the point of being gauche.

The marquess decided to take matters into his own hands. "Yes, Clary and Caro met when we were driving in the park. I should think Clary would be delighted to have a friend who will not only encourage her to take the air, but who is capable of carrying on an intelligent conversation at the same time—certainly a rarity in London. Perhaps I can drive the two of them the next fine day." He bowed in Caro's direction, thoroughly enjoying her conspiratorial smile. There, that should prove to her that he was not under the cat's foot, even if it were a foot as beautiful as the Countess of Welham's.

For her part, Caro was highly amused, and felt something else besides, that she could not quite put her finger on. Clearly, the man was not at all stupid. He had picked up on the undercurrents of her exchange with Lavinia, had read the innuendos correctly, and come immediately to her defense. He needn't have done it. Caro considered herself more than a match for her cousin any day, but she was oddly touched by his concern for her welfare and his willingness to take her part against someone who so very obviously considered him to be her territory. Unable to help herself, Caro smiled. Looking up into the twinkling blue eyes, she realized how very pleasant a thing it was to be understood and how very attractive this sympathy and camaraderie made a person appear.

A hand tugging at her skirt broke into these disturbing reflections.

"Cousin Caro, you said we could take some sugar to your horses because they are ever so fond of it. May we?"

The conversation among the three grown-ups, though short, had been significant enough to make them forget the existence of Ceddie and Clarence who, abashed by their mother's presence, had remained remarkably quiet. Now, however, Cedric had had more than enough of such inactivity.

Caro came to with a start. "Oh, goodness! Clarence, Ceddie, I quite forgot you were standing there. Dreadfully impolite of me. Yes, do let us go and feed the horses and you can tell me all that you know about Astley's. Let us bid good day to the marquess and then be off."

Smiling gratefully at Nicholas, Caro hurried from the

room, leaving the marquess thinking once again that he had never met a woman who left his presence so precipitately and with such apparent eagerness.

"Well, that's fixed then. I shall look forward to seeing you this evening, Lavinia." Nicholas snatched his hat and cane, leaving Lavvy, who had been preparing for a few moments of flirtatious tête-à-tête, seething with frustration.

However all signs of ill temper had been wiped away by the time she arrived at Daventry House that evening. She looked as enchanting as ever in pale pink satin which was nearly as delicate as her pink-and-white complexion and somehow made her appear as young and fresh as a girl in her first Season. Seeing her, the marquess hurried over with gratifying alacrity. "Lavvy." He bent over her hand, inhaling her heady perfume, and once again he was struck by the thought of how truly beautiful she was.

"I am come alone, Nicky. I hope no one is disconcerted, but I could see that Miss Gray truly preferred to join the schoolroom party at Astley's. She and Caro are so devoted to my two boys that it is quite touching to see, though entirely understandable. But you must forgive the prejudice of a fond mama."

This pretty speech, designed as it was to lay to rest any qualms the marquess might have after her previous display of annoyance, succeeded to some extent. Indeed, seeing the boys with their mother and Caro and observing the way they naturally turned to Caro for support and understanding had made it plain again to Nicholas that for Lavvy, the happiness, admiration, and comfort of the Countess of Welham was still her major preoccupation.

"That was kind of you, Lavinia. We shall do our best to see that you are well taken care of and do not lack for companionship." Nicholas smiled meaningfully down at her.

"I appreciate that, Nicky. I knew I could count on you to support a poor widow," Lavvy replied, an answering smile dimpling her bewitching mouth. Everything was proceeding to her satisfaction. In truth, Miss Gray would have preferred hearing the celebrated Clementi perform. Caro, knowing this, had urged her to accompany her cousin. But Lavvy was so insistent that the musicale would be very dull and that the boys truly needed the attention of both women because Tony was such a corkbrain that he might suddenly take it in his head to leave them while he went to talk to the riders or performers, that Caro had capitulated. However, it was not before her suspicions were thoroughly roused as to the motives behind Lavvy's uncharacteristic solicitude. Highly aware of her cousin's stratagem to have Nicholas to herself as much as possible, Caro oddly enough felt a degree of sympathy for the object of such a concerted campaign. She even had a thought to spare for his welfare as she and the others sat spellbound in the amphitheater.

Caro would have been astounded to know that at that particular moment, the Marquess of Everleigh himself was thinking about the little group at Astley's, and rather enviously at that. He had just led the Countess of Welham over to the alcove where his mother and sister were sitting and Lavvy was exclaiming her pleasure at seeing them again in tones designed to carry the message to all and sundry that she and the marquess's family were on the best of terms. The Marchioness of Everleigh beamed at her, but Nicholas could see that Clary was not fooled in the least. Nor could he help noticing that while Lavvy expressed her delight that Clary was able to make the trip to London, hoped that the constant activity was not too much for her, and assured her that she was most eager to hear her play, somehow she could not bring herself to look directly at his sister.

Nicholas was not deceived. He knew that Lavvy, cosseted as she had been her entire life, protected from every possible pain and unpleasantness, could not bear to be confronted with it now and was made excessively uncomfortable by the thought of his sister's disability, invisible as it was at the moment.

For some reason, this brought Caro to mind with her ever-ready sympathy, whether it was for rejected lovers or small boys leading a stifling existence. Thinking of small boys made him wonder how they all were enjoying themselves and he wished most desperately that he were there watching Mr. Ducrow's amazing feats of horsemanship and seeing the wonder of it all through their eyes. The marquess resolved to call at Grosvenor Square first thing the next day so he could share in some of the enthusiasm.

Nicholas was entirely correct in his picture of the little group. In fact, Helena was the only one not hanging breathlessly over the edge of the box as Mr. Ducrow, in the manner of Philip Astley himself, was prancing around the ring perched on the bare backs of two horses and looking for all the world as though he were doing nothing more unusual than walking in the park.

"How can he do such a thing!" Caro gasped.

The viscount grinned. "Practice, and a great deal of it, I should say, though you can see it is owing as much to the training of the horses as the skill of the rider. Magnificent beasts, aren't they?"

"But how do the horses know what to do? They can't talk, so how do they know?" Ceddie piped up.

"Oh, Mr. Ducrow knows how to talk to them, lad, never fear," his uncle assured him.

"He does?" Ceddie was round-eyed.

"Well, after all, you talk to Argos, don't you," Caro replied reasonably. "He knows when he is not supposed to do something. I expect Mr. Ducrow began with his horses in a very similar fashion."

"Oh." Ceddie digested this thoughtfully before continuing in a wistful little voice. "I wish Mama would let us have ponies."

"Your mama loves you very much and, as she is not a great rider herself, perhaps she is afraid you will hurt yourself on a pony," Caro responded, defending her cousin. Privately, she thought it had more to do with the countess's wish to have two docile children who were both clean and always at her beck and call. Caro vowed that she would continue to see that Ceddie and his brother were allowed to live more as little boys and less as accoutrements to their beautiful mother.

12

CARO HAD RECKONED without the Marquess of Everleigh in her plan to win Ceddie and Clarence more freedom. The very next morning at an unfashionably early hour she was sitting in the breakfast room perusing the *Times* and drinking her coffee—much to the disgust of Susan who stoutly maintained that one was not a true lady unless one had one's morning chocolate in bed—when the marquess was announced. "Oh goodness!" Caro strove madly to straighten her dishevelled curls, but not before the marquess had seen her struggling to smooth them and pin them in some sense of order.

He grinned. There was something very comfortable about coming in on a woman this way, knowing that she was completely herself, at ease and absorbed in something that interested her instead of having her enter beautifully gowned and coiffed with everything arranged in a manner designed to appeal to him. Actually, he reflected, he saw his mother and sister this way quite often, but it was so refreshing and somehow delightfully intimate to discover someone entirely unrelated to him in this state.

Nor did Caro blush and dissemble or make vain excuses when she was surprised thus. Looking him straight in the eye she remarked in a friendly fashion, "Good morning, my lord. Would you care for some coffee? I presume you have had breakfast, for no Englishman worthy of the name would stir abroad without it. However, if you have not, or would like a second helping, I should be happy to request some bacon and eggs. I expect the boys to be in at any moment and they, of course, will be simply ravenous."

Nicholas took the chair she indicated. "Thank you. As you have so correctly divined, I have been treated to a more than ample repast already, but I should like some coffee."

"Very well then, so should I. And I think, as I detect my

cousins' gentle tread upon the stairs, that I shall order
something substantial enough to keep them quiet. I . . .''

The pounding of feet cut her short and two fair-haired
bundles of energy rushed into the room. "Cousin Caro,
Cousin Caro, do you think we could go for a drive in the
park today and do you think Dimmock would let me hold
the reins for a little while?" Ceddie burst out.

Caro smiled. "Why I believe he could be persuaded to
do so. But come, have some breakfast and say good morning to our visitor."

"Good morning, sir," the boys chorused before plunging
into enormous plates of eggs and bacon that the footman
had brought in along with the fresh pot of coffee he set in
front of Caro.

"Good morning." The marquess accepted the steaming
cup of coffee Caro handed him. "I am particularly pleased
that you lads are here because I came to Grosvenor Square
expressly to see you. I have brought something that I think
you might find amusing."

"You brought something for us?" Clarence found it difficult to believe that a personage as exalted as the Marquess
of Everleigh had even noticed two small boys, much less
spared them a second thought.

Less bashful than his older brother, Ceddie was not going
to allow himself to be impressed until he knew more.
"Thank you very much sir, but what did you bring us?" he
demanded cautiously.

Nicholas grinned. Ceddie was nobody's fool, and he was
not about to be won over so easily. Obviously he had been
offered useless gifts before from adults eager to win his
favor.

"Oh, I expect it will meet with your approval, but I am
afraid you must step outside," he replied airily.

"Outside?" three voices echoed and three pairs of eyes
were riveted on him. Ceddie was encouraged. This seemed
more promising and in truth, all along he had never doubted
that the marquess was a regular Trojan.

"Yes. Come along, that is, after you've finished your
breakfast." But before the marquess had even completed his
sentence the boys were out the door, leaving their plates
virtually untouched.

"May I come too?" Caro wondered. "I confess that you
have piqued my curiosity quite as much as the boys'."

"But of course." Nicholas stood aside as she hurried out, only a shade less eagerly than her cousins.

"Ponies!" Caro echoed the ecstatic exclamations of Ceddie and Clarence as she stepped through the door held open by a disapproving Wigmore.

"Cousin Caro, Cousin Caro, just look what he has brought us!" Ceddie bounded back up the steps to urge his cousin along.

No less excited than his brother, Clarence beamed. "Thank you, sir. They are the most bang-up present anyone has ever given us. How did you know we'd been longing for ponies forever?"

Nicholas's blue eyes twinkled. "Call it a lucky guess."

"Oh, thank you, sir, ever so much." Ceddie, halfway down the stairs again, remembered his manners and came rushing back. "But,"—his small face clouded—"what will Mama say?"

Nicholas laid a reassuring hand on his shoulder. "You leave your Mama to me. I feel certain I can persuade her to see the wisdom of allowing her sons to become bruising riders. Now off with you, and mind you check them on all points to see that they are the fine horseflesh their owner assured me they were."

The marquess turned to find Caro looking at him, a bemused expression on her face. He cocked a quizzical brow.

"How," she paused in some confusion, "how very kind you are," she murmured huskily. Somehow she could not find words adequate for the feelings washing over her at the moment. Nothing could quite express her surprise that such a man of affairs as the Marquess of Everleigh should take the time to notice two small boys, much less divine their dearest wish and then fulfill it. It was nothing short of extraordinary. The man was a strange mixture: arrogant canal builder, a man-about-town who was by turns satiric and appreciative of her beautiful cousin's machinations, someone of obvious intelligence, yet one who despised bluestockings. But he was also an affectionate brother, and now a champion and friend of the young Welhams. Caro wanted to say more, to tell him how much she admired him for this generous gesture but, for once in her life, she found herself at a total loss.

As she stood there trying to collect her thoughts, the door swung open again and Lavinia appeared. "Good heavens what a commotion! I could even hear the noise in my dressing room,'' she complained in a peevish tone which altered considerably the minute she caught sight of the marquess. ''Why, Nicholas, whatever are you doing here?'' Though accustomed to being the object of slavish attention, the beauty did have her standards, and they did not include admirers who appeared on one's doorstep before the middle of the afternoon.

''Mama, Mama, look what the marquess has brought us!'' Ceddie could bear the suspense no longer and, preferring that matters be brought to a head sooner rather than later, he pointed to the curved drive where two glossy chestnut ponies stood docilely surveying their new home.

Observing the frown beginning to cloud her cousin's brow, Caro deemed it time to intervene. ''How fortunate for you, Cousin, that you have an admirer who takes such a *fatherly* interest in your boys. After all, a gentleman must be an accomplished rider and I am sure neither you nor I would have the least notion how to begin to find mounts for Ceddie and Clarence, much less teach them.'' Caro spoke hastily, completely disregarding for the moment the existence of Uncle Tony who would have been eminently suited to the task.

The frown was replaced by a speculative expression and then, as the full import of Caro's words sank in, a delighted smile lit up Lavvy's face as she swept over to Nicholas. ''Of course, you are in the right of it. How dreadfully stupid of me, but I do so worry about my boys as they are all I have.'' She allowed her voice to break pathetically before continuing. ''Thank you, Nicky.'' Laying her hand on his arm she looked up at the marquess, her blue eyes glistening with unshed tears.

Unimpressed by this byplay, but vaguely suspecting that somehow Cousin Caro had made everything all right again, Ceddie broke in, ''Does that mean we can keep them?''

''Yes, dear, you may keep them.''

''Hooray! Hooray! I am going to call mine Duke.'' And Ceddie skipped down the steps to share the wonderful news with his brother.

''Come Lavvy,'' the marquess started down the steps toward the boys who were becoming acquainted with their new friends. ''Let me reassure you as to the quality of these animals.''

"Oh, I trust your judgment implicitly," she replied hastily, remaining firmly fixed on the top step as Nicholas had known she would. Even as a child, Lavinia had never had any use for horses—nasty things that snorted, stamped, and made one dirty. Then, having satisfied herself as to the cause of the disturbance, and wishing to continue the toilette which had been so rudely interrupted, she turned towards the door.

"Come, let us look at the ponies." Nicholas turned to place a firm hand under Caro's elbow, shepherding her out of earshot. "Thank you for coming so quickly to the boys' defense. It was cleverly done, but certainly has left me with a great deal on my plate."

Though it had been quickly suppressed, Caro had seen the horrified expression on the marquess's face when she made her remark and she had been highly amused. In truth, she had been unaccountably relieved at his patent dismay over being cast in the role of the boys' stepfather. "But I thought I was helping you as well." She gazed up at him, her gray eyes wide and innocent.

Nicholas was not fooled in the least. "You thought no such thing, my girl, and well you know it. All you were concerned with was choosing the best strategy to win Lavvy's approval of my gift and I give you your due. You were brilliant. However, I do not relish the role of sacrificial lamb."

Caro chuckled. "Pooh! I have seen how you work things to your advantage. I have not the slightest doubt that you are well able to take care of yourself."

"In the main, yes," he admitted, "but I doubt my abilities to withstand the machinations of *two* beautiful women."

Caro stared. No one had ever called her beautiful before, even in jest, and though she didn't believe it for a moment, she realized that nobody had ever even bothered to offer her Spanish coin either. It was a novel experience and she was not at all sure how she felt about it.

For his part, as he watched her expression and detected the delicate blush that tinged Caro's cheeks, the marquess was both amused and touched that such a casual remark had elicited such a response. Most women took such compliments as their due, expected them, in fact. Few females of his acquaintance would have even noticed that he had called them beautiful or given it a second thought. Not only was

Caro thinking about it, she was shaking her head in disbelief.

All of a sudden, Nicholas found himself wanting to reassure that she *was* beautiful, as beautiful as her cousin and with far more reason because her heart matched the promise of her lovely face with its wide gray eyes and generous mouth. But he knew that such reassurances would only serve to make her more uncomfortable. Smiling down at her, he continued, "But come, I really do want your opinion of these ponies. Tony says you are an exacting judge of horse-flesh. I hope they meet with your approval."

"I am certain they will. Having seen your own cattle, I trust you completely." Caro glanced up to encounter such a look of understanding that she was completely taken aback. Truly, the man sometimes appeared to be omniscient—recognizing the boys' fondest wish and now noticing her confusion and helping her to recover. She had not expected such a thing. Most of the men she encountered were either overbearing like Colonel Ffolliot—Smythe or blithely unconscious like the viscount. But here was someone at least as skilled at all the masculine pursuits as they were, but possessed of intuitive powers she had hitherto known only in a few women. Caro was intrigued in spite of herself.

"Come see, come see." Ceddie, impatient with their slowness, had come running back and was now tugging Caro towards the newly christened Duke.

She ran a practiced eye over the shiny chestnut flanks, the strong neck, and the dark intelligent eyes before gently stroking the soft nose. The pony whickered and she bent down to get a look at its mouth.

"Well?" The marquess prompted her.

"You have done excellently well, and to find two so remarkably similar. It was extraordinarily well thought of on your part. No matter how amicable the relationship between Ceddie and Clarence, it is bound to be strained if they are treated differently."

"Thank you. Though the credit for locating them must go to my coachman, Watkins. I did look them over thoroughly, but I merely seconded his choice," Nicholas replied modestly.

Caro liked the marquess better for this disclaimer, but her attention was immediately claimed by the more practical

Clarence who wondered, "But we have not the slightest notion how to ride. And where will we keep them?"

"Have no fear," the marquess assured him. "Before I embarked on this impulsive gesture, I spoke to John Coachman who not only made sure that he had ample stabling but insisted that he or one of the other lads would be delighted to take you to the park for lessons any time you wished. If the truth be told, I believe he would infinitely prefer that to driving your mother's carriage. I thought we might begin tomorrow morning by meeting in the park. My sister delights in driving there, but she prefers an unfashionable hour when it is not so crowded that one can barely move." The marquess turned to Caro. "Will you join us? I feel certain that as a reluctant Londoner, you have brought your own mount, but if you need one, I shall be happy to supply you with one from my stable."

Caro thanked him, assuring him that even had she not been able to ride him in London, she would have wanted Xerxes with her simply because she could not be gone so long from such an old friend and she had been eager to get out ever since Tim had returned to London with her mount.

Seeing that the boys were on the best of terms with their new companions, and confident of Lavinia's begrudging acceptance of the new additions to her household, the marquess fixed a time for meeting in the park and then rode off, congratulating himself on a morning's work well done.

13

THEY WERE UP betimes the next morning in Grosvenor Square. Ceddie and Clarence, who had been practicing the previous day in the stableyard, were bursting to show the marquess the progress they had made and scarcely allowed Caro a minute to swallow her coffee before they were charging off to find Dimmock to bring round the horses. It was a glorious day with sun glinting off newly washed flowers and trees, and the air was fresh with the promise of spring—a perfect day for a ride. But the boys, interested only in their newly acquired ponies, were oblivious to it all.

"See, Cousin Caro, I don't even need a block to get on Duke," Ceddie declared proudly as he swung himself into the saddle.

Caro laughed as she allowed Dimmock to throw her up, "Already you put me to shame."

"Oh, but that's because Xerxes is a stallion. I wager he is as large as the marquess's horse," the little boy replied admiringly. Count on Cousin Caro to have a real horse and not some tame mare appropriate for a lady.

Much the same thoughts were going through Nicholas's mind as he watched the trio approach. Xerxes had not been ridden for days and he was itching for a gallop, sidling restlessly as Caro kept him in pace with the ponies. Watching the firmness with which she handled the huge black stallion, the marquess was impressed in spite of himself.

"What a magnificent horse! You must be a splendid rider to keep such an animal in check." Leaning out of the carriage to greet them, Clarissa Daventry gave voice to her brother's thoughts.

"Why, thank you. At the moment, Xerxes is a bit impatient, but in general he is the most complete gentleman and makes me look far more skilled than I truly am," Caro replied "But speaking of accomplishments, I understand that you study the pianoforte with Signor Clementi. One hears praise of him even in the depths of the country. You must be very talented to have such a teacher."

"Oh no." Clarissa blushed. "I am the veriest amateur who enjoys music immensely and, leading the circumscribed life that I do, perhaps devote more time to practice than others who possess more natural abilities."

This, in fact, had been precisely the opinion that Lavinia had voiced when lamenting the tedium of the evening to Caro the day before. But having recently accustomed herself to seeing the world through her cousin's eyes, Caro had divined the true cause of her boredom: the celebrated performer and his student had been the focus of attention, leaving Lavinia with little to do but tap her foot in annoyance and appear as interested as possible. Without being precisely aware of her own feelings and motivations, Caro had resolved to do what she could to make Clarissa a more active participant in situations where she would be appreciated for her accomplishments and her intelligence.

"I am afraid that I quite disagree," Caro responded firmly, "for I am persuaded that he only takes on those pupils who show a great deal of promise. I know of several people he has quite kindly but most definitely refused to teach and rustic that I am, even I have heard that he declined an invitation from the Royal Family itself. So you see I am not at all inclined to take you at your word. In fact, I should very much like to hear you play. I am a less than indifferent musician myself, but that only adds to my appreciation of the skill in others. I . . ." But here she was interrupted by an exuberant Ceddie who came trotting up, his back very straight, hands holding the reins at the correct angle.

"Look Cousin Caro, the marquess taught me how to trot and I can do it already."

"So I see." Caro smiled at him. "And very well you do it too." She cast an eye about for Clarence to see how he was faring, knowing him to be somewhat more cautious than his intrepid brother, but he was eagerly questioning the marquess about his experiences on the Peninsula and was oblivious to the rest of them.

Catching a phrase here and there—"the wagons and cannon bogged down in the mud . . . and then we charged up the hill with no thought but to get to the top"—Clary chuckled. "I am afraid that those of you who come to the park for exercise will be sadly disappointed. Once Nicholas had begun his stories, he will hold his audience spellbound.''

"How well I know," Caro replied remembering back to a winter evening long ago when she had been as enthralled as Clarence was now. "How lucky men are to lead such adventurous lives," she sighed. "How lovely to be able to go wherever one chooses without having to be accompanied by a respectable companion."

"Yes, it's dreadful to be dependent upon others," Clary agreed. "I love the fresh air, but in order to indulge myself, I am forced to cause such a fuss that I feel quite shockingly selfish ordering a carriage and a coachman just for a quick turn around the park."

Though her words were uncomplaining, there was a wistful note in her voice that made Caro realize how she must chafe under her enforced reliance on other people. If the rest of the *ton* spoke of Clarissa Daventry in the same pitying tones as Lavinia had, calling her "a poor crippled thing and such a worry to her dear brother", then Clarissa's life must be frustrating to no end. She appeared to have an active mind and, if Caro's impressions were correct, a great deal of talent. To be dismissed by someone like Lavvy as though she were a hopeless invalid or feebleminded must be galling in the extreme.

Struck by a sudden thought, Caro inquired, "Why do you not ride then? To be sure, one must still send for one's horse in the stables and be accompanied by a groom, but it is less of an undertaking for all involved."

"Ride? Why I can only walk with the greatest of difficulty and in the most ungainly manner." Clary was staring at her companion as though she had calmly suggested she take to the air and fly.

"But that is just the point," Caro insisted. "You say you can walk, so that means you must have the use of your legs, however awkward, and when you sit there is nothing to distinguish you from anyone else. Therefore you ought to be able to ride a horse," she concluded triumphantly and cocked her head in such a quizzical, friendly way that Clary, ordinarily wary of discussing her disability, was forced to smile.

"To be perfectly honest, I had never thought of it," she began hesitantly. "However, I suppose I might be able to." Clary remained thoughtful for a moment, trying to picture herself in the role and realized that she liked it very well indeed. To someone who had always compensated for her physical awkwardness by burying herself in books and music, the idea of moving as gracefully and easily among her peers as others was extraordinarily appealing. "Well, I shan't know unless I try," she responded firmly. "I shall inquire if we have any mounts docile enough to handle not only a novice, but a cripple as well. I doubt that my brother possesses any such horseflesh, but we shall see."

"Wonderful! I should be delighted to help you if you need it and I look forward to having someone to share my morning rides." Caro was impressed at the decisive way Clarissa had reacted upon being introduced to the idea. From her experience, females, with the exception of herself and Helena, were not inclined to show the least resolution and she found herself warming to the marquess's sister.

For her part, the more she considered it, the more Clary was becoming enamored of the idea. Not the least of her pleasure arose from being treated like an ordinary person rather than a helpless invalid. Caro's confidence in her gave her faith in herself and she was most grateful. "Thank you so much. If it works, it will be a splendid idea. How very clever you are. However shall I repay you?" she wondered shyly.

"Oh, as to that, you could do that by allowing me to hear you play," Caro replied.

Recognizing from her insistence that Caro's interest was genuine, Clary responded, "Very well, then. Why do you not follow us home? The boys can proceed to Grosvenor Square with Dimmock, and Watkins or Nicholas can accompany you later."

"A splendid idea, but why not allow Clarence and Ceddie to enjoy the treat as well? I am sure that they will be worn-out enough from the excitement and exercise to be on their best behavior."

"But will they not find it deadly dull?" Clarissa was skeptical. The marquess's sister enjoyed the company of Lady Caroline Waverly, but she did come out with the oddest suggestions.

"Why should they? Even animals are soothed by music. They have no friends their own age so how are they to know that the rest of society expects little boys to be heartily bored by such things? Besides, how else are they to discover music? Not from their mama, I'll wager."

Remembering the fixed expression of polite attentiveness that had never varied on Lavinia's face during Signor Clementi's entire performance, Clary had to agree with her new friend. She laughed. ''Very well then, but I leave it to you to extend the invitation.''

They rode along in silence enjoying the fineness of the day and the sight of the boys trotting along so happily and proudly next to Nicholas, who seemed to be enjoying himself as much as they were.

In point of fact, he was. There was something so refreshing about Ceddie's forthright candor and Clarence's shy admiration, both untinged by any of the ulterior motives that so often governed the behavior of adults. He found the boys to be interesting and curious companions whose questions about his life as a soldier were as intelligent and probing as adult's. And their reasons for asking them were inspired by a more genuine desire to know about life in Wellington's army than any he had yet encountered except, perhaps, that of Lady Caroline Waverly. The thought of her made him turn in his saddle to see the two ladies progressing slowly along, deep in conversation. He smiled to himself. Nicholas had not seen his sister looking so animated in years, but he had known how it would be. There was just something about Caro that encouraged people to relax and be themselves around her.

The piping sound of Ceddie's voice recalled his attention to his companions. ''I am sorry, Ceddie, I was not attending. What did you ask?''

''I was wondering, if you were fighting all over the countryside for so long, where you got food?''

''A crucial question, my lad. In an extended campaign, finding supplies is almost as important to the final outcome as winning battles. You must ask Thompson how he did it. He was my batman and a perfect genius for discovering a chicken or onions or flour in what you would swear was a totally deserted and barren countryside.'' Then, seeing that the reins were beginning to slacken and that some of the rigidity had gone out of the boys' spines, he continued, ''But, come, I think the ponies have had enough exercise for one day. After all, they have been standing idle eating their heads off until now and they are unaccustomed to all this activity.'' He turned Caesar around and headed back to his sister's carriage.

''I can see you have ridden your mounts to a standstill,''

Caro greeted them. Then turning to Ceddie and Clarence, she remarked casually, "It seems a shame to end our outing so soon, though I can see the ponies are quite done up. Lady Clarissa has graciously consented to play the pianoforte for me and she has even more graciously included the two of you in her invitation."

"The pianoforte?" Ceddie was patently skeptical about the dubious pleasure of such a treat.

"Why yes. I feel quite certain you have never heard such a talented performer as the marquess's sister. Her teacher is the celebrated Clementi. I have heard that he even played for Marie Antoinette—before she had her head chopped off, that is."

Overhearing this last, Nicholas could not help smiling at Caro's clever appeal to the bloodthirsty tastes of a six-year-old.

"He did?" Ceddie's eyes were round. "Was he in the revolution too?"

"No," Caro apologized. "I am afraid he was here in London during all the upheaval, but he was in a pianoforte contest with Mozart at the court of Marie Antoinette's brother."

"Someone who knew Mozart teaches Lord Daventry's sister?" Clarence, intent on proving his worldly, knowledge, broke in.

"Yes," Caro replied. "So you see, Lady Clarissa must be very skilled. But come listen for yourselves. I am persuaded you will enjoy it."

Ceddie remained unconvinced. However, Cousin Caro had never steered them wrong before so he acquiesced and dutifully joined the little cavalcade which soon came to a halt in front of the curved steps flanked by *torchères* that marked the marquess's imposing residence in Berkeley Square. A bevy of grooms and stableboys hurried out to take care of the assorted equine companions while the butler, somewhat surprised by the party on the doorstep, ushered them in.

Watching Clarissa make her awkward ascent of the stairs on her brother's arm, Caro understood why she so assiduously avoided life in a society where grace and beauty were such necessary prerequisites for success. A young woman, no matter how well-born or how well-endowed with a handsome portion, was unlikely to attract an eligible *parti* if she could not dance. And any appearance in the fashionable world would amount to an invitation to the inveterate gossips of the *ton* to comment pityingly on her unfortunate condition. Such a situation would be intolerable to one as intelligent and sensitive as Lady Clarissa Daventry. Small wonder, then, that she preferred her isolated existence in the country. But it was such a dreadful shame to think of such a charming person without companions who could appreciate and encourage her. Caro became more determined than ever to do just that.

By now they had reached the music room and Clary, seated at the pianoforte and running her hands lightly over the keys in preparation, already looked a different person. She was happy, assured, and aglow with a special radiance that attracted her listeners even before she began to play. Accustomed to a life of quiet observation, Clary had remarked on Ceddie's lack of enthusiasm and so began with a series of jolly country dances and a march or two. From there she proceeded to the *Harmonious Blacksmith* and ever so gradually into the more complicated keyboard works of Mozart and Beethoven.

Even though she had expected a skilled rendition, Caro had been unprepared for the magnificence of Clary's performance. Her technique was flawless, and the feeling with which she managed to imbue the works would have moved the most indifferent of listeners, as indeed it did.

Perched uncomfortably on the edge of a footstool, Ceddie was the picture of resignation, while his brother's face wore an expression of polite interest remarkably reminiscent of his mother's. As the music flowed around them, they gradually relaxed and ever so slowly were drawn into the performance until they were completely absorbed in Clary's playing.

Only Nicholas, accustomed as he was to his sister's skill, retained enough sense of detachment to observe the little group. Leaning his broad shoulders against the door of the music room, he smiled at the picture of rapt attention the three of them presented as, chins on their hands, Caro and the boys sat spellbound. It seemed impossible that the two little bodies recently so active could be so still and attentive. Once again, Caro had known how it would be and had somehow phrased things in just the right way so as to encourage everyone.

There was a rousing finale, and with a resounding chord, the performance ended. Immediately the little audience burst into applause as Clary, flushed from her exertions, smiled happily at them. How did Caro accomplish it? Nicholas wondered. Without seeming to do anything, she had brought together the unlikely group in such a way that they all brought each other pleasure and enriched each other's lives. He had seen her do it before—a remark here, some encouragement there—and even people as rigid as Lavinia were doing the strangest things: welcoming stray dogs into their well-ordered households and allowing their children to ride in the park.

"Ride in the park." A voice echoed his thoughts and Nicholas realized that it was his sister speaking. He looked up as she added, "That is, if Nicky can find me a horse."

Nicholas stared. "Find you a what?"

"A horse, brother dear," she continued serenely.

"A horse. But what for?"

"Don't be obtuse, Nicky. To ride, of course. Caro has pointed out, and very cleverly too, that although I cannot walk very well, I can sit beautifully. However ill-suited to each other and to the rest of me, my legs are strong enough to allow me to remain on a horse. I cannot think why it had not occurred to us before."

Nicholas was dumbstruck. And why had it not? It was a perfectly obvious conclusion, but it had taken someone with a different view of the world, someone unaccustomed to accepting things as they were, to point it out to both of them. The marquess turned to catch Caro watching him with a guarded expression in her gray eyes. He smiled and the wary look was replaced by an answering smile that left him feeling oddly comforted and reassured, as though he had rediscovered a long-lost friend.

"Thank you," he whispered softly so that only Caro could hear. "An excellent idea. I shall be delighted to find a mount for you, but only if you promise not to follow in your brother's reckless footsteps." He winked at his sister who had also been waiting uneasily for his reactions.

"Hooray, then we all can go riding in the park," Ceddie clinched the matter and the group from Grosvenor Square soon departed, well satisfied with the morning's accomplishments.

14

HOWEVER, SEVERAL DAYS LATER in his next encounter with
Caro, at the Duchess of Beckford's ball, it was borne in
upon the marquess that there were also distinct disadvan-
tages connected with those who took an individual and original approach to life. Having seen how the briefest of
appearances at the Countess of Mortmain's rout had revi-
talized his mother, Nicholas had offered her his escort to
another of the Season's most brilliant events. He expected
to be thoroughly bored. Here the most hopeful of the Upper
Ten Thousand appeared religiously—mothers with unmar-
ried daughters to dispose of, fathers hoping to advance or
repair the family fortunes by introducing their child to an
eligible bachelor, young misses certain they would be hailed
an incomparable if they could only attract the attention of
the Earl of This-and-That or Lord Such-a-One. Ordinarily,
Nicholas found these affairs tedious in the extreme, if not
ludicrous. But the chance of feasting his eyes on Lavinia
and indulging in a mild flirtation with her while sharing his
delight at his sister's equestrian progress with Caro made
the prospect bearable—attractive even—and with these
cheering thoughts, he sought out the Countess of Welham's
party the moment he entered the ballroom.

The marquess identified them almost immediately. Despite the crush of people, Lavinia, as always, drew the eyes
of everyone who entered. She was standing a little apart
with Tony, Helena, and Caro in a small alcove next to a
torchère that cast a halo of warm golden light around her.
Her curls glistened and the glow of the candles caught the
sheen of the magnificent strand of baroque pearls draped
over the beautifully rounded bosom revealed by her décolle-
tage. Their shimmer drew the eyes downward to the blush-
colored satin slip which clung to her figure underneath a

white lace dress. In spite of himself, Nicholas caught his breath.

His mother glanced up and, following his gaze, smiled grimly to herself as she saw the look of welcome on Lavinia's face at the sight of them. In the main, the Marchioness of Everleigh adored her son. He had always been her favorite. Far more intelligent and adventurous than her staid firstborn, he had been more responsive and loving as well. But where Lavinia Mandeville was concerned, he had always been a fool—more so now because he knew her for what she was and still he seemed to find her irresistible. So it came as no surprise to her when Nicholas casually pointed out the Countess of Welham's coterie and suggested they exchange a few words with their country neighbor.

In fact, Nicholas himself was pondering the reasons that Lavinia drew him to her. First and foremost was her undeniable beauty, and the marquess, possessed of a highly developed though carefully concealed aesthetic sensibility, simply delighted in feasting his eyes on the straight nose, delicately sculpted lips, and perfect figure. There was no denying that the Countess of Welham was a work of art. Every movement was grace itself, every gesture called attention to pearly teeth, dainty hands, and beautifully molded arms, while every article of dress, every ornament was precisely selected and designed to enhance this exquisite creation. Not the least of her attraction was her absolute confidence in her capacity to draw all eyes and hold them. True, this assurance was somewhat self-centered, but it also made her irresistible. For what man could be indifferent to someone whose entire existence was devoted to enslaving and charming him and other members of his sex? Lavinia's blithe assumption that, despite her former rejection, Nicholas Daventry was as besotted as ever, worked a remarkably powerful and persuasive effect even on someone as accustomed to running his own life as the Marquess of Everleigh. There was a certain bravado in her absolute conviction of the power of her beauty and he could not help being drawn to her.

Lavinia's cousin, on the other hand, did not seem to be the least bit appreciative of this as she stood surveying the scene, a look on her face that only barely escaped being scornful. Caro glanced over at Lavvy as she eagerly greeted the marquess and his mother, and the ironic glint in her eye became even more pronounced.

Nicholas should have ignored it, but for some reason he could not help remarking on her lack of enthusiasm. "You do not appear to be deriving much amusement from all this, Lady Caroline."

"Oh, this," she indicated the entire brilliant assemblage with a derogatory wave of her hand. "It is merely an arena for those intent on making a splendid marriage to show themselves off and for those who have already done so to prove their continued attractiveness by collecting adoring cicisbei."

"A remarkably cynical view for one so young. Do you not believe in love, then?" he asked, forgetting entirely that he had been entertaining very similar thoughts himself as he had mounted the stairs to the ballroom.

"We were not speaking of love, sir, but of marriage," Caro responded tartly.

"Presumably they become one in the same." Her patent expression of disbelief irritated Nicholas for some inexplicable reason and he continued, "You speak as though it were all some desperate sort of charade, but I find that it can all be very agreeable—pleasurable in fact." He shot a challenging look t her.

"Undoubtedly you find it so, but then, you are a man," Caro responded. Her tone was low, but there was a bitterness in it that took him by surprise.

"This is unarguably true, though I am not at all certain, given the tone of your voice, that it is a state to be wished." Then, seeing that she was deadly serious, he dropped his bantering tone. "Would you care to elaborate? Are you so scornful of the male sex in general or only of some of its particular members?" The marquess could not picture Caro having suffered some unrequited love in her past, but he supposed it was possible. It was certainly an interesting thought and offered a plausible explanation for her cynical outlook.

Catching the drift of his thoughts, Caro was highly incensed. "My views have been formed entirely apart from my personal experience," she responded stiffly, "and even if I had been so stupid to have endured some disastrous *affaire de coeur,* I am not such a poor creature as to let it color my opinion of the entire sex."

Taken aback by the intensity blazing in her eyes, he could well believe it. "No, I don't suppose you are," he agreed mildly, glancing over at Lavinia who was carrying on a desultory conversation with his mother, all the while surveying the ballroom with an eagle eye.

But Caro was not about to be so easily dismissed. For some reason she could not explain, she wanted desperately to prove to Nicholas that her opinions sprang not from some disappointment, but from a high moral level. "It is not that I am so critical of men: they are all very well in their own way. It is society in general and the behavior it engenders in both sexes that disgusts me. Women are led to believe that the only way they can excel or provide for themselves is by marrying well, and this puts an unnatural burden on both men and women. Women devote their entire existences to dressing, flirting, and acquiring accomplishments purely to attract the attention of the most eligible males for which they compete with their sisters. Thus, they can be friends neither with other women, whom they view as a threat, nor with men, whom they view as their quarry. The men, in turn, measure themselves in terms of the incomparables they can win with their social address or the diamonds of the first water they can lure with wealth and position. It becomes no more than a competition, with each side viewing the other as some prize to be won or lost. And, of course, the entire performance is only significant if it can be conducted in full view of the Upper Ten Thousand."

The marquess was not at all accustomed to having young ladies state their opinions with such fervor, and somewhat nonplussed, he stared blankly at her.

In spite of herself, Caro was the tiniest bit disappointed that someone who seemed, from the concern he exhibited for his sister and the attention he lavished on Clarence and Cedric, to be different from the rest of his empty-headed peers, was no more perspicacious than the rest of them. She sighed to herself and turned to Helena, hoping for a sympathetic look or some show of support for her beliefs.

"I had not looked at it quite that way, Lady Caroline," Nicholas's chastened voice broke into her thoughts. "I can see that you, along with Mary Wollstonecraft, believe that the capacities of women are neither fully appreciated nor utilized by our present society. But how would you suggest we remedy such an unfortunate situation?"

It was Caro's turn to look blank. Not only had he listened to her little emotional diatribe, he appeared at least to be familiar with her point of view. "Actually, I believe that if women were given a proper education it would be better not only for them, but for society as a whole. Instead of being merely ornamental, they could aid in the instruction of their children and their servants, be greater helpmates to their husbands and, in short, by their example, they could contribute to the moral well-being of those nearest and dearest to them." She blushed. "Forgive me, my lord, this is not the time or the place to advance such radical opinions, even for a bluestocking. It's just that I cannot help but feel sorry for so many people here who seem to think that their entire existences rest on the approval accorded to them by the leaders of fashion."

Nicholas smiled in spite of himself. At first, hearing the ironic note in her voice, he had been prepared to write Lady Caroline off as just another future ape-leader who, embittered by lack of social success, had turned against the *ton,* cloaking her anger in moralistic criticisms. But then he had realized that the undertone he had heard in her voice was not so much bitterness as passion and he had begun to reconsider. After all, as an independent woman in her own right, thanks to a considerable inheritance from her mother, and mistress of the estate left to her by her father, she was not likely to have been subject to the pressures she described with such vehemence. Recalling their contretemps in the library at Berkhamstead, Nicholas realized that, to do her credit, the only way Lady Caroline Waverly wished to win acclaim or satisfaction was as an agriculturalist and a landlord. As his eyes took in the glossy black hair, the compelling gray eyes, and the elegant figure, he was forced to concede that she was not precisely an antidote either. Then why was she here if she harbored so strong a distaste for such things? Casting back, Nicholas remembered an offhand remark uttered by the viscount about Caro's immediate, though unwilling, compliance to Lavvy's demand for her support. If that were true, he had been misjudging her for some time and she was a creature of rare generosity and loyalty, even to those whose mode of existence was abhorrent to her. Reluctantly, Nicholas was forced to revise his opinions of Lady Caroline Waverly and accord her a begrudging respect.

He was not allowed the luxury of such serious reflection for long. Annoyed at the amount of time Nicholas was forcing her to converse with his mother—really, it was more than politeness warranted—Lavvy glanced peevishly around. There he was, kind-hearted to a fault, expending far more attention than was necessary on her cousin. Nicholas had always had a sympathetic spot for those weaker and less privileged than himself, but he was carrying it to the extreme in his efforts to make Caro feel at ease. Was he not able to see that her cousin would never feel comfortable until she had returned to that rustic retreat of hers and tromped around the village hobnobbing with the greasy locals and exchanging the latest farming news with the squire?

Lavvy snorted in disgust. It was time to rescue Nicholas from his own good intentions. Smiling sweetly at the marchioness she began, "I can hear them striking up the waltz and Nicholas made me promise the first one with him. Excuse me." And she glided over to where Nicholas was deep in conversation with her cousin, arriving in time to hear him respond in a most serious tone.

"I quite agree with you that universal education is the best, most lasting way to ensure the dignity of our fellows and the true progress of mankind. I have seen that you are reading the article entitled ''The Causes and Cures of Pauperism'' in the *Edinburgh Review* and no doubt you subscribe to the views expressed by the author that education is essential to alleviating the condition of the poor."

Caro's eyes widened in astonishment, "Why, yes, as a matter of fact I do, but . . . ."

The rest of her sentence was lost as her cousin, taking Nicholas's arm, smiled entrancingly as she cooed, "This is the waltz you promised me, Nicky, and I am longing to escape this crush for the dance floor."

The marquess was not altogether certain he had promised any such thing, but he was no proof against the imploring look in the big blue eyes. "Then, by all means, let us make haste to join the rest of the couples. You will excuse us, ladies?" He bowed to Helena, his mother, and Caro, who nodded absently, her mind still reeling from Nicholas's last remark. She knew him to be an intelligent man, but to discover that he read and discussed topics such as the article on pauperism was something of a surprise and she began to look at the marquess in a new, more appreciative light.

"There, you see, Nicky, I can play the knight errant too," Lavvy teased as she followed him to the floor.

"Oh?" he responded vaguely, his mind still on the previous conversation.

"Why, yes. There you were caught in dull conversation with Caro and I could see you were never going to extricate yourself without some help. Of course I love Caro dearly, but she is sadly blue and forgets that other people do not wish to exhaust themselves in long tedious discussions of elevated topics."

"Just so," Nicholas agreed, thinking how very boring Caro must be finding London if her cousin's acquaintances were all of the same opinion. It had taken Lavvy's artless prattle to make him realize just how unusual Caro was and to make him appreciate how very stimulating serious conversation with an intelligent woman could be—far more enjoyable, in fact, than the empty exchanges one was usually treated to. It was a most intriguing thought, and continuing to consider it, he led his partner unconsciously around the floor, replying mechanically to her sly animadversions on various other members of the *ton*.

Observing the marquess's bemused expression and misinterpreting its cause entirely, Caro was experiencing a variety of emotions, none of which was particularly comfortable. First and foremost was incredulity that any person could apparently be so besotted over another, especially over someone as vain as Lavvy. But mainly she felt distaste, disappointment, and something else that was too upsetting to identify. How could the marquess, who had experienced firsthand Lavinia's self-centeredness, still count her a friend, much less look at her as he was looking at her now? How could a man who was familiar with the writings of Mary Wollstonecraft bear to associate with the epitome of all that noble authoress condemned? There was only one conclusion and that was so dispiriting that Caro rebelled mightily against acknowledging it. However, it did appear, unfathomable though it was, that no matter how intelligent or worldly wise a man might be, he was at the mercy of his baser instincts where a pretty woman was concerned. But why did it have to be a man whom she had begrudgingly grown to like? True, this state of affairs did not negate his kindness to the boys, his affection for his sister, or even his appreciation of such serious concerns as education of the poor, but such blindness did render him suspect.

Caro sighed. It all seemed so unfair. There was Lavvy with no thoughts to recommend her receiving admiration from men like the marquess. No matter that other women were genuinely concerned for their fellow creatures, no matter that they tried to cultivate their minds instead of their physiognomies. In the end, it was a beautiful face, no matter what emptiness lay behind it, that spoke to men. How hopeless it all seemed.

And then, quite suddenly, Caro was angry. Why should someone as vapid as Lavvy have everything she wanted? She never should have come to London. She had known how it would be. Hang Lavvy and her obligations! Caro resolved to return to Berkhamstead as soon as possible and forget her disillusionment. Disillusionment? The word stopped Caro short. If she had never aspired to the fashionable world in the first place, then why was she feeling this way? It was a question she did not like to consider, but, never one to suffer illusions, Caro forced herself to examine it. As she half suspected, it had to do with the marquess.

Somehow she had hoped he would be different from all the others. Certainly he had seemed so that evening so long ago when, dressed in his regimentals, half a head taller than everyone else, and carrying himself with the pride of a military man, he had made all the other young bucks look like the merest Bartholomew babies. When he had vowed to return to the Peninsula and cover himself with glory, she had felt sure of it. Truth to tell, she admitted shamefacedly to herself, she had secretly kept him in her mind as a hero—not one to fall in love with and sigh over as the other girls at school did, mind you—but someone she could look up to who would be brave and idealistic, just as Caro herself wanted to be. She had suffered a shock when she had discovered the identity of the grasping Marquess of Everleigh, so anxious to get his greedy hands on her lands, but as she had come to know him, that image had receded and the heroic one, the one that was attentive and kind to those weaker or more unfortunate, had begun to reassert itself.

Had she but known it, Caro would have been extremely surprised to learn that much the same thoughts were occupying the marquess's mind as he whirled his partner around the floor. Responding at random to Lavinia's idle remarks, he reflected how unfortunate it was that those who used all their arts to attract won the acclaim of society. Perhaps that was why he had always been so bored by it all and why he had done his best to absent himself during the Season and to escape to the more honorable existence of a soldier.

Nicholas could not help smiling at the irony of it all. Here he was lamenting over the fact that he was forced into the position which so many years ago would have given him his dream—Lavinia. And now he could hardly wait to escape so he could continue his discussion on female education with her cousin. The more he thought about it, the more he agreed with Caro, and, being a man of action, the more he determined to remedy the situation.

Knowing full well that Lavvy would never allow him further opportunity for rational conversation or even a chance to talk to Caro, he resolved to call in Grosvenor Square the next morning at an hour so unfashionably early that he was likely to encounter only congenial companions. That decided, Nicholas returned Lavvy to her companions and, much to the disgust of a significant number of the Duchess of Beckford's female guests, devoted his attention to his mother.

15

ACCORDINGLY, Nicholas arose at the crack of dawn the next day, ate a leisurely breakfast, perused the papers, and rode around to Grosvenor Square as early as he thought such a country riser as Caro could be counted upon to be up and abroad. But he had apparently underestimated even this particularly unusual young lady, for when he requested Lady Caroline Waverly, Wigmore, barely able to hide his disapproval under the customary mask of impassive dignity, informed my lord that she had gone riding. Really, what was the world coming to, the butler wondered, people calling on people at such awkward hours. Was there no sense of decorum left?

"Thank you, Wigmore. I shall catch her in the park, then," he replied, turning to descend the steps. But something in the butler's face gave the marquess pause. There was an uneasy look, a look that seemed entirely incongruous in someone who was the soul of propriety. The marquess stopped and was trying to fathom the meaning of it all when he heard shouts of encouragement and boyish laughter issuing from the direction of the stables.

On impulse, Nicholas left his horse and sauntered towards the commotion. He reached the stableyard to find Ceddie, Clarence, several of the stable lads, and one pony all breathlessly watching a youth, carefully balanced on the back of the other pony, ride slowly 'round and 'round the pump in the center of the yard. Judging by the looks on the boys' faces, he could only suppose they were to be next to essay this feat and he shuddered to envision the tongue lashing in store for the viscount were Lavinia to discover the outcome of the excursion to Astley's.

There was a cheer and he looked up to see the youth leap lightly off the pony's back, remarking, "You see, it only takes a little practice, but I believe you boys should wait to try until you have something more forgiving underneath you than cobblestones.''

With a shock, the marquess recognized the voice as that of Lady Caroline Waverly. He looked again. Yes, the black hair escaping from underneath the concealing cap was definitely Caro's, but the slender figure clad revealingly in breeches that he presumed had once belonged to the viscount, was disturbingly unfamiliar. Knowing her views on the emancipation of women, the marquess tried to put the enticing line of her thigh out of his mind, but it was with difficulty that he tore his eyes off the gentle curves revealed under the thin cambric shirt which, hastily thrust into the top of the breeches, also enhanced the tiny waist. He took a deep breath and looked down into the clear gray eyes which betrayed not the least hint of self-consciousness at being caught in such a compromising position and such outrageous attire.

The expression with which Caro greeted him was unabashed and friendly. ''Good morning, my lord. We are discovered. As you can see, one visit to Astley's has had a most deleterious effect on all of us. At least, though, I have kept Clarence and Ceddie from running away to join them.''

''A fortunate thing which must have demanded considerable tact on your part. Have no fear, I shall ensure that not a whisper of this reaches Lavvy's ears,'' he responded, correctly reading the mute appeal in Caro's dark-fringed eyes.

A brilliant smile lit up her face. ''Famous! I knew I could count on you.'' Her brow wrinkled worriedly as she continued, ''I confess to some concern that I have an unsettling influence on the boys. Of course, I don't wish to, but I do so want them to enjoy themselves.'' Caro paused to reflect a moment, but then a thought struck her and she looked quizzically up at him. ''I don't suppose you know how to ride standing up on two horses,'' she inquired hopefully.

Nicholas burst out laughing. ''You are incorrigible! Caught in a situation which would make most females faint with mortification at the mere thought of it, you not only exhibit no discomfiture, but you wish to ask how to accomplish something even more outrageous than you are already doing.''

Caro had the grace to blush and hang her head. ''I warned Lavvy how it would be. I told her it was no use for her to try to establish me in the *ton* for I should only come a cropper. Sometimes I wonder if I avoided society more because I knew I should lose my reputation before I even had gained one to lose, than because I disapproved of the vanity of its ways," she confided.

She looked so dejected at this dreadful admission that Nicholas had to smile once again. What an absurd child she was, so critical of society and critical in such a high-minded way that it made her subscribe to unpopular political principles, yet so kind that she would sacrifice her comfort to support Lavvy in her particular social aspirations, and lastly, so rigorous in her own moral system that she even questioned her own motivations. All the while she was blithely participating in the innocent amusements that so entertained Ceddie and Clarence and encouraged his shy sister to enjoy herself and share her very special talents. There was no question that Lady Caroline Waverly was an original, and he very seriously doubted that the world was ready for her. However, Nicholas himself was becoming more intrigued.

"Do you really think you could ride both ponies, sir?" a young voice piped behind him. The marquess turned to find Ceddie looking up at him expectantly.

"I don't know." Nicholas surveyed the two ponies, his shining Hessians, and then Caro, still slightly flushed from her exertions. There was no mistaking the challenging look in her eye. "But I expect I could if I took off my boots," he replied nonchalantly.

" 'Ere, I'll take care of your boots, guv'nor. Won't even get no smudges on them neither." Grinning from ear to ear, Caro's groom, Tim, strolled over leading the ponies.

There was nothing for it but to prove himself. Suddenly the marquess felt absurdly youthful. The stable yard faded away and he saw himself on a dusty parade ground in Spain, cheering soldiers encouraging him. How alive he had felt then. How much more exciting life had been when each day it was one's skill and daring that commanded attention and respect and not one's rank or income.

Vaulting lightly into the saddle, he caught the reins, tossed his boots to the waiting Tim, and pulled the ponies in until they were standing docilely side by side. Then, raising himself to a crouch, he gingerly placed one foot on the back of each pony and carefully straightened, keeping the ponies in check all the while. The onlookers held their breaths while he gently flicked the reins and set his mounts in motion, slowly at first until he had made one turn of the yard, and then faster until they began to trot. The audience, swelled by the addition of Dimmock and several lads from the neighboring stables broke into applause. The marquess stopped, bowed, and leapt gracefully down, forgetting entirely that he was in his stocking feet.

"Hurrah! What a Trojan!" Ceddie burst out, while his brother's eyes positively glowed with heroworship.

"And I am entirely cast in the shade," Caro complained, but she could not keep the admiration our of her voice. Indeed, the marquess had made an impressive picture, his lithe athletic figure perched effortlessly on top of the ponies, controlling them and attuning himself to their motion until the trio moved as one living being. She too had glimpsed for a moment the young soldier from so long ago and was delighted to see that the adventurous spirit had not entirely disappeared, but had merely been obscured by the responsibilities the marquess had been forced to take on. Caro stopped. Perhaps the assumption of these duties had been as onerous to him as her concession to Lavvy's demands had been to her. Unexpectedly, Caro felt a rush of sympathy for the man who leaned over and ruffled her hair.

"You're young yet, Waif. Wait until you've had more practice. Why, when I was your age, I too could only ride one horse standing up. But I feel confident you'll improve," he teased, his blue eyes twinkling down at her.

Looking up into them, Caro could not help thinking what a singularly attractive smile he had—no wonder that everyone from small boys to society's most illustrious hostesses were drawn to him.

"How did you know what to do? Could you show us?" The babble of eager questions broke in upon them.

"Whoa! One question at a time. Don't forget that I too have been to Astley's, and at an even tenderer age than you. And I had a brother who was a good deal older than I who was already, to my great envy, allowed to ride a horse. So, desperate to prove to my father that I could ride, I practiced every day in the paddock at Everleigh with only a groom, who was sworn to secrecy."

The marquess continued to reminisce, explaining the method of his progression, but Caro no longer heard, too busy with her own thoughts which were running in much the same vein as Nicholas's had only a few minutes earlier. How different he was from the other people she had encountered in the *ton*. Why he hadn't so much as blinked an eyelash upon discovering her in male attire or indulging in a ridiculous activity that even most men above the age of fifteen would be embarrassed to be caught in. Not only had he made no comment, but he had immediately shed his own boots and entered in with a gusto that made it all that much more enjoyable for the rest of time. Caro was not even sure that Tony, madcap that he was, would have joined them so blithely and Tony, never one to claim that he had much in the old brain box, was someone whose ramshackle ways were already suspect.

A loud halloo, which could only have come from the viscount himself, broke into these reflections. "Aha! I thought I should find you here. Wigmore told me you were riding, but as I had just come from the park, I knew he was having me on, the old devil. Why Lavvy must employ that stiff-rumped pillar of propriety, I haven't the foggiest notion. It ain't as though any of you has a shred of reputation to be ruined in the first place. And it ain't as though I'd let slip that you were cutting up a lark. Why, I am more like to object that you did it without me, which I think was dashed churlish of you," he complained, looking at them all with an injured air.

"I do beg your pardon, Tony, I simply never thought . . ." Caro began.

"How could you, Caro, when you know I'm always up for a bit of sport, especially here in town where life is so dashed flat." He sighed lugubriously, but there was a twinkle in his blue eyes. "I see you kept your fencing clothes. You'd better not let Lavvy catch you in that rig if you know what's good for you. Or me, for that matter," he concluded darkly.

"Uncle Tony, we've been practicing to ride like Mr. Ducrow, and Caro rode 'round and 'round standing on Prince's back and then Lord Daventry came and he rode two horses standing up," Ceddie interrupted eagerly.

"Oh Lord!" Tony looked rueful. "Now I am in the basket! Don't let word of this get to your mother, lad. She'll lay blame for it at my door for taking you to Astley's and I shan't be allowed to set foot here again."

"As if I would," Ceddie began scornfully. Then, not

wishing to exclude his beloved uncle from all the fun, he continued, "Would you like to have a go?"

"What? After you've watched the likes of two such equestrians as Caro and Nicky? You must be all about in the head if you think I am going to try to compete with them. I've my own reputation to maintain after all." He peered at Nicky. "Taken to riding without boots, have you man? That ought to cut quite a dash in the park."

"Oh Lord!" Nicholas looked rueful. "No, but I was so intent on maintaining my form that I quite forgot I was without them. Thank you." He took the boots from Tim, who was eyeing the marquess with new respect. There was no doubt about it, his lordship was a proper gentleman all right, not one of those town beaux he had seen so much lately who were so obviously better acquainted with their tailors than their horses. Now, here was a man for her ladyship, the groom thought to himself.

Though fully aware of Lady Caroline's wish to remain independent and entirely respectful of that wish, Tim couldn't help hoping that she would find someone who could share life with her. Miss Gray was a nice sort of lady, all very well as a companion for talking about books and such, but she was an indifferent rider and did not care about horses above half. The Countess's brother, could offer more sporting companionship, but anyone could see that he had nothing in his cock-loft and that would never do for his mistress who, as far as the groom could see, knew more than most men. Tim had seen the way the marquess, try though he would to fix his eyes elsewhere, had looked at Caro in her breeches, and he felt encouraged. In truth, Lady Caroline was a rare armful, but most people never stopped to consider it because she dressed so plainly and did so little to call attention to herself. For his part, Tim thought she was far more beautiful than his mistress's cousin who spent half the day primping and fussing so that she looked more like an overdressed doll than a real woman. The groom smiled to himself. The situation would bear some watching. His mistress was as yet unconscious of all this, but she appeared to like the marquess well enough, and no female could be in the presence of such a fine figure of a man without being affected. Yes, this would definitely bear watching.

Meanwhile, Clarence, silently observing the scene as he usually did, had worked his way over to his cousin. "Did

Uncle Tony teach you to fence, Cousin Caro?'' he asked shyly. Truly, there was no end to the surprises where this new relative was concerned.

"Why yes, he did,'' Caro smiled down into the big blue eyes. "Whenever I visited at Mandeville Park, we would sneak into the barn where he very kindly initiated me into the intricacies of swordsmanship. But you mustn't say anything about that to anyone.''

"Why ever not?'' Ceddie demanded. "If I could fight with swords, I should certainly want everyone to know.''

"Yes, dear, but you are a boy and it's all very well for boys to do such things, but the world frowns upon it if ladies do.''

"I don't think that's fair. I am glad I am not a lady. They don't have any fun,'' Ceddie declared stoutly.

"Precisely. But one is not allowed a great deal of choice in such matters,'' his cousin replied.

"You see, Ceddie, you must always make sure to see that the females of your acquaintance have as much fun as you do, and the world will be a better place for it,'' a deep voice remarked.

Caro whirled around to find the marquess, once again properly shod, standing next to her. "And do you shoot as well as fence, Waif?'' he inquired with some amusement.

"No,'' she replied wistfully. "And as I've only just learned to fence with any sort of confidence, I . . .''

"And a remarkably good swordswoman she is, too. You want to watch yourself with her, Nicky. I don't believe I've ever seen a quicker eye or a defter wrist,'' Tony volunteered with pride. He fell silent a moment, frowning in concentration. "Needs to improve the footwork, though. Yes that's it.'' His brow cleared. "She's light enough on her feet, but not fast enough.''

"If you possess a good eye and a steady hand, no doubt you will enjoy shooting a pistol. It isn't as elegant as fencing, but there is a greater challenge to one's concentration. I should be most happy to teach you,'' Nicholas offered. Thinking about it, he could not be quite sure why he had. Certainly he had no wish to encourage a ferocious bluestocking to be even more eccentric than she already was, but there had been something about Tony's possessive manner in speaking of Caro's fencing prowess that had irked him. Not that he didn't consider Tony to be the best of good fellows, but though a competent swordsman, he had been bested by Nicholas himself upon several occasions. Nor could the marquess imagine that someone who thought as seriously and deeply about things as Lady Caroline Waverly would have much to say to any purpose to someone whose lighthearted insouciance in the face of all disaster was legendary. The viscount was the best of companions if one were downing pints of ale at a mill, following the hunt, or looking for sport of any sort, but beyond that and his cheerful, handsome countenance, he had little to recommend him. It was difficult for Nicholas to fathom what Caro and Tony would have to talk about or why she should smile at him quite so fondly when he praised her swordsmanship.

"Oh, thank you ever so much. I have been wanting to learn, but Tony was not very forthcoming." Caro directed a teasing glance at her cousin. "And I did not like to ask. I should enjoy it of all things, but . . . but, how did you know?" Caro's gray eyes were alight with expectation. Truly, she was as pleased and excited as if he had just given her a set of jewels. In fact, she was more delighted with this simple offer than his mistress, Suzette, had been by the diamond necklace he had recently bestowed on her. Caro's happiness made Nicholas feel more fully appreciated than Suzette's professions of gratitude had. Apologizing in his heart to Caro for such an unflattering comparison, he replied, "Something told me that a person who risks her neck riding erect on ponies and fencing with Tony would naturally be drawn to more dangerous sport, and the best way to keep such a person from coming to the bad end that seems inevitable, is to ensure that they have an excellent teacher." He raised a teasing eyebrow.

Caro made a face. "And where ever are you going to find such an exemplary instructor?" she wondered.

"You imp!" He laughed. "I have it on the best authority that Nicholas Daventry is accounted a fair shot. But more important, he is possessed of *infinite* patience."

"Oh, you couldn't do better than Nicky," Tony blithely assured her. "Why he even beat Weatherby at Manton's the other day."

Caro appeared to consider, tilting her head to one side and scrutinizing the marquess. "Very well, then, but only if I truly am getting an expert."

"You are." Nicholas grinned.

Suddenly uncomfortable at having her wishes so easily divined and fulfilled, Caro reached over to rub Duke's nose before glancing shyly up at the marquess. "Thank you," she whispered. "I am truly grateful for, for . . ." She struggled for the words. What was it that touched her so about his offer? Was it that he treated her as a special person, that he seemed to understand Caro Waverly and to realize that her interests were different from those of other women? Was it that he accepted her odd quirks and appeared to like her, even respect her in spite of them? Or was it simply that he was offering her friendship, something that was very precious to one who had led such a solitary life? She sighed. It was too difficult to capture in a few words. "For so many things," she finished lamely.

Caro cursed her inarticulateness, but looking up into his face at last, she could see that Nicholas knew what she was trying so unsuccessfully to say. The grin had softened into a sympathetic smile and there was a look of appreciation, almost of fondness in his eyes as he replied, "You are most welcome."

They stood for several seconds this way, transfixed, as if isolated from the rest of the world by this mutual understanding and esteem. Then the irrepressible Ceddie broke in, "Pistols! Famous! Oh, Cousin Caro, how lucky you are," he sighed enviously knowing that a mother who disapproved of dogs and ponies would never countenance such engines of destruction.

Nicholas, hearing the sigh, was touched. "I am afraid Ceddie that you have not quite grown into them, but you are more than welcome to watch so that when your hands are a little larger, you will already have some feeling for the sport."

Ceddie was so ecstatic that for once in his life he was entirely bereft of speech and it was left to his cousin to say, "Thank you. Somehow you seem to anticipate all our wishes. You are most kind."

Nicholas looked up at the sun. He wanted to stay, to reassure her that he was not being kind, that he truly enjoyed her company, and that it made him happy to gratify such simple wishes, to watch faces and eyes light up with enthusiasm. He could see that for too long Caro and the boys had been unappreciated or misunderstood. The extraordinary pleasure they exhibited at the least offer of friendship was touching in the extreme. All of a sudden, the marquess found himself wanting to give them everything, in order to keep those looks of happiness forever on their countenances. Also, oddly enough, he wanted to thank them for including him in their escapade, for making him feel alive and appreciated for something besides his exalted place in the *ton*. The words would not come and he was forced to content himself with, ''I shall look forward to it, but I must be off. I promised Holworthy I would spend the rest of the day going over accounts with him, but I did want to invite Lady Caroline, Lavinia, and Miss Gray to *Guy Mannering* tomorrow evening. I have convinced Mama and Clary to go and lured them with the promise that I would try to secure rational companionship for them.''

Caro felt foolishly flattered. He truly did seem to wish for intelligent conversation, or else he would have spoken to Lavinia first. Since Lavinia had made no mention of such a thing, he must not have broached the subject with her. ''Why thank you. I can only speak for myself, of course, but I should be delighted.''

''Good, then.'' He leapt onto Caesar and, with a wave to the assembled company, headed off in the direction of Daventry House.

16

WHEN INFORMED of the marquess's invitations, Lavinia was decidedly cool. Not only was she miffed that it had been extended to her in a most offhand manner—through her cousin, no less—but also that that the marquess so obviously expected her to be free. In a more socially aware person, this would have been a calculated insult. Coming from Nicky, it was merely another indication that, though he might now be one of the leaders of fashion, he was not so far removed from the brash young officer who had not only expected her to marry a younger son, but a soldier at that. Really, he could be almost as obtuse as Tony at times.

Therefore, the countess found herself in something of a quandary. She truly did welcome any opportunity to be with Nicky, for whatever his faults, he was devastatingly handsome, not to mention the most eligible bachelor the *ton* had to offer. On the other hand, it would do her case no good to be taken so much for granted that a belated invitation was as casually extended to her as if he were asking a sister. In Lavvy's experience, gentlemen who treated one as a sister were unlikely to consider one in the light of a wife. Eyes narrowed for a moment, she plotted swiftly. "Aha! The perfect thing," she exclaimed after a moment's thought. "We should be happy to join the Daventrys in their box, but the honor of escorting us has been secured by Sir Evelyn Willoughby."

"But Lavvy, that is not true! He hasn't invited us." Caro was horrified.

"Well, not in so many words," her cousin conceded, "but he has most certainly begged us time out of mind to join him at the theater. And we have just accepted," she concluded triumphantly. "I shall just pen him a short note." And before Caro could respond, she had disappeared from the room in a swirl of lemon-colored muslin.

Recovering from her surprise, Caro shrugged. She should have expected no less from Lavvy, she supposed, but really, these social machinations were so exhausting! How much easier it would all be were she simply to accept the marquess's invitation since that was the person whose company she appeared to be after, if the flirtatious behavior she always exhibited in his presence were any indication. Shaking her head, Caro went off in search of the soothing companionship of the *Times* and the progress of the seditious meetings bill.

A note delivered some time later and addressed to Lavinia in the marquess's careless scrawl went a little way to raising that gentleman in the lady's affections. Some time later, in search of a better quill, she invaded the drawing room. "At least he had the decency to send 'round an invitation, even if it is unconscionably late. Why he should think we are so readily available is more than I can say," she remarked, sniffing audibly.

Her head buried in the paper, Caro grinned. So that was what was behind her cousin's annoyance. It would do Lavvy good to be taken for granted once in awhile instead of forever making men dance to her tune.

Nor was the countess necessarily the center of attention once they reached the theater. Remembering Lady Caroline's original and perspicacious remarks from their encounter at the opera, Sir Evelyn, having carefully seated the ladies and assured himself of their comfort, leaned over and addressed her. "Having enjoyed your comments on *Figaro*, I am most curious to hear what you hope from this play, Lady Caroline."

"I?" Caro was astonished. "You flatter me, sir. I have no expectations in particular. Ordinarily, I do not read a great deal of Scott as I oftentimes find him too romantical to my taste. I am afraid that I prefer Miss Austen's novels. For what they may lack in sentiment, they make up for in her ironic touch and skilled observation of the world. However, I would be the first to admit that they would not lend themselves to dramatic production as do Mr. Scott's, which are full of incident and color."

"I am surprised at you, Lady Caroline. I should have thought that a young lady who preferred *Don Giovanni* to Mozart's other operas would appreciate the same power to move in the sublime Mr. Scott."

Caro cocked her head, an intent look in her eyes as she considered for a moment. "Yes, I suppose that would make a deal more sense. But while I respond to the sublime in music, I find my taste in literature rather tends in other directions and I, for one, do not wish for the picturesque at the expense of character, though I expect that such a point of view is eccentric enough to the point of being heretical."

"I should think that the subject matter of Miss Austen's novels more closely resembles your own cynical view of society. In some respects, reading her novels must be like sharing a conversation with a kindred spirit," Nicholas broke in.

"Oh dear," Caro was distressed. "I had not meant to appear cynical in the least. Far from it. It is because I believe that society can improve that I am so critical of it."

"Oh? And now do you propose to carry out this ambitious scheme? As a devotee of Mary Wollstonecraft, you no doubt have a plan." There had been an earnestness in Caro's tone that had caught Nicholas's interest. It was so rare that anyone in the *ton,* and young ladies in particular, was passionate about anything, that he found her idealism both a refreshing change and extraordinarily appealing.

It was not, however, appealing to some other unwilling members of the party. "Nicky, Caro, it is too bad of you. We are here to enjoy ourselves and you insist upon discussing the problems of the world. Surely they can wait another day to be solved." Lavinia laid a hand on the marquess's arm and smiled up at him.

Unable to resist the entreaty in her eyes or her whispered, "Please, Nicky, it is so long since I have been able to enjoy myself", he smiled back.

"We shall consider ourselves properly rebuked, Lavvy, and promise to speak of nothing but the most amusing and trivial of topics for the rest of the evening. Now, what would you have us discourse upon?"

"Don't discourse upon anything." The beauty pouted enchantingly. "After all, we are here to be entertained and . . . oh, do look at Lady Heatherington. What possesses a harridan like that to ape the manners and dress of a young lady in her first Season, I cannot say. But it begins. We must stop our idle chatter and see what Mr. Scott has to offer us. I adore his books, but it is so much nicer to have them

presented to one instead of having to shut oneself up in
one's library and read. Do you not think so, Nicky?''

''Idle chatter,'' Caro, now thoroughly disgusted, muttered to herself. As if she weren't the queen of ''idle chatter''! Doing her best to shut out the affecting scene of
Nicholas's dark head bent towards Lavvy's fair one, his blue
eyes gazing appreciatively into her imploring ones, Caro
rigidly concentrated her attention on the stage. But her mind
was in a turmoil. Was it truly possible that he could contin-
ually fall for such transparent ploys and insipid conversation? Did intelligence, either the obvious abundance of his
and the equally obvious lack of hers count for nothing? Apparently not. If so, how was it possible not to be cynical
about life?

Caro was so wrapped up in her own unpleasant reflections
that she did not observe Nicholas's gaze transfer itself to her
the moment the play began. Using Lavinia's own strategy
to disengage himself from their *tête-à-tête,* he murmured,
''There, the curtain is up.'' And once he was sure that the
countess's attention, such as it was, was focused on the
action below, he turned back towards Caro, hoping to catch
her eye and signal his interest in continuing the discussion.
But Caro was staring intently at the scene on stage and there
was something about the stiffness of her posture that suggested her disapproval of the entire episode with Lavvy.

Again the marquess felt a surge of annoyance that she
should set herself up as some sort of judge of her cousin.
After all, Lavvy was merely a product of her world, and a
charming one at that. Just because Caro subscribed to im-
possibly high moral principles was no reason to condemn
others out of hand.

A tiny sigh caught the marquess's attention and he glanced
again in Caro's direction, more observantly this time. Now
it seemed to him that the shoulders which had been so
straight a moment ago drooped. Her dark brows were drawn
tighter together and her brow was wrinkled in unhappy puzzlement. From what he could see, there was a hurt look in
the gray eyes which he could not quite fathom.

Nicholas frowned, wondering at the change in her. Unlike other women in the *ton,* Caro was entirely transparent
and one had the feeling, looking into her clear eyes, that
one was peering directly into her soul—a condition that was

both reassuring and disturbing. It was reassuring because one could always count on her to be honest, disturbing because she demanded the same sort of honesty in return and would not be fobbed off with easy answers or charming smiles. She was a funny little thing to be sure, prickly and proud, but in the main, somehow, he felt infinitely comfortable with her.

The marquess was not the only person focusing more attention on Lady Caroline Waverly than on the stage. Sir Evelyn had been an interested observer of the entire scene, had read the annoyance in Lavinia's eyes when Nicholas's interest had strayed from her, and had remarked on the determined set of her head as she coquettishly reclaimed it. He had also remarked on Caro's determined effort to ignore her cousin's machinations and had sensed something of the conflict within her. For all her obvious intelligence, Lady Caroline had much to learn about the world and herself. Sir Evelyn had correctly interpreted Caro's disappointment in the marquess's immediate capitulation to her cousin's charms. But unlike that young lady, he, with his vaster experience of the world in general and the *ton* in particular, recognized Nicholas's response for what it was—the purely reflexive action of a gentleman whose attention is required by a lady. He had noticed the marquess's reluctance to interrupt his conversation with Caro and he had also seen how quickly his interest returned to her once politeness to Lavinia had been satisfied.

Inveterate and enthusiastic social observer that he was, Sir Evelyn smiled to himself. This situation would bear some watching and, with a little outside help, might possibly develop into something quite entertaining, to say the least. He suspected that Lady Caroline Waverly and the Marquess of Everleigh had more in common than they might have imagined. Endowed with abundant and active intellects, they were obviously concerned with the improvement of their society, and both were equally untroubled that such interests were considered to be most dreadfully unfashionable.

The middle-aged exquisite had known Nicholas Daventry ever since the gallant young officer had appeared briefly one Season before departing for a brilliant career on the Peninsula, leaving a trail of broken hearts behind him. Sir Evelyn knew well his taste for adventure and his thirst for glory. If he was not much mistaken—and Sir Evelyn rarely was about such things for he collected people the way his cronies collected snuff boxes and walking sticks—Lady Caroline was possessed of an equally ardent spirit. There was something about the flash in her eyes and the vibrant tone in her voice when she spoke of things she held dear that hinted at a passionate nature. And he, Sir Evelyn, was going to help her uncover these depths to the delight of some and the chagrin of others. He much suspected that, given the proper encouragement, she would blossom into a truly captivating woman, possessing the warmth and intelligence that her cousin lacked, and would give the Countess of Welham a run for her money. Not that Lavinia wasn't all that was enchanting. Personally, he infinitely preferred a woman of her highly cultivated and delicate sensibilities. They were much more predictable and passion—though irresistible and involving—could be so thoroughly fatiguing.

Meanwhile, the entire episode had not gone unnoticed by other occupants of the box. Though perhaps less astute than Sir Evelyn, Lady Clarissa Daventry, always highly perceptive wherever her brother's happiness was involved, had also noticed the eagerness in Nicky's eyes when they rested on her friend. And when she too had realized that he was merely being polite to Lavinia, she had been greatly relieved. Catching his glance straying back to Caro at the first possible moment, Clary was highly gratified that the very real attractions of Caro's mind and person outweighed the more obvious and superficial ones of the Countess of Welham.

A germ of an idea began to form itself in her mind. Accustomed to seeing women fling themselves at her brother's head, and concerned lest someone unworthy of him should somehow manage to ensnare him, she had never given the least thought to the type of person she would choose for her adored Nicky. Now, the more she thought about it, the more she realized that Lady Caroline was just such a one as she would choose. Equally as energetic as Nicholas, she also applied her mind to as wide a variety of interests as he did and she exhibited the same unobtrusive kindness and concern for others that set her brother apart from the rest of society and made him so beloved by his household.

It was Caro's inquiring mind and refusal to accept things as they were that had been responsible for one of the most exciting changes in Clary's circumscribed existence. All be-

cause Caro had paid attention to her and extended her ready
sympathy, Lady Clarissa was growing stronger and more
self-confident with her daily rides in the park. Caro had
been able to see beyond the frail invalid and had somehow
appreciated the spirit that lay beneath. Like Nicholas, who
threw himself into a problem the minute he perceived it,
Caro, in her own quiet way, had set about encouraging and
freeing that spirit until Clarissa felt quite like a new person.

Clary's observant gaze had also taken in another fascinating aspect of the scene: that Lady Caroline had seemed
to become more animated whenever she was conversing with
her brother. Even if the discussion was confined to the most
general of topics, she appeared to look to Nicholas for stimulation of her own thoughts on a given subject. It was his
comments that spurred her to further reflection and response, and it was clear to anyone who cared to pay attention that Caro relished the challenge of debating with him.

A secret smile crept over Clary's face as she too resolved
to bring these two together. Not only would it give happiness to Caro and Nicky, it would also save Nicky from the
clutches of Lavinia and that alone would be worth the effort.

Clary had never had any particular love for Lavvy, who
only paid attention to her when she wished to advance her
cause with Nicky. Nor did Clary relish the way Lavvy had
always looked upon Nicky as though he were some posses-
sion, carefully selected to enhance her reputation—whether
it was as the wounded hero from the Peninsula or the Marquess of Everleigh. Clary loved her brother dearly and she
was not about to have him become a mere accessory to a
lady of fashion. Besides, with Lavinia, he would be bored
within a fortnight. Beautiful though she was, the Countess
of Welham was not precisely stimulating company. Though
Nicky might have been forced to abandon existence as the
dashing Captain Daventry, he was not about to take his place
tamely in the *ton,* at least not the way Lavinia would expect
him to.

It was obvious from the half-wary, half-interested way
that Nicky and Caro dealt with one another and from the
concerted effort that Lavinia was mounting to capture the
marquess that Nicky, usually more than able to fend for
himself, was in need of assistance from an outside source.
But how was Clary to begin? To one who had lived most of
her life apart from that sea of gossip and intrigue that was

the *ton,* the plotting and contrivance required by the situation was entirely foreign to her. For the first time in her existence, Clary began to wish she had acquired the skills of a normal young lady of rank to whom such machinations were part of daily life.

Fortunately for all and sundry, fate, in the form of two of Almack's most illustrious patronesses, was about to take a hand. The curtain had hardly fallen on the first act when the door to the box opened to admit Princess Esterhazy and Lady Jersey.

"Caro, my dear, how charming to encounter you in London. I had quite despaired of seeing you here after you resisted all my efforts to entice you. But then, you always were the most willful child and the very image of your handsome papa. We miss him dreadfully still. But tell me how you go on." Barely pausing to acknowledge the other occupants of the box, the princess, her face alight with welcome, sat down next to Caro and immediately engaged her in lively reminiscences of foreign courts and past political intrigues.

Lady Jersey, who had come more to see the new Marquess of Everleigh than to accompany her friend, advanced on that gentleman with a flirtatious glint in her eye. "So, Nicholas, you are forced to give up your madcap ways and join the rest of us dull respectables. How very fortunate, to be sure. We shall do our utmost to see that you remain amused." She smiled wickedly at him while noting gleefully the countess's rigid posture and frozen smile.

Though loquacious to a fault, Sally Jersey was no fool and her bright chatter hid a keenly observant mind. She had noted the look of annoyance, quickly concealed, that had crossed Lavinia's face at the princess's obvious preference for her cousin. This ill humor had not been improved by the princess's cool acknowledgement of the Countess of Welham nor by Nicholas's pleasure in seeing Sally. The Countess of Welham was accustomed to being the center of attention and did not take gracefully to a subsidiary role. Well, it would do her good. It was time someone took Lavinia down a peg or two and Sally Jersey was precisely the one to do it.

Smiling sweetly, she turned to Lavvy. "How charming to have your cousin for a companion this Season. She appears quite enchanting, and with her fortune should do exceedingly well. She is a taking thing, and if she is anything like her dear papa, she will soon have the *ton* flocking around her.'' There, that should do it! Having lighted the spark, Sally sat back to see if it would catch.

A frown, quickly banished, crossed Lavvy's face. Her lips tightened and her blue eyes were icy. Then, taking a breath, she forced her lips into the semblance of a smile. ''Yes, of course.'' She leaned forward confidingly though keeping her tone of voice loud enough to be overheard. ''But she is shockingly blue, you know. At times I quite despair. She *will* spend so much time with her books and her journals that, as you can see, she hardly has a moment to spare for her toilette. Of course, I try to help, but she seems determined to become an antidote. If I drop so much as the slightest hint that she is on the path to becoming an ape-leader, she merely smiles and says that it is very well with her. You, aware as you are of the ways of the world, can sympathize with me I am sure.'' Lavvy shrugged prettily, adopting a look of patient resignation.

''Just so, my dear countess. Well, we shall see what we can do to bring her more into fashion.'' Sally's eyes sparkled maliciously. ''Come along, Therese. We must return to our seats before the play resumes.'' And thus, having planted these seeds of conflict, she exited serenely leaving turmoil in her wake.

17

As usual, Lady Jersey's strategy had been highly successful. Without exception, each occupant of the box was left with certain reflections, some more unsettling than others. Lavinia was positively fuming. That the princess should so obviously snub her in favor of her scrubby little cousin was outside of enough, but to have that odious Sally Jersey gloating over it and flirting with Nicholas was beyond all bearing! She turned a dazzling smile on the marquess and picked up the thread of her flirtatious chatter, which had been so rudely interrupted.

For her part, Caro was almost as upset as Lavinia. That Lavvy, for whom she had sacrificed her freedom and the delight she took daily from the freshness of the countryside around Waverly Court, should consider her such a liability to her standing in the *ton* when Caro accompanied her from one stultifying gathering to another was so infuriating that it was not to be thought of. For one brief moment, Caro had the most insane desire to grab her cousin's slim white throat, shake her until her teeth rattled, and tell her precisely what she thought of her spoiled and selfish ways.

Fortunately, before she could commit such an act of violence, Sir Evelyn Willoughby intervened. Well-accustomed to the ways of Sally Jersey, he saw what she was about and stepped in smoothly to pick up where she had left off. Smiling benignly, he continued as though there had not been an ominous silence after the ladies' departure. "I can see you are a great favorite with the princess. Small wonder, for she rarely finds someone with enough wit to keep her amused for long. It is her esprit and intelligence which distinguish her from the rest of the members of the *ton* and attract so many admirers. Compared to all the exquisite but vapid women of fashion, she is a refreshing change and her charm is all the more potent because it is unique. You are very like her, you know.''

"I?" Caro gasped, thinking that there could be nothing further from the truth. That anyone who had just been stipulated an antidote could be compared in the same breath with one of Almack's most brilliant patronesses seemed ludicrous in the extreme.

"Why, you are every bit as clever as the princess and, as far as your person goes, you are far more lovely." Casting a swift grateful smile at Sir Evelyn, Helena came stoutly to the defense of her protegée.

"Indubitably. I am glad that you agree with me, Miss Gray. I can see I was not mistaken in thinking you a woman of great good sense." Sir Evelyn bowed gracefully in her direction. "But, Lady Caroline, you do your sex a disservice by depriving the *ton* of your stimulating conversation. Why should those who devote their existences to their outward appearance succeed at the expense of those who put their energies into higher things? You will do society no good at all, you know, by burying yourself in the country and allowing such women to rule the *ton*."

The flash in Caro's eyes was indication enough that Sir Evelyn had struck a responsive chord. Good! He had thought her well and truly roused by Lavinia's shabby treatment. All she needed now was the tiniest bit of encouragement.

"I hadn't quite thought of it that way," she replied thoughtfully. She remained silent for some minutes, struck by the novelty of the idea. Then, giving herself a shake, she continued stoutly, "And I shan't allow such a state of affairs to continue. It is not enough merely to read tracts about such things. One must put one's beliefs into action. The only way to change the way of the world is to best it at its own game." Her chin went up and the light of battle shone in her eyes, only to disappear an instant later. "But how shall I begin? I haven't the least notion of how to go on. If it weren't for the help of Susan, I should barely be presentable." She waved an apologetic hand over her serviceable evening gown of white tulle over white satin. Like the rest of her wardrobe, it was appropriate but uninspired. Caro was conscious of the lack of *éclat* in her toilette, but heretofore, she had not thought much about it, nor had she particularly cared. Now, all of a sudden it seemed imperative that she stun the *ton* with her style. For after all, how was she to convince them of the superiority of her ideas if she could not convince them of the superiority of her taste—an interest that appeared to be a consuming one in the fashionable world. If that meant that she must look like someone out of *La Belle Assemblée,* then so be it.

It was the entree Sir Evelyn had been waiting for. "Oh, as to that," he dismissed her objection with a graceful wave of one white hand, "that is the merest nothing. Why I know the very person you must consult on these matters."

"You do?" Caro and Helena spoke as one.

"But, of course. When one is a slave to the world of fashion as I, one knows these things." He gave a deprecatory shrug, but there was a twinkle in his eyes. "I don't base my entire happiness on it, but I do derive considerable amusement from being *au courant.* I have a dear friend from ages ago, Violette, who for many years kept her family alive after their escape from France with her skill as a needlewoman. She is respectably married now to a merchant of great wealth and position so has no need to earn her way, which is unfortunate because she is possessed of a truly extraordinary talent. And while I am most delighted at her well-deserved good fortune, as a connoisseur, I am saddened that the world has lost a creative genius. She is truly an artist and, given the proper inspiration, I believe she could be persuaded to return to her craft. I shall see what I can do to convince her of the worthiness of the endeavor."

"You are too kind. Thank you. I should be most appreciative of your help, Sir Evelyn." Caro smiled brilliantly at him. Scorn her cousin though she would for her coquettish ways, Caro was perfectly capable of flattery when it was employed in the promotion of a noble cause. Nor was Sir Evelyn proof against the gratitude he read in the big gray eyes, and he resolved to call on Violette Winwood the very next day.

Thus it was that he spent the following morning in Henrietta Street employing every ounce of charm he possessed attempting to convince Mrs. Winwood that he was in a such a desperate case of need only her particular skills could save him.

"It is too bad of you, Evelyn," the lady scolded him smilingly after he had carefully put forth the entire situation for her consideration, "when you know how busy I am with

John and the children, to try to tempt me into such a thing. Your Lady Caroline sounds like a perfectly charming young person whose ideals I most earnestly support, but truly I cannot. Timothy, who is recovering from a fever, is dreadfully fretful. And Mary, my maid has just had the most unfortunate fall and broken her leg. I truly would like to help you, but I fear I cannot.''

Sir Evelyn sighed gently and played his trump card. "I understand, Violette, but it is the greatest shame to stand by and let Lavinia Mandeville have it all her way.''

"Lavinia Mandeville? You never told me that Lady Caroline's cousin is Lavinia Mandeville!'' Violette was all attention now. She had not forgotten an evening many years ago when as a poor *emigré* desperate for the cultural stimulation she had once enjoyed, she had accompanied her kindhearted patroness, Lady Frances Knightley, to the opera. There, the beautiful Lavinia Mandeville, seeing one of her beaux take a kindly interest in the shy little French girl, had sniffed quite audibly and wondered out loud what the world was coming to if people in trade were to be seen absolutely everywhere.

Her visitor repressed a victorious smile. "Yes, is it not sad? As far as the fashionable world is concerned, she is a mere babe compared to Lavinia and quite without resources. I had been hoping that with your help . . .'' he allowed his voice to trail off a moment before continuing briskly, "but I quite see you are taken up with affairs here and I shan't trouble you further.'' He turned to pick up his walking stick.

"No, stay awhile.'' His hostess held out a restraining hand. "Let me ring for some refreshment and we shall see what can be done. After all, it is time that the Lavinias of the world be checked in their absolute sway over society.''

It was nearly a good two hours later when Sir Evelyn quitted the slim elegant house on Henrietta Street and, a congratulatory smile on his face, directed his coachman to drive him to Grosvenor Square. There he found Caro and her companion, with a volume of *Guy Mannering* open before them on the table, deep in a discussion of the previous evening's performance.

The ladies were delighted to see him. "The very person! Do sit down. Helena and I were just talking about last night's play and checking to see how faithfully Mr. Scott's work was put before us. We have reached a small area of disagreement and, being absolutely convinced of the merits of our own arguments, are in want of a third party to offer a disinterested view,'' Caro greeted him with flattering enthusiasm.

Sir Evelyn bowed. ''I should be delighted, as I am loath to think of any disharmony between two such lovely and spirited ladies. But first, I must put aside such lofty discussions in favor of more mundane but pressing affairs to inform you I am come from Violette Winwood's with an invitation to take tea with her in Henrietta Street. She is intrigued by Lady Caroline's dilemma and is most anxious to do what she can for her.''

Caro thanked Sir Evelyn prettily enough for his efforts on her behalf, but she remained doubtful both as to anyone's capacity to transform her into an enviable figure of fashion and as to the possibility that she might like such a person well enough to trust her to do so.

Caro's face, always vividly expressive, was a mirror of these thoughts and Sir Evelyn hastened to reassure her. ''Violette is the dearest soul imaginable and had she not been forced to turn to dressmaking to support her mother and younger sisters, I feel sure she would have become an artist of some note, perhaps another Angelica Kauffman—with the proper training of course. If I were not quite certain that you two would deal famously together, I should not have suggested such a thing in the first place, believe me, Lady Caroline.''

Caro blushed at her transparency, disclaimed any such mistrust in Sir Evelyn's judgment, and promised to accompany him to the Winwoods' the next day.

Any remaining misgivings were banished the instant she was ushered into Violette's drawing room where everything, including the lady herself, was in restrained but exquisite taste. Everywhere she looked there were objects that not only delighted the eye, but also caught the interest of the beholder, making one wish to know more about the character of their owner. Unusual and beautiful Oriental porcelains were displayed on the delicately carved Adam fireplace. Small, deftly arranged bunches of hothouse flowers were unobtrusively placed to enliven the airy apartment with color and fragrance. Caro found its chief inhabitant to be as pleasing as the drawing room itself.

Violette Winwood was a diminutive creature whose pleasant but unexceptional features were lent distinction by a pair of expressive brown eyes and a mouth about which a friendly smile always appeared to be hovering. Her dress of jaconet muslin was of an unusual canary color and, like the rest of her toilette, while it at first appeared unremarkable, once it had caught the observer's eye, proved to be of original and elegant design quite unlike anything Caro had seen before. In spite of herself, she was intrigued.

"I am so glad you have come." A welcoming smile lit up her hostess's face as she motioned her visitors to chairs on either side of the fireplace where a cheerful flame took the slight chill off the air. "Sir Evelyn painted a portrait of you as such a woman of character that I was not altogether certain you would consent to call on me, but I am delighted to make the acquaintance of a reader of Mary Wollstonecraft. I am quite an admirer of her work and only sorry that economic necessity forced me to participate in a small way in the creation of the types of female she deplores. But, from what Sir Evelyn tells me of you, perhaps I can be of assistance in promoting the reputation of a woman who will serve as an example to our sex and then, in some way, I shall make amends." And so, by degrees, Violette proceeded to put Caro at ease and discover more about her.

There ensued a most agreeable afternoon spent discussing a variety of topics ranging from the agricultural practices of Mr. Jethro Tull to Mr. Owen's plan for the relief of the manufacturing and laboring poor. For Violette, having had to earn her living from a young age, could not forget all those other unfortunates who were still in the same situation and likely to remain so for the rest of their lives.

"I honor you greatly for your sentiments, Mrs. Winwood," Caro assured her hostess earnestly as she bid her adieu. "And I cannot but acknowledge that I feel slightly ashamed at never having suffered such hardship and therefore never having experienced the conditions which I am endeavoring to correct. It must seem to you that on my part this is the greatest piece of impertinence."

Violette laughed gaily. "Never fear, Lady Caroline. It was an accident of birth that allowed you to study the philosophical, moral, and legal systems which will correct the ills of society that I have learned about through another equally capricious accident of birth. Suffice to say, all that matters is that we are persons of sensibility who wish to correct the injustices of the world. In that we are equals and we understand each other. I am delighted to have made your acquaintance, and I hope to prove just that by putting my skills at your service.''

''Thank you so much for your offer. I have enjoyed myself excessively, but I can't think how anyone, even someone as intelligent as you appear to be, can transform me into what I need to be.'' Caro gratefully pressed the lady's hand before allowing Sir Evelyn to escort her to the carriage.

That experienced observer of mankind was thoroughly enjoying the sense of satisfaction that any social being must experience after having introduced two kindred spirits. Nor could he resist treating himself to a few congratulatory remarks. ''I trust you found Mrs. Winwood to be congenial, Lady Caroline.''

Caro turned to him with shining eyes and a happy smile that was a reward in itself. ''Oh yes, thank you, Sir Evelyn. I enjoyed myself immensely. What a delightful person she is, to be sure. But how can someone such as that possibly understand what I needs must acquire in order to win the acclaim of the *ton?*''

Her mentor smiled enigmatically. ''Never fear. Violette is a woman of parts. She will have taken your measure and no doubt will create a wardrobe for you accordingly.''

''A wardrobe?'' Caro exclaimed in surprise.

''But, of course. Why else do you think I introduced you to her?''

''But . . . but she didn't take any measurements or push me and pull me and pin and chatter,'' Caro protested.

''Ah, but Violette does not need to, and therein lies her art. She looks at a person, absorbs her personality, and translates it into the appropriate garments. Have no fear. You will see. Of course, eventually she will have to subject you to the tedious business of final fittings, but for the moment she will concentrate on designing gowns that capture and express your own distinctive character.''

18

THOUGH SIR EVELYN was obviously a man who devoted a considerable amount of his time to his tailor, Caro was skeptical at his lavish encomiums. She need not have worried, for where matters of taste were concerned, that exquisite peer could be relied upon absolutely not to exaggerate—far too much was at stake. Much to her surprise, Violette's sketches were delivered early the next morning by a likely looking lad who refused to give them up even to the imposing Wigmore, insisting as he quaked in his boots before that august personage, "Miz Winwood told me as I wuz only to give 'em to Lady Caroline herself, nobody else nor even if it was the Queen of England as asked for 'em."

And he was amply rewarded by a grateful smile from the lady in question who, seeing him hungrily eyeing her breakfast muffins, instructed that he be taken to the kitchens for something to refresh him for the return journey. "Please convey my compliments to your mistress for choosing such a reliable messenger and extend my thanks to her for her efforts. May I know your name?"

The lad, though momentarily stunned that one of the Quality should know he even possessed such a thing, much less inquire about it, replied forthrightly, "It's Bill, mum. Bill Small."

Caro, fully aware of Wigmore's horrified stare behind her and relishing his discomfiture, smiled again. "Well, thank you, Bill Small. Now run along and see what Cook can find you." There, that should give the odious prig something to think about. She congratulated herself with smug satisfaction, knowing full well that the story would be repeated to interested audiences in both Grosvenor Square and Henrietta Street.

"She will never command that respect of the lower classes which is so necessary to the consequence of a true lady,"

Wigmore sniffed to the sympathetic housekeeper. "I am only glad I am employed by someone who knows what is owed to her rank and keeps a proper distance."

Meanwhile, Caro was examining Violette's sketches in the privacy of her boudoir where she could be sure her cousin would never seek her out. Besides, she was eager to discover Susan's opinions of Violette's efforts. For her part, Caro was mightily impressed. Somehow, Sir Evelyn's friend had managed to capture her taste for simplicity and comfort and her preference for garments that allowed one to move easily without forever worrying that one would stumble over a flounce or tear a delicate sleeve that was molded too tightly to the shape. There were sketches of a ball gown, carriage dress, and a walking dress—each more breathtaking than the last. Even Caro, who could not get very excited about such things, was enthusiastic over them while Susan was beside herself. "Oh, Ma'am, they're beautiful—and so unusual too. You'll be the first stare of fashion."

"I am not at all certain I shall like that," Caro admitted ruefully, "but I shall do my best not to put Violette and you to shame. They are lovely though, are they not?" From a purely artistic point of view, Caro was entranced by the skill and originality of the designs. Created to enhance rather than overwhelm the wearer, the gowns owed their distinctiveness to elegant flowing lines and exquisite materials instead of being overloaded with distracting frills, ruchings, rouleaux, and lozenges. And Caro was also forced to acknowledge that she was quite looking forward to seeing whether the dresses could actually transform her as much as Violette's sketches seemed to suggest.

"Well, what do you say, Susan? Will they do?" She cocked an inquiring eyebrow at her maid.

"Oh yes, Ma'am! This lady seems to understand just what sort of person you are. She won't force you into something that will make you feel as though you're wearing the Countess of Welham's cast-offs nor will you look just like everyone else. When you wear these, you will still feel like Lady Caroline Waverly—just as individual as ever only a trifle more *à la mode*."

Caro laughed. "What a trial I must have been to you, Susan, eccentric that I am. I shall try to do better, I promise."

"Oh no, Ma'am." Susan was aghast. "You aren't

strange—leastways not like the Duchess of Oldenburg is, only you are just different.'' Worried lest she be misunderstood, Susan hastened to add, ''But it is a good sort of different. Your mind is on higher things, and that makes you ever so much more interesting. You know about so many things and can do so many things. Why you know as much as most men. Besides, it makes you so much kinder than most ladies. It's just, it's just . . .'' the maid hesitated, knowing the elevated nature of her mistress's principles in certain matters.

''It's just what? Don't be shy, Susan. You are a bright observant girl and I value your opinions.''

The little maid blushed with pleasure. ''Why, thank you, Ma'am. It's just that you are so lovely too, but you don't know or care about it. Ladies like the countess who spend every waking moment trying to be as beautiful as possible are the ones who attract all the attention when you're so much nicer than all of them. 'Tisn't fair. Why should they have all the beaux? I know you don't wish to have lots of admirers and you don't wish to be married, but . . . but, it would be nice to have someone—as a friend at least,'' she finished up in a rush, fearing that perhaps she had gone too far.

Caro remained silent for some time, a pensive look clouding the gray eyes. ''Perhaps you are right, Susan,'' she replied at last. ''It would be nice to have someone.'' There was a wistful note in her voice that Susan had never heard before. It saddened the little maid greatly to think that someone as selfish as the Countess of Welham never lacked for admirers while someone as loving and generous as her mistress always seemed to be alone. *Not any longer if I have any say in the matter,* she promised herself. *I must have a talk with this Mrs. Winwood privately and make her see how important it is that my mistress attract the admiration that is due her.*

Resourceful as she was, Susan was not at all certain how this plan was to be put into effect, but fortunately Caro herself paved the way for the scheme. Looking just the slightest bit sheepish, she admitted, ''Mrs. Winwood knows that I wish to keep our relationship private, so I am to visit her for my fittings. I do hope you'll accompany me, though, as I rely on your judgment to make sure I am not being led astray. And perhaps you will be able to think how I should dress my hair, for I feel certain that the way it is done now will not answer if I am to burst forth on the *ton* in a completely new wardrobe.''

"Of course, I shall be happy if I can assist. Thank you, Ma'am.'' Susan was so flattered by her mistress's regard for her abilities, so enchanted at the prospect of watching the transformation, and so eager to see a real modiste at work, that she was at a loss for ways to express her gratitude. But the excitement in her eyes and the joy in her voice were more than enough for her mistress, who herself was becoming more enthusiastic by the minute. For Susan, who had at first aspired to no greater glory than that of maid to a lady of fashion, seeing the sketches which showed what dress could do to make a face and figure appear its most elegant and attractive, now set her sights on becoming one of those women whose art and skill gave their patronesses such power in the *ton*. Nor did she plan to stop at merely working in one of the elegant establishments she had seen while doing errands on Bond Street. She was determined one day to own one. Susan was not precisely sure how this was to come about, but she vowed that one day ladies would be vying with one another to have a gown created by Mademoiselle Suzanne.

In fact, by the time they arrived at Henrietta Street, Caro was quite looking forward to an experience she had customarily viewed as something of an ordeal. Violette welcomed them cordially. "Lady Caroline, I am delighted you are come, and so soon. I take it that you approve. And this is the Susan you made mention of.'' She smiled warmly at them both and led them to a spot in the drawing room that was bathed in northern light. "There.'' She placed Caro in the center. "Now I am afraid you must endure the rest with as much patience as you can muster while Susan and I take care of the details. Susan, do you come here and hold this, and mind, stop me if you see anything amiss.''

Thus, without having to put herself forward in the slightest, the little maid found herself not only invited to join her mistress, but consulted from time to time. At first, she hesitated to offer her opinion, but as time wore on, she was solicited more and more frequently for her thoughts on this material or that particular draping. It soon became clear to her that there was no need for her to voice her sentiments to Mrs. Winwood for she could see that their hostess had taken her mistress's success as closely to heart as Susan had. Indeed, there was a leading tone to the questions with which Violette plied her customer that made Susan wonder if perhaps their hostess had as great a stake in Lady Caroline's transformation as the lady did herself.

Did the Countess of Welham still enjoy her customary ascendance over the *ton?* Were the admirers as plentiful as ever? Who was her modiste? And, when informed of this person's identity, she gave a deprecatory Gallic shrug but there was no hiding the sly smile. Susan wondered at this and hoped against hope that this meant Mrs. Winwood felt secure in her abilities to outshine this high priestess at whose altar the countess was a devoted worshipper.

Some hours later, as they emerged exhausted but triumphant from the Winwood's elegant abode, Caro turned to her maid and, flushed with enthusiasm, the light of battle in her eyes, demanded, "Well, Susan, what do you think? Am I like to take the *ton* by storm?"

"Oh yes, Ma'am!"

Caro laughed. "I most certainly shall not, but at the very least I shall no longer be labeled as antidote. And to be quite honest, I feel a good deal more inspired than I was. Violette was so kind that I feel I must make a push to do credit to her inspiration."

But Susan was not to be put off. "Mark my words, what with the dresses Mrs. Winwood has created, the new coiffures I picture, and your own elegant conversation, you will be the latest sensation, I predict."

Once again her mistress could not contain her mirth. "It is not likely to happen, but I thank you for your faith in me."

We shall see, Lady Caroline. Susan smiled smugly to herself. *When Mrs. Winwood and I have finished, no one will be able to look anywhere else and won't that just make the Countess of Welham sit up and stare.*

The little maid had grown more accustomed to life at the rigidly formal Welham house, but she was no more enamored of its inhabitants than she had been at the outset and resented their lack of appreciation for her mistress as much, if not more than, their coldness to her. A quick and clever girl with neat ways about her and a willingness to help, Susan had finally recommended herself to the redoubtable housekeeper and that guardian of propriety, Wigmore, so that she was now able to elicit a "good morning" from these two pillars of the establishment. But she longed for the easy intercourse of Waverly Court and the cozy evenings spent around the kitchen fire with William and Mrs. Crawford discussing all manner of things. Then, too, it was strange, though the servants at Welham House talked of nothing but "my lady must have this" or "my lady always does it that way", they did not appear to care for her at all—quite the opposite in fact. They were proud of the whims and caprices, the exacting demands that made their lives so difficult and attested to the fact that their mistress was the spoiled darling of the *ton*. Such slavish devotion made no sense to Susan. How could one possibly devote one's entire existence to someone who barely knew one's name and cared less? But the reflected glory of the Countess of Welham seemed to suffice for Wigmore and his minions. Susan was glad her mistress was a human being instead of a demanding goddess and she longed to prove Caro's superiority to all these toadies who, taking their mistress's lead, discounted her as nothing but a dowdy bluestocking.

19

FOR THE TIME BEING, however, the fashionable world was forced to await the appearance of a rival to the claims of such an incomparable as the beautiful Countess of Welham. Lady Caroline had a far more important social commitment, which was to take the air with Ceddie and Clarence.

"For we have been waiting forever to ride with you, Cousin Caro," Ceddie volunteered as they headed for the park that afternoon.

"You have?" she asked in some astonishment. "But I thought you were enjoying yourselves with Tim and John Coachman."

"Oh, them. They're the best of good fellows but they are rather cautious because Mama is so worried about our riding in the first place and they don't want to offend Mama. She can be a trifle sharp at times, you know," Clarence explained in a shy undertone.

"Mama is a worrywart." Ceddie, more forthright than his brother, was not one to beat around the bush.

"Oh, ah." Caro, being in complete agreement, was left without a thing to say. Fortunately, before she was forced into indiscreet comment, a shout broke out from Ceddie.

"Look! It's Uncle Tony and Lord Daventry and his sister." He waved vigorously and trotted off to join the group of riders heading purposefully in their direction.

"Hello Ceddie, Clarence, Caro. Bang-up day isn't it? Your seats are improving a great deal, lads, but look at Clary, would you? She's on her way to becoming a true horsewoman," Tony greeted them jovially.

"How you do go on, Tony! You always were given to hyperbole," Clary laughed. "However, I admit to having become an enthusiastic equestrienne, thanks to Caro," she concluded softly, smiling gratefully in Caro's direction.

Seeing the happiness in her face and observing the confidence with which Lady Clarissa maneuvered her mount, Caro could not help feeling pleased with herself. Though Caro might command fewer admirers and less attention than Lavinia, she was at least able to bring happiness to those who deserved it.

Such a thought was not unique to Caro. Nicholas took the earliest opportunity to move Caesar in next to her. "I have not yet had the opportunity to thank you properly for all you have done on my sister's behalf. She is a changed person. Thank you."

There was such warmth and gratitude in the deep blue eyes that, unaccustomed as she was to attracting attention, Caro did not know where to look. "Oh, it was nothing, my lord. I may be a 'ferocious bluestocking,' but I am not without human feeling you know. And when I see people who, but for a little encouragement, could more fully enjoy their lives, I make a push to help them do so."

"I am sure you do," Nicholas responded. "And do you always set about putting the world to rights with such reforming zeal?"

There was something in his voice—the slightest hint of amusement perhaps—that set Caro's back up. "Not at all, my lord. I do it merely when others are too blind to see what needs to be done," she retorted stiffly. Caro knew she sounded like the worst sort of prig, but she could not help herself. She could not bear to have genuine sympathy for her fellow creatures written off as though it were the queer start of some moralizing spinster who had nothing better to do with her life than offer advice about everyone else's.

Nicholas could see that he had inadvertently struck a nerve. He had only intended the lightest of remarks but had not counted on Caro's prickly defensiveness over her role in society. It was a great deal too bad because he genuinely liked and admired her, finding her ready enthusiasm, intelligence, and quick wit quite charming. "Relax, my girl. I was merely observing that you exhibit more concern for your fellows than the average citizen. It is to be commended." Bother! He sounded as stiff as she did. Why was it that he was able to converse lightly and easily with the likes of Lavinia and Sally Jersey, but when it came to discussing serious matters with this woman, who had something of purpose to say, the two of them seemed to circle each other like wary animals.

Observing their mutual discomfort, and concerned that both Lady Caroline and the Marquess of Everleigh reveal to each other only their most attractive sides, Clarissa hastened to rescue the situation before it could deteriorate any further. "You are privileged to see Nicky today. Since perusing the debate in the *Edinburgh Review* on the "Causes and Cures of Pauperism," he has been burying himself in discussions and readings of the Poor Laws which, though it proves him to be a most responsible citizen, makes him a nonexistent escort and an exceedingly dull companion," she complained teasingly. But though the remark and provocation were directed at her brother, Clary was closely scrutinizing his companion.

Clary was not disappointed. Caro was oddly moved that he should be reading the same thing and her eyes lit up. "I believe you mentioned before that you had read such an article, but we were interrupted. I had not thought to find someone such as you concerned with such things. I . . ." She colored when she realized the infelicitous nature of her comment. "I *do* beg your pardon. I didn't mean it to sound so odiously condescending. It's just . . ."

"It's just that you didn't expect that from such an arrogant constructor of canals," Nicholas teased. Then, seeing that she truly was embarrassed, he continued, "Don't refine upon it too much, Lady Caroline. I quite understand. If there were more people who were concerned about the desperate straits of many of the people in this country, we shouldn't be in the fix we are in now. I am not by nature a politician, but I cannot bear to see the gallant fellows who fought with me tossed back on the streets with no hope of earning their keep with the price of bread as high as it is. That is why I feel it imperative to put to peaceful use the industry which had its inception in the war and my canal is just one way to cheapen and improve the transportation of the materials we need." His eyes twinkled ruefully. "And now *I* sound as odiously condescending as the best of self-righteous reformers."

Caro wrinkled her brow. "I quite agree that something needs to be done, but it will take years for industry to raise the general level of the poor's condition. I believe that with just a little attention paid to our agricultural practices, we could do much more to the purpose to help by producing more abundantly and for less. Then people will not have to leave the land and their villages in order to earn more in the crowded cities where life is so wretched.''

Though Nicholas did not entirely agree with Caro, there was something in the earnestness of her look that he found infinitely attractive, quite apart from the ideas she was putting forth. ''Quite possibly you are in the right of it.'' Catching the stubborn lift of her chin, he paused. ''Now don't poker up at me. I quite agree that in theory 'tis an excellent scheme, but who is to say that farmers who adopt your principles—and knowing the way such people resist change, they will be few and far between—and are able to produce more, will not try to increase their price as well, so the poor laborer will be left with the same, if not a higher price, for bread. Not everyone is as high-minded as you are, you know.''

The kindling look in Caro's eye made Nicholas realize that somehow he had managed to insult her again when he had only meant to applaud her good intentions. For someone who cared little about the approbations of the *ton*, she was extraordinarily sensitive about some things—though just what those were, he could not fathom.

For her part, Caro could not precisely say what it was that bothered her. Perhaps it was the tone in his voice when he called her high-minded that reminded her of his opinion of her as a bluestocking; perhaps it was that she had hoped he would regard her more as a kindred spirit rather than an intellectual oddity. Whatever it was, she could not help bridling. ''I am not some 'high-minded' reformer with my head in the clouds, my lord. I have seen such a scheme work. It is purely a matter of the market, and when one person is successful at producing more from the same plot of land, the others are forced to follow suit. It is merely a matter of self-interest.''

Nicholas grinned. So that was it! It was his vision of her as one of those fearsomely intellectual women that somehow rankled. He was glad to know that his opinion counted for so much. So often he had felt inadequate when her clear gray eyes had happened to catch him pandering to Lavinia that he could not help being grateful that he could make her uneasy too. There was no doubt that encountering Lady Caroline Waverly was becoming an increasingly unsettling experience for him and, inexplicable as this was, he did not wish to be the only one rendered uncomfortable by this.

"You're a regular little Benthamite, are you not, Lady Caroline?" he teased. Then, seeing that he truly had upset her, his eyes softened. "I did not mean in the least to call into question your opinions. It is just that I have been looking at the same problems from such a very different angle," he apologized.

Caro was somewhat mollified. He certainly did appear to be in earnest. No doubt, after Lavinia's disparaging remarks, she was just being overly sensitive. And he really did seem to be genuinely interested in effecting the same changes as she. It was Caro's turn to excuse herself. "It's only that I am not used to being taken at all seriously, you see," she explained. "I am far more accustomed to being derided than listened to."

There was something about the quiet way she said it and the half-defiant, half-pleading look in the big gray eyes that touched him. His heart went out to her. Lord knows, few enough people gave his ideas the least respect, and he was a peer of the realm. How difficult it must be for her to win any sort of acknowledgment, either from her sex who mistrusted someone of her interests and intellect, or from his who mistrusted her sex. Realizing this, the marquess resolved that he, at least, was bound and determined to respect and encourage all of her intellect, her wit, and her courage. Before he was through, he intended that others would too.

Nicholas smiled tenderly down at her. "Would that we could have you in Parliament, Lady Caroline. The country has need of such as you. Unfortunately, I cannot even make my fellow peers vote as they should, much less influence them to accept a woman in their midst, but I can invite you to hear the debates and perhaps counsel me as to how I should vote on various issues. Could I interest you in allowing me to escort you tomorrow? There is to be evidence given on expenditures on the poor by the high bailiff of Birmingham—a topic which should interest you exceedingly, I am sure."

Caro was speechless for a moment, overwhelmed by a rush of emotion such as she had never before experienced. It was such a mixture of emotions that she was left bewildered as to their causes and astounded at their intensity. Though she was always concerned for the welfare of her fellow creatures, and did her utmost to remain sensitive to

the needs of those around her, ordinarily, she remained personally unaffected by them. It was true that she and Helena
enjoyed a rewarding friendship, but it was a companionship
built on mutual respect for each other's intelligence. With
the marquess, that respect, though in its infancy, was there.
But there was something else besides, which she had only
barely sensed before but which now struck her full force.
He cared about her. He truly appreciated who she, Lady
Caroline Waverly, was, what she believed in, what she was
trying to do, and he was not only letting her know that he
recognized and valued that, he was offering to help her realize those ideals. No one, perhaps with the exception of
her beloved father, had offered her such help and understanding before and the effect of it was unnerving to say the
least. Caro had spent so much of her life looking after others that she was slightly taken aback at being looked after
by someone else.

With an enormous effort, she gathered her wits about her
enough to reply tremulously, "Th . . . Thank you. How
very kind you are. I should like it above all things." When
she finally had the courage to look up at him, she wished
she hadn't. There was a smile in the deep-blue eyes that
gazed down into hers, but there was something more—a
special light—an intensity which she found faintly disturbing. Suddenly shy and unsure of herself, she glanced quickly
away to where the boys and Tony were engaged in earnest
discussion of the various bits of horseflesh on display. Tony
was pointing to a flank here, a neck there, while his companions listened with open-mouthed attention. "Well, I
must be going. I promised Lavvy I would have the boys
back in time for their lessons." Caro gathered her reins and
prepared to depart in her usual precipitous manner, but as
Xerxes pricked up his ears and headed eagerly towards the
boys, she could not help turning around to whisper shyly,
"And thank you again," leaving Nicholas to remark to himself once again that though this adieu was abrupt as far as
adieux went, it was far less so than was customary where
Lady Caroline Waverly was concerned.

The marquess smiled to himself. The sudden shyness had
not been lost on Nicholas and it had both amused and gratified him—amused him to see that the coolly self-possessed
Lady Caroline was not immune to less intellectual emotions, and gratified him because he felt that it was precisely

because she trusted him intellectually that she had allowed herself to let her emotional guard down. After all, it was a rather lowering thing to have beautiful women constantly throwing themselves at your head while the truly intelligent ones appeared to be no more moved by your presence than they were by your other companions'. Stop it, Nicky, my lad, you will be in a fair way of turning into an insufferable coxcomb if you continue to think of yourself as being irresistible to the female sex. But that was just the point. He didn't consider himself irresistible. It was just his position and his wealth that were. And now, when someone to whom these attributes were as meaningless as they were to him seemed to be affected by him—well, it did give a fellow pause. Nicholas began to wonder if he had perhaps been in the *ton* too long and was beginning to adopt its exaggerated opinion of him as a highly eligible bachelor. But, no. The marquess grinned, remembering the delicate blush stealing up the slender neck and the confusion in the gray eyes as they had looked up into his. So he made Caro uneasy did he? Well good! She had been intruding into his thoughts far too often herself and the unsettling vision of her slender figure attired in breeches was upsetting his peace of mind more than he cared for: which was to say, more than once since their encounter in the stable yard.

A tug on the reins broke into these disturbing reflections. Caesar, never the most patient of mounts, was becoming restive and was making it plain that he did not take kindly to this dullness on the part of his master. Nicholas came to with a start. "Very well, Caesar, it is time for us to be gone. Are you ready Clary?"

It was fortunate for the marquess's already distracted state of mind that he did not notice the look of amused satisfaction on his sister's face. Ever an interested onlooker, Clary had been delighted to observe both the frown that clouded her brother's brow at Caro's hasty departure and the look of tender bemusement that followed it. She could not refrain from giving herself a secret congratulatory hug for her part in it all. "Well done, Clary," she whispered to herself as she turned her horse toward Berkeley Square, and in truth, she did feel as though she had done a good day's work.

20

IN FACT, not only was the marquess unaware of his sister's efforts where he was concerned, in the ensuing days he was less than his usual perspicacious self. Now that Nicholas was uncomfortably aware of just how often Caro occupied his thoughts, he was not able to put her out of them any more successfully than he had before this revelation. In fact, she was present in them more than ever and he was chiding himself severely for this as well as for the pleasurable feeling of anticipation as he mounted the steps of Welham House the next morning. By now Wigmore had abandoned all hope that his disapproving expression would encourage the marquess to confine his visits to a more fashionable hour, one that was more acceptable to the countess, and he greeted Nicholas with an impassive stare. If possible, his demeanor became more rigidly correct when he discovered that it was not Lavinia for whom the marquess was inquiring and there was a distinctly frosty note in his voice as, conducting the visitor to the drawing room, he promised to send someone to alert Lady Caroline as to his lordship's presence.

"Certainly, you wouldn't compromise your dignity so much as to do it yourself, you starched-up old Cerberus," Nicholas muttered to himself as he searched among Lavvy's elaborate furnishings for a chair that did not look likely to collapse under his weight. He had just selected a sort of stool that appeared to stand upon both claws and talons while supporting a fairly sturdy looking seat on folded wings, when he heard a light quick step in the doorway.

The welcoming smile died on his lips as he glanced up to see not Caro but a fresh-faced attractive girl shyly approaching him. Nicholas looked again. The cautiousness that he at first had ascribed to timidity was belied by the observant brown eyes and he realized, to his amusement, that he was being carefully assessed by a highly critical young person. She stood so quietly that he wondered, in an unusual moment of self-consciousness, if he were found to be wanting.

"Lady Caroline is not here, sir." The voice was low and pleasant.

"Not here? But . . ."

"She asked me to extend her apologies and to beg your forgiveness but there were"—Susan wrinkled her brow as she sought to remember her mistress's precise words—"there were extenuating circumstances."

"Oh." Nicholas, suddenly deflated, could not keep the disappointment from his voice.

"But she wouldn't have missed this for the world. She was that excited about going to Parliament," Susan hastened to assure him. Though her beloved Lady Caroline deserved the best, Susan had hardly dared hope for such an out-and-outer for her ladyship. The marquess was extremely handsome with a muscular physique, black hair, and those deep-blue eyes now crinkling at her in an encouraging fashion. The little maid was determined to do her utmost to advance her mistress's cause with this truly splendid gentleman. "Well, you know how she is, sir, tenderhearted to a fault." There, that should set her apart from the countess who, if the rumors belowstairs were anything to go by, had designs upon his lordship. "And when Argos turned up missing, she was so distressed for the young masters that she would find him before they were through with their lessons, which I hope she can do soon," she finished, catching a glimpse of the clock on the mantel.

"Perhaps your mistress is in need of assistance," he ventured.

"That she is, sir." Convinced that the marquess was a right one and someone worthy of Lady Caroline, Susan bestowed a dazzlingly grateful smile on him. "She is as clever as they come and will stop at nothing, but that dog, though he usually hides in the stables, could be anywhere and she is all alone. The rest of the staff is kept too busy by the countess to be able to spend any time looking for Argos whom her ladyship doesn't like above half anyway." And that should fix that, Susan concluded triumphantly to herself as the marquess hurried off in the direction of the mews behind Welham House.

He did not have to go far before he heard Caro's encouraging tones issuing from a loft above Xerxes' stall. "Relax, Argos. I shall have you out of here in a trice. To be sure, you were very clever to climb the ladder, but however did you propose to come back down?"

Nicholas reached the door as Caro, clutching a much subdued Argos, was descending a less than sturdy ladder. "Here, hand him to me." He hurried over to grab the ladder with one hand while reaching up with the other.

"Oh dear." Caro turned to smile ruefully down at him. "You must think I spend most of my time here in the stables indulging in odd behavior, but truly there was nothing for it but to find him and assure him that he was not to be cast out in the streets for thoroughly dismembering the under housemaid's feather duster. Mrs. Blethersop is not one of Argos' admirers and she can be rather hard on him. There. Thank you." Caro hopped down from the last rung and accepted the disheveled little dog who licked her gratefully.

The marquess smiled down at her as the pink tongue licked across a cheek. "You seem to have encountered a few cobwebs in your rescue mission." He whipped out a clean handkerchief to wipe a smudge off her cheek only to pause as he tilted up the firm little chin and encountered the wide gray eyes looking trustfully up at him. There was something about her as she stood there, flushed from her exertions, the scent of rosewater rising from the dark hair, which had escaped here and there to curl softly around her face, that made him want to pull her into his arms and kiss the generous half-parted lips. Nicholas stood transfixed by the suddenness and intensity of the unexpected impulse and might have done so forever if Argos, his nose full of straw dust, had not taken the opportunity to sneeze violently several times.

The marquess came to with a start. Kiss Lady Caroline? He must be all about in the head! Why that woman didn't appear to have the least use for men much less for any sort of dalliance with one. He sighed. It was a pity really for she did look utterly enchanting clutching the dirty little dog, bits of straw clinging to the hem of her dress and the smudge of dust emphasizing the purity of her complexion. Gathering his scattered wits about him, he dabbed again gently at the dirty spot and delicately removed a few wisps of straw from the silky dark hair. "There. Once you have shaken out your skirts you ought to be able to return to the house with no one the wiser.''

Caro looked up guiltily. "How did you know I wished to remain undiscovered?''

Nicholas grinned. "Years of surreptitious behavior on my own part has taught me to recognize it in others. Never fear, I shan't betray you, though, in return for keeping your confidence, I shall insist on your keeping your original promise to accompany me to the discussion of the poor laws.''

"Still?'' Caro could not hide her surprise.

"But, of course. I feel reasonably certain that you are not one of those females who must needs spend hours to repair their toilette and that you can be ready to join me momentarily.''

It was Caro's turn to smile. "I fear that you are in the right of it. Susan informs me that I am a hasty dresser because my mind is on higher things. But I am not at all sure that it is merely that I am too impatient or too lazy to expend the effort,'' she finished apologetically.

"Susan? Is that the likely looking lass that came to offer your excuses? I quite liked her—a most observant and intelligent girl she appears to be.''

"Yes. I should be quite lost without her. The fact that I am able to show my face in polite society at all is entirely due to her efforts at making me presentable.''

"I doubt that,'' he replied, serious for a moment as he realized once again how attractive she truly was. "But she seems devoted to you. I was subjected to the most intense scrutiny. Mrs. Drummond Burrell could not be more exacting in her tastes.''

Caro laughed. "Yes, Susan has her standards, and very high they are too. She appears to be a most talented seamstress and has aspirations to be a modiste to the fashionable world one day. I can serve only as a poor advertisement, but I intend to do my utmost to further her ambitions. She is extremely bright and capable and it would be a great shame if she were to waste away as a lady's maid. But excuse me, I shall go see what I can do to make myself fit to be seen.'' And Caro hurried off straightening her unruly curls as she went.

It was not long before she rejoined the marquess, having washed her face and changed from her simple morning dress of lemon-colored cambric muslin to a walking dress and spencer of blush-colored figured sarcenet, whose delicate hue set off the tinge of pink in her cheeks and emphasized the glossy dark hair, while its short tight cut revealed the supple figure beneath it. Taking in the picture she made standing on the threshold, the light of anticipation in her eyes, and her whole attitude of eager expectation, Nicholas could not think when he had seen Caro looking so lovely.

"I hope I did not keep you waiting. I confess your last remark put me rather on my mettle. But I could not go on such an important outing without at first changing my clothes. I have wished to see Parliament in action forever and I can't thank you enough for taking me."

Her enthusiasm was infectious and he could not help but reflect, as he explained to her the various precedents and, later, watching her absorb every word of each speaker, how much more enjoyable and exciting everything was when shared with someone who was curious and intelligent. Her questions tested his own knowledge of the issues at hand and forced him to think things through to their conclusions while her opinions, cogently expressed, expanded his own views of the problems being discussed.

Later, on the way home, encouraged by an eager and sympathetic listener, Nicholas found himself confiding dreams and plans for the improvement of the lot of the common man that he barely knew he possessed. But there was something about the encouraging tilt of the head, the light in the dark-fringed gray eyes, and the way Caro wrinkled her brow in concentration as she listened to him expound on the need to provide more work for the returning soldiers, and opportunities for the poor to earn their livings and retain their dignity, that inspired him to share his fondest hopes with her.

Nor did her eyes glaze over, as did most everyone else's when he waxed eloquent over the implementation of his plans. On the contrary, she was well and truly intrigued, listening carefully, offering an opinion here, a comment there until Nicholas was forced to admit he did not know when he had enjoyed a conversation more. How wonderful it was to be judged on the merits of his ideas alone instead of his eligibility as a husband or lover. Perhaps there was something to this bluestocking thing after all. Certainly it was all very comfortable to be discussing matters with a female who wasn't forever dimpling provocatively up at him or fluttering her eyelashes. He hadn't realized until he had met Caro how very wearing it was to be constantly sought after. It was most novel, but he found intensely serious conversation with a woman as blithely unself-conscious as Caro to be far more restful than the lightest, most amusing of flirtations with her cousin.

However, her next words gave him some pause and he began to wonder if perhaps he ought not to stop and reconsider the advantages of escorting an empty-headed beauty who avoided the rigors of a social conscience at all costs.

"Yes, I agree that the plight of the poor in the nation, especially those in the cities, is become absolutely desperate. Why even I, who have always made it a point to inform myself of such things was absolutely shocked when I saw the living conditions in Spitalfields." Realizing what she had said, Caro clapped a hand over her mouth.

"Spitalfields?" Nicholas stared at her dumbfounded. "When? How? What were you doing in Spitalfields? Why even *I* would never venture near there and I have been in some uncomfortable spots in my life."

"Perhaps you would do, but in a way that would cause comment. I prefer to observe as unobtrusively as possible." Caro spoke haughtily, forgetting entirely that there had been numerous times in the Peninsula when he had not born the least resemblance to the elegant peer sitting across from her.

Enlightenment dawned. "Tony's breeches!" Nicholas exclaimed.

"Well, no one pays the least mind to another grubby lad, though I did get asked to lend a hand to pull out a cart that was stuck," she defended herself. "Besides, how else can one of the Quality learn what it is like to be poor unless one relinquishes the trappings of wealth? So I . . ."

"Stop! Don't tell me. I do not wish to know. For I should either worry myself to death thinking you will do it again, or be forced to tell someone in order to stop you." Nicholas shook his head. "You are incorrigible, Waif, you know. Will you stop at nothing?"

She tilted her head, a mischievous smile tugging at the corners of her mouth. "I think not." Then suddenly serious, she paused as if to examine her conscience. "At least not if it is in a good cause," she concluded seriously.

Hearing the anxious note in her voice, he raised a reassuring hand. "Make no mistake about it, I find this extremely admirable, if a trifle unusual."

Caro sighed and hung her head. "Yes, I know. I never try to get into scrapes, but somehow I find myself forever at odds with the rest of the world."

Nicholas reached out one finely shaped hand to tilt up her chin. "Never change, Waif," he admonished her gently. "The world has need of people such as you."

They sat thus, bright blue eyes gazing intently into soft gray ones until the carriage, free at last from the press of traffic blocking the road, lurched forward and Nicholas leaned out to see what was happening.

21

THEY ARRIVED AT their respective dwellings in reflective moods. Caro, wondered at herself for thinking more of the way Nicholas's eyes had become a darker blue when he spoke of the issues that truly absorbed his interest and attention than for attending to the issues themselves. There was an energy about him, an intensity of purpose that permeated his entire being and set him apart from the other fashionable men of the *ton*. While the other town beaux moved languidly here and there, evincing only a tepid interest in their surroundings, Nicholas plunged headlong into the activity of the moment, whatever it was, investing it with his own peculiar brand of vitality. Caro had witnessed time after time how the boys, his sister, Tony, not to mention Lavinia, seemed to come alive when he appeared. Each in his own way looked to Nicholas for that zest for life that heightened their own, each one feeling special and appreciated because of the attention he paid to them. After all, wasn't she, Caro Waverly, thinking even at this moment that no one had ever understood her half so well or participated in her interests half as much as Nicholas Daventry? For shame, Caro, she scolded herself. You have seen firsthand how he can charm even the most sophisticated and *ennuyee* of society's matrons. Why even Sally Jersey and Therese Esterhazy were not immune to the lazy appreciative smile that hovered around his mouth and wrinkled the corners of his eyes. And, conjuring up the most salient points of today's debate in order to relate them to Helena, Caro resolutely put the marquess out of her mind.

As for the marquess, he was having no more success at ignoring Caro's effect on him than she was. Having left her off at Welham House and finding himself prey to a thousand confusing thoughts, he had Watkins drop him off at Gentleman Jackson's in hopes that a good bout with the master

would be just the thing to set things right again in a world
that suddenly seemed topsy-turvy. All at once, Nicholas
Daventry, the formerly ineligible younger son more appreciated and more accepted by his men than by members of
the fashionable set, more accustomed to seeking out adventure and danger than avoiding them, was now the responsible head of a noble family and preaching propriety and
discretion to a mere slip of a girl who was no more impressed by him than she was by Cedric and Clarence. It was
a role he had previously scorned and certainly managed to
avoid. Now, somehow, without his wishing it in the least,
it had been thrust upon him, and the only compensation for
it was that women who had previously avoided him were
now casting themselves at his feet while ones he ordinarily
wouldn't have given a second thought—bluestockings with
an interest in problems political and social, for example—
were cutting up his peace of mind.

He sighed as he mounted the steps to Gentleman Jackson's select establishment, but brightened perceptibly as a
tall fair-haired young man in a scarlet coat caught sight of
him and stopped to exclaim joyously, "Nicky Daventry!
Where have you been old fellow? Been looking for you this
age! Heard you'd sold out to turn respectable. Dashed
shame, eh what?"

"Tubby! What are you doing? Up to no good, I'll be
bound." Nicky clapped him on the back, cocking an inquiring eyebrow at the young guardsman whose immense
height and well-knit frame belied his name.

"Nothing in particular. We're back in our old quarters in
Portman Square for the time being and, except for a lark or
two here and there, it's dashed dull without Boney on the
loose, I can tell you. There's nothing left for a fellow who
wants a spot of adventure. Oh, there's always India, I suppose, but it ain't the same thing. What's a person to do?"
He paused ruminatively. "Ran across Totteridge the other
day. Remember the lad who scouted across the lines for us
at Vitoria? Poor chap. He was holding horses for the odd
bit or two, has nowhere to go. I tell you, Nicky, it's a
damned shame to see such splendid fellows cast aside the
way they are. But come along. I want to see if the most
punishing left in the 18th has been dulled by the soft life of
a well-breeched swell."

Nicholas, his mind still absorbing the idea of the intrepid

Totteridge reduced to cadging a stray coin here and there
from unconscious members of the *ton*, was immeasurably
saddened by the picture and resolved to concentrate more
than ever on effecting a means for such men to earn their
livings and retain their dignity. Caro was only partly right.
It was necessary to provide more food cheaply in order to
feed the poor and it was important to educate them in order
to accomplish lasting change, but nothing gave a man his
self-respect as quickly and effectively as work. Having seen
the way Britain had been able to arm itself against Napoleon, the marquess was convinced that it could turn that
same effort into manufacture and trade, employing the same
men who had been defending it on the battlefields of Europe. "Eh, what's that?" Nicholas came to as he realized
he was being addressed.

"Wondered if you'd seen the bay that Weybridge is selling. I'm thinking of putting old Champion out to pasture.
He's a magnificent creature, but slowing down a bit. Never
be able to replace him. We've been through so much together, but I'm in the market for a mount and I saw this at
Tatt's the other day. You always did have an eye for a pretty
piece of horseflesh. Wonder if you'd care to cast a glance?"

"Happy to," Nicky replied, nodding as Gentleman Jackson himself came over to greet them.

"Glad to see you back, sir. It's been too long since we've
had any true skill around here. These young lads," he said,
nodding at Tubby, "they're all very well, great strapping
fellows, all bounce and go, but no science. It takes patience
to develop that and they're all in such a hurry." And commenting on this young peer's footwork and that one's high
cut, he led them over to a special corner reserved for favored patrons.

As he followed the champion, Nicholas was struck again
by how much he missed the simple life in the regiment.
Tubby and Gentleman Jackson had, each in his own way,
recalled the old times when he was sought out and consulted
for the knowledge and skills he had developed on his own,
not for the privileged position in society that he happened
to have inherited.

He missed that sort of camaraderie. His mind slid back
to Caro again, perhaps because he knew that she too appreciated him for himself and though she might not always
agree with his ideas, she accorded him respect for having

come up with them and thought them out. It was very reassuring to have a friendship built on that rather on something that fashion or circumstance might deprive him of at
any moment. In the army, Nicholas had known he could
count on his men because he had earned their esteem and
their trust. As a result, they were concerned for his welfare.
All sense of that mutual trust and respect had disappeared
when he had returned to take up the title and its attendant
responsibilities. Now, seeing Tubby brought it all back and
made Nicholas realize that Caro, in her own quiet way, gave
him that same sense that he could count on her. From time
to time, he had caught her looking at him, summing him up
with those big gray eyes that saw so much and saw it all so
clearly. That someone who scorned the petty trappings of
the *ton* appeared to consider him a friend made him feel
both flattered and assured of his own worth.

Caro. His mind dwelt on her appreciatively, tenderly, in
all her facets. She was so many things: proud mistress of a
successful estate, enchanted observer who was childlike in
her appreciation of the theatrical delights London had to
offer, impish mischief maker setting Welham House about
its ears the moment she arrived, active intelligence taking
in and evaluating everything, and passionate reformer who
extended as much interest and concern to the nameless
masses whose lot she wanted so desperately to improve as
she did to those immediately around her. He couldn't think
when he had enjoyed himself more, and all he had done was
spend a morning sharing something important to him with
someone who felt the same way. Or, at least he hoped she
did.

All of a sudden, the possibility occurred to Nicholas that
she might not think of him as he thought of her and the
thought was so upsetting that he threw himself with renewed
energy into the bout, earning a reproof from the master.
"Hold on there, sir. You've lost your concentration and
you're all abroad." Nicholas put his head down and focused
on his opponent, eventually losing himself in the effort to
get beneath his opponent's guard while maintaining his own.

In the meantime, the object of his reflections was trying
equally hard to immerse herself in her own distracting activities as she pored over accounts that had just arrived from
Waverly Court. The numbers swam before her eyes, and
every time she tried to fix on a suggestion from William

or a report from one of the tenants, she thought of the marquess and how much she had relished their morning's outing.

Accustomed to being alone in her interests and aspirations, Caro had never taken into account the pleasure that could be derived from sharing these with another person. To be sure, she had Helena who was able to converse intelligently on a wide variety of topics that were of interest to Caro; but though Helena was possessed of a fine mind, she lacked Caro's passionate intensity and her sense of purpose. While Helena was quite content to inform herself on the issues of the day and reflect seriously on them, she lacked her companion's compulsion to right the wrongs so manifest all around them.

The marquess, it seemed, was driven by the same forces that Caro herself was subject to. Like her, he took an active view of the world. And like her, he set himself apart from the rest of the *ton* in his concern for the issues of the day with which most of his peers were not even conversant, much less involved. Confronted by a situation, whether it was Bonaparte laying waste to Europe, two boys who longed for ponies, someone stuck at the top of a ladder, or the poverty of many of England's citizens, he did not stop to consider the consequences of involving himself, but immediately applied his considerable skill and energies to the solution of the problem.

Caro smiled to herself as she thought of this energy. Never before had she felt so alive and so immersed in the scene around her as when he was there, enjoying the same things, picking up the same nuances, interpreting them in a fashion that was similar enough to hers to make her feel encouraged in her own opinions but different enough to challenge her and enlarge her perspective. Heretofore, Caro had never quite understood why people did things together. To be sure, she had Helena, but that friendship had sprung up more because society dictated that a young woman could not live alone respectably than because of her need for companionship. Now, having experienced the pleasure of sharing and communicating so closely and intensely, Caro realized just how solitary, and in some ways, barren, her previous life had been.

She sighed. Passionately proud and protective of her independence and self-sufficiency, she did not like to think that she could come to rely on anyone for anything, even if that were something as simple as companionship. Especially disconcerting, though she could not even acknowledge or admit this to herself, was that the company she so enjoyed was that of an attractive and highly sought-after man. No! This was the merest foolishness. This train of thought was getting her nowhere. It was time she cleared her head of these silly fancies. Nothing could accomplish this quite as effectively as a vigorous ride in the park, or at least as vigorous a ride as was permissible in the restricted atmosphere of the *ton*. Resolved on this, she looked forward to donning her new riding habit—the first of Violette Winwood's creations to arrive at Grosvenor Square.

At the first sigh, Helena, who had also been reading, glanced up quietly and smiled to herself. She could not ever recall having seen her young friend look quite that way before. There was a softness in the eyes that stared off into space. Ordinarily, Caro would pore over her work, twisting one dark curl around her finger as she devoured it, never moving a muscle or changing position until she had read it from beginning to end. But now, when Caro was no more than a third of the way through the papers sent for her perusal, she abandoned it altogether and sent word to the stables that she wished to ride. That was another odd thing. Ordinarily, Caro avoided the fashionable hour in the park like the plague, condemning it as an exercise in equestrian frustrations. Perhaps, at the moment, she was too abstracted to pay attention to the hour?

Helena nodded wisely. She had been unable to accept the marquess's very kind invitation to join them in their visit to the nation's lawmakers, having made prior arrangements to visit an old friend, but she had seen the light in Caro's eyes and the vivacious expression on her face when she returned and had no need to look very far for the cause.

To be sure, Lady Caroline Waverly had a strong interest in the affairs of the nation, but it was not the opportunity to witness these firsthand which had given her the glow in her face. Well, it was all very well. The marquess was as fine a person as Helena could wish for her former pupil. He was a true gentleman: kind, courageous, intelligent, and, if Helena had read aright, not entirely impervious to her young friend. What the Countess of Welham would have to say to such a state of affairs, Helena shuddered to think.

Helena was not the only one aware of a change. Upstairs, Susan, helping her mistress into the riding habit, was quick to notice a certain uncharacteristic trend to reverie, a dreamy look in the gray eyes which ordinarily took in even the slightest detail.

More fiercely attached to her mistress than Helena was, and possessed of a more romantic soul, the little maid could hardly keep from hugging herself with delight. She's in love, she crowed to herself and it's with his lordship. Oh, I knew how it would be. He's far too nice for the likes of madam, though she's not one to give up such a catch without a fuss. Here's some fun, I'll be bound. And she longed once more to be back at Waverly sitting around the table sharing her secret with Mrs. Crawford and William, for it was too wonderful to keep to herself. However, she was not about to betray, by so much as the flutter of an eyelash, her suspicions to the countess's high-and-mighty retainers. Let them boast of their mistress to their hearts' content. They would soon see who was the real lady at Welham House. Tucking a wayward curl under the jaunty hat, Susan smiling triumphantly, remarked, "There! You are as pretty as any of those ladies in *La Belle Assemblée* and look far better on a horse, I'll be bound. You'll take the shine out of everyone in the park."

"Oh, Susan, I could not, even if I would, but you are a dear for saying so." Caro snapped out of her abstraction long enough to bestow a brilliant smile and a quick hug on her henchwoman, and then she was off, tearing downstairs with unladylike haste in her urge to be gone, and out in the fresh air clearing her mind of its disturbing thoughts.

22

BUT THOUGH Caro had laughed it off, Susan's comment stayed with her as she clattered towards the park with Tim following discreetly behind her. The habit was something slightly out of the ordinary and was unusually becoming. Its material, a particular shade of purple popular this Season, was molded tightly to her figure revealing the elegant lines which were usually obscured by the comfortable loose-fitting garments she ordinarily selected. The richness of the color emphasized the whiteness of her skin and the glossy darkness of her hair where it escaped from underneath the dashing cap, and gave a violet tinge to the big gray eyes. The severity of the cut only served to call attention to the delicacy of the straight nose and the generous lips that needed no artifice to give them color. It was a costume as simple as the drapery seen on statues of Greek goddesses and, in truth, mounted on the splendid Xerxes, Caro made all the chattering women trimmed with ruffles and lace, crowded together in their carriages, appear like so many silly butterflies flitting aimlessly through the park, stopping a moment to flirt with this gentleman or smile coquettishly at that fashionable beau.

Glancing neither right nor left, concentrating only on her mount, Caro looked like a severe young Diana as she cut her way through the mass of horses and carriages in search of space to give Xerxes his head and allow him a little exercise. "There, free at last, no more stupid cart-horses or showy mindless equines pulling carriages," she remarked as they pulled away from a gaudy yellow barouche that was impeding rather than proceeding in the crush. "Now you can at least move," she sighed, wondering just precisely what would happen if she were to urge her mount into anything more than a respectable trot.

"Don't even think it, Miss Caroline. It's as much as my

place is worth to let you give that there horse his head. William told me how it would be with both you and Xerxes chafing at the bit. 'Mind you don't give either one of them their head when they go in the park or it will be the ruin of both them, Tim,' he says to me. I know as how you don't give a jot for this society sort of thing, but William knows what he's about and he told me to watch out for you, so I am.'' The groom surveyed her anxiously.

''Very well, Tim,'' Caro acquiesced with a considerable show of reluctance. ''But it is so very tame riding in London that one could scarcely call it exercise.''

''That's the truth for certain, Miss Caroline.'' The lad's ordinarily good-natured countenance wore almost as woe-begone an expression as his mistress's. ''But look on the bright side. Where else could you see so many bang-up pieces of horseflesh.''

Caro brightened perceptibly. ''You are right, Tim, and I stand corrected. It's rather self-indulgent to feel sorry for myself, but I . . .'' Whatever she planned to say in her own defense was cut short as her name boomed out across the park and she turned to see Tony at the head of a group of young men in scarlet coats, seated on magnificent mounts, waving vigorously as he made his way slowly in her direction.

''Caro! I'm that glad to see you. I've been wanting to ask you what you think of Ajax here.'' The viscount patted the neck of the powerful gray that sidled skittishly up to her side. ''Got him for a song off Trevylan because old Trev's a timid rider and Ajax is a bit short on manners. But we'll come to an understanding. Not an ounce of vice in him, really. Poor thing's a bit frisky and what with Trev for a master, it's no wonder.'' Tony looked around anxiously. ''Say, you ain't here with Lavvy are you? She don't understand such things exactly and is forever complaining to the Pater that I shall go to wrack and ruin all because of my stable.''

Caro laughed and assured him that she was quite alone. Then, unable to ignore the group of young men milling eagerly around her cousin while they cast meaningful looks—first at Caro and then at the unconscious Tony—she continued, ''What? Have you just purchased him on the advice of these gentlemen? If so, you seem to have been well served.''

Tony broke into a gratified smile, ''Yes, and a good thing

they were with me. Why Bedford would have beaten me to it if Charles here hadn't had the forethought to distract him with an inquiry about the mill in Clapham on Friday.'' A cough and a significant look on the part of the aforementioned Charles recalled the viscount to his duties. ''Oh, eh.'' Tony looked blank and then grinned sheepishly. ''Sorry, Caro. This is Captain Charles Allen, Lieutenant William Forbush, and Lieutenant Edward Collings. My cousin, Lady Caroline Waverly.'' Tony waved airily at the assembled group. ''But Caro, I must ask, do you think he's a bit short in the hindquarters?'' Tony continued earnestly, forgetting his companions entirely in his concern over the latest addition to his stable.

''Tony you are becoming a dead bore. Can't you think of anything else but your confounded horse? You must forgive Tony, Lady Caroline. When he is involved with a horse he can think of nothing else. As his cousin, you no doubt have suffered this single-mindedness more than once. But you yourself appear to be no mean judge of horseflesh,'' Captain Allen praised, his eyes dwelling only a little less appreciatively on Xerxes than they had on his rider. ''Tony tells me that you are an accomplished horsewoman besides being a devoted agriculturalist and that it is only because of singular circumstances that we are lucky enough to have you with us in the metropolis. I must say it is a blessed relief to meet a woman who can discuss something besides scandal and fashions. But tell me about Waverly Court. Tony says that you are setting the worthy country squires about their ears with your progressive notions.''

By dint of his ingenuous admiration and friendly curiosity, the captain soon overcame Caro's initial wariness of sharing her ideas with others. She watched suspiciously to see the expression of boredom or censure that soon appeared on the features of those to whom she had unwittingly confided her cherished projects, but all she saw in his open countenance was genuine interest and, oddly enough, a look of respectful appreciation that made her feel as though the captain found her attractive.

This was such a novel sensation that, for a moment, Caro was completely silenced by it. Then, realizing that she had paused in the middle of a sentence while Captain Allen waited attentively for the rest, Caro blushed, looked conscious for a moment, and then continued, little knowing how charmingly transparent and endearing was her confusion.

Accustomed to women who wished to converse on no other topic but themselves, Charles Allen was entranced both by the fact that Caro was able to converse knowledgeably on a topic entirely unrelated to the world of the *ton,* and by her evident embarrassment at his admiration. Truly, she was, as Tony Mandeville had claimed, a most unusual and companionable female.

Shyer than their friend, and somewhat bashful in the presence of a lovely young lady, the other two gentlemen had refrained from entering the conversation, but upon hearing how sensibly Caro spoke and how unconscious she was of her own beauty, they soon relaxed and began asking questions. Where had she purchased Xerxes? Who was his sire? Did she raise her own livestock? In no time at all, they found themselves in as lively and enjoyable a conversation as they could have had with one of their brother officers, but with the added attraction of being able to feast their eyes on Caro's animated countenance and graceful figure.

It was truly an unusual and delightful experience and one the four could have enjoyed for the rest of the afternoon had not an elegant barouche that was slowly making its way by them come to a dead stop. Its beautiful occupant, carefully shading herself with a delicate parasol, leaned forward to exclaim in accents of some surprise, "Why Tony, you here? I had not thought you still in town, it's been such an age since you have called. The boys have been asking after you." Lavvy could not keep a hint of displeasure out of her voice.

Upon discovering her brother happily engaged with what looked to be yet another set of gay young blades in scarlet coats instead of dancing devoted attendance on his widowed sister, Lavvy had not been best pleased. But when a second look had proven them to be paying court to another woman, she became thoroughly vexed with him. Now, to her intense annoyance, she discovered the identity of the equestrienne to be none other than her Cousin Caro, and a Cousin Caro who suddenly appeared to be unusually attractive.

Narrowing her eyes suspiciously, Lavvy scrutinized her cousin's new riding habit. Where had she come by such fashionable attire? Why the chit never gave the least thought to what she was wearing. It was entirely unfair that she looked so stunning. "Caro, I . . ." Thoroughly irritated by the entire situation, Lavvy was at a loss for words. "I had thought you back in Grosvenor Square reading one of your boring reviews, not gallivanting about the park."

If Lavvy had meant to deflect attention from her cousin, she did quite the opposite. The touch of animosity in the countess's tone as she referred to Caro's reviews only caused the gentlemen to look at Caro with renewed interest. Tony's cousin must be quite the unusual female if the Countess of Welham, who was notorious for confining her attentions to members of the male sex, could be unnerved by her. Though unsophisticated in the ways of the *ton* after their years in the army, the three officers were wise enough in the ways of mankind in general to recognize jealousy when they saw it, and there was very definitely an air about the lovely countess that suggested she disliked competition of any sort for the attention that was her due—even competition from a country cousin.

Another observer was coming to much the same conclusion and, having had a hand in its inception, was consequently enjoying himself hugely. "Hello Tony." Approaching on a well-mannered bay, Sir Evelyn nodded languidly in the viscount's direction before turning his attention to his cousin. "Lady Caroline, you are looking charming and what a magnificent animal. You quite take the shine out of every other woman in the park," he remarked with gentle malice. "It is a rare creature indeed who can appear to advantage on a horse. You are to be congratulated. And here is Lady Jersey who will back me up, I am sure. Will you not, Sally?" Without appearing to have raised a finger, Sir Evelyn had caught that inveterate mischief-maker's eye and caused her to instruct her coachman to drive up alongside the countess's barouche.

"Oh, indubitably. To appear graceful and yet maintain control of one's mount, especially such a one as Lady Caroline is riding, is unusual indeed. You are to be commended, Lady Caroline." Lady Jersey, whose sharp eyes never missed a thing, smiled slyly as she observed the compression of Lavinia's delicate lips and the rigidity of her spine. One who relished byplay as much as Sir Evelyn, Lady Jersey was highly appreciative of the entire episode and would have been willing to bet that that exquisite gentleman had somehow been at the bottom of the entire thing. Glancing quickly under her lashes, she saw the ill-concealed look of satisfaction on Sir Evelyn's face and she was sure of it.

Very well, then. Her name wasn't Sally Jersey if she weren't ready to make a push to help him. Smiling benevolently at Lavvy, she began, ''I have not seen you at Almack's this Season, my dear Countess. It is too cruel of you to deprive the world of your lovely young cousin.'' Sally laid the most delicate emphasis on the word ''young.'' ''I shall send you a voucher directly. But there, I see Lady Sefton beckoning to me. I must be off. I count on seeing you Wednesday next, Lady Caroline. We shall see if you command the same devoted attention there that you so obviously do here.'' And smiling warmly at Tony's three handsome companions, she was off again having given a further shove to the chain of events Sir Evelyn had set in motion.

It was at this critical juncture that Nicholas, agreeably tired from his session at Gentleman Jackson's and strolling casually through the park with Tubby, caught sight of the little group clustered near the elegant barouche halted in their path. Not so far removed from the military life that he did not look to see what formed the center of attraction for a group of scarlet coats, Nicholas glanced idly in their direction. Because they were fellow soldiers, he was perhaps more curious about the woman who commanded their attention than he might ordinarily have been.

In truth, she was a woman to make the pulse quicken—tall and slender, sitting her mount with such careless grace that she seemed to be at one with the magnificent animal beneath her. The rich color and elegant cut of her riding habit emphasized the exquisite lines of her figure which seemed to flow directly into those of her horse. Standing somewhat aloof from the crowd, barely restraining their wish to break free and indulge in headlong flight, horse and rider seemed possessed of an energy and vitality that made those around them appear petty and insipid. There was something in the proud tilt of the woman's head under the rakish hat and in the impatient gesture with which she brushed a stray lock of black hair from a soft cheek that struck a familiar chord. Where had he seen her before? Nicholas shook his head. Women who held themselves with such distinctive independence were virtually nonexistent in the fashionable world.

Then, one of the attentive group of admirers made some

comment and she raised a gloved hand to her mouth to stifle a laugh. Caro! It was Lady Caroline Waverly! And yet, it was not Caro. Where had she learned to tilt her head so provocatively? No. She was above such things. She despised women who played the coquette. Nicholas looked again. No, it remained true. She was above such things. Caro was not consciously flirting with the besotted captain. It was just that she invested every gesture with an innocent sensuality that was enough to drive a man mad. The marquess's mind harkened back to the day he had come upon her in her breeches, standing boldly on Duke's back as she rode him around the stableyard. She had been entirely unconscious of her effect on him then—as unconscious as she was of her effect on the admiring group surrounding her now, and therein lay part of her power to attract.

Nicholas ground his teeth. It was all very well to appear thus in the privacy of her cousin's stableyard, but to be exercising that same magnetic attraction here in full view of the entire world? Well, it just wasn't proper. Nicholas was on the verge of marching over to tell her so when he was stopped dead in his tracks by his virtually forgotten companion.

"By God, what a lovely creature!" Tubby exclaimed reverently. "Who is she? Surely she cannot have been on the town that long and not be the toast of the *ton*. With that face and that figure, why . . ." At a loss for words, the hapless Tubby was content to stare as Caro leaned forward to calm the impatient Xerxes who, tired of standing, was beginning to take exception to all the idleness.

"Who? Oh, that's Lady Caroline Waverly," Nicholas replied in as noncommittal a tone as he could muster. "Quite above your touch, Tubby. She's a bluestocking of the most ferocious sort."

"You know her? Will you introduce me?" the young guardsman begged eagerly.

"Yes, I know her," the marquess responded impatiently. "But I am not at all sure that you wish to. You're a great gun, Tubby, but you haven't all that much in the brainbox, old fellow, and this is a woman who interests herself in politics and worthy causes," he continued in a dampening tone.

"That's as may be, but by God, she's magnificent! Furthermore, if it's as you say, what's Mandeville doing with her? Why he's got less in his cock-loft than I have!''

Nicholas frowned. Of course, Tubby was entirely correct. Somehow, despite her clever intellect and serious pursuits, Caro managed to make everyone feel comfortable around her, even the insouciant Tony, who was looking at her again with that damnably possessive air. Insolent puppy! What chance did he have with someone like Caro. And furthermore, she was his cousin. Tubby was correct for once in his life. She was magnificent, but it was not purely a superficial thing. There was something majestic in the way she approached life—a nobility and generosity that were all too rare among men and virtually nonexistent among the fairer sex.

Nicholas could not have said whether it was Tubby's unabashed admiration or Tony's air of almost paternal pride that prompted him, but all of a sudden, he found himself pushing his way over to the spot where Xerxes was restlessly pawing the dust. Completely ignoring all the others, he addressed Caro. "Lady Caroline, how delightful. After this morning's outing, I had not thought to have the pleasure of seeing you again." There, let Tony Mandeville stare. "I can see that Xerxes is longing to be gone so I won't detain you any longer than to ask you and any young companions you might happen to know to join me at the balloon ascension in Hackney tomorrow afternoon."

Caro's face lit up in a way that caused the other men there to wish they had thought up such a fortuitous suggestion. "Why thank you, my lord. I should love to. I have been longing to see a balloon, and I am certain that nothing could keep Ceddie and Clarence away."

"Very well, then. I shall look forward to it." Then, realizing that no matter how much he might wish to establish his friendship with Caro, it behooved him, for her sake at least, to remain on good terms with his hostess, Nicholas turned to Lavinia with a dazzling smile. "That is, of course, if their enchanting mother will entrust them to me." Seeing the gathering frown on the beauty's brow, he hastened to add, "Of course, I should be charmed if you could accompany us, Countess, but knowing how sought after your company is, I should not dare to insult you by inviting you at such short notice," effectively making it impossible for Lavinia to join them and relieving her of the unpleasant choice between losing Nicholas's company or having to enjoy it as best she could among a crowd of cits gawking at a ridiculous spectacle.

Trapped, and with all eyes upon her, the beauty was forced to smile as graciously as she could. "That is very kind of you. I appreciate your taking them when you know the delicacy of my sensibilities. I really cannot support these rude public gatherings, pain me though it does to deprive children of amusement. Besides, as you so correctly surmised, I am otherwise engaged." The emphasis Lavinia placed on the word "children" was not lost on any of the principals at whom it was directed, but far from having its desired effect, it served only to amuse the marquess and Caro and bring a sly twinkle into Sir Evelyn's eyes.

23

IN FACT, it could have been said that Caro was nearly as excited by the prospect as were the boys when she relayed the marquess's invitation to them.

"Hooray, hooray! What a lark." Ceddie cried, bounding around the room with Argos yapping exuberantly at his heels.

"I say, it's very kind of the marquess, isn't it, Cousin Caro?" Clarence, though more restrained than his sibling, was just as thrilled for more scientific reasons. "I have been reading of the early attempt by Lunardi, but I find it all rather difficult to picture. I hope we shan't be too much trouble for his lordship. I shall do my best to see that Ceddie behaves himself. He isn't at all naughty, as Mama thinks, it's just that he is sometimes carried away by his own enthusiasm."

"I appreciate your concern, Clarence." Caro was hard put to keep her lips from quivering. "But I expect that among the three of us, we can keep Ceddie from falling into mischief."

In fact, it appeared that the person Nicholas considered most likely to fall into a scrape was not Cedric, but Caro. As he watched her lean forward in the carriage, her eyes eagerly absorbing every detail of the colorful scene, the marquess could not help smiling. It was obvious from the moment she caught sight of the gaily colored ball of silk that Caro was entirely captivated.

"Oh how lovely!" she gasped as the red-and-white striped mass slowly took shape and rose majestically into the air. Entirely forgetting her companions or the discussion she had been in the midst of with Clary—convinced to accompany them by her brother's repeated appeals—she gazed entranced as the balloon filled and rose gracefully like some magnificent bird until it swayed aloft over the awed spec-

tators tugging gently at its tether ropes. "How I should love
to see what the world looks like from there. We humans
must appear so insignificant compared with the vast view
one must have from such a lofty perch. It must be wonderful
beyond all imagining to fly as free as the clouds over the
countryside."

"I daresay you will think me a dreadful coward, but I
confess I should think it would be excessively uncomfortable up there at the whim of the least little puff of air, with
the wind whistling about one and never being certain of
where one was going to land," Clary protested mildly. "I
admire your courage, Caro, indeed, I do."

"But how glorious to descend into a completely unknown
place. It would truly be an adventure." Caro clasped her
hands around her knees, fixing her eyes above on the balloon and its occupants.

Sitting there, enraptured, in much the same pose in which
he had first come upon her, she reminded Nicholas of nothing so much as the enchanting eleven-year-old who had won
his heart with her curious mixture of innocence, enthusiasm, and world-weary cynicism. All of a sudden, he found
himself wishing that he could gratify her every little wish.
Assuring himself that everyone in the party was completely
absorbed with the spectacle at hand, he slid carefully down
from the carriage and strolled over to the area where one of
the balloonists was keeping the most curious of the onlookers at bay.

"I say, my good man, is it possible for you to take a
passenger up with you?"

The man looked skeptical. "I—I couldn't say my Lord,
that is, the risk involved and it's still being in the nature of
a scientific experiment. Besides, it's not very comfortable
and all."

Nicholas, recognizing the fellow's distrust of the Quality,
smiled in a friendly fashion. "I quite understand your reluctance, especially as the passenger I propose is a lady.
No," he held up a conciliatory hand, "this is a lady accustomed to a life of adventure, who scorns discomfort and
courts risk for the sake of acquiring knowledge. In fact, she
has not the least idea that I came over here to burden you
with such a preposterous request. But, see for yourself how
she concentrates on your every move with the alert eye of a
truly scientific observer. She has admitted to me that her

understanding of the physical principles behind ballooning is sketchy at best and she is eager to discover more.''

Scrutinizing the balloonist carefully as he glanced over to where Caro sat mesmerized, Nicholas could see him beginning to weaken and seizing upon this he continued, ''But there, I shall let the lady speak for herself and you will see what I mean.'' He beckoned to Caro who, tearing her eyes away from the preparatory activity aloft, caught his gesture and nodded, smiling.

''Oh sir, a young lady, I don't think . . .'' the man began, only to be interrupted.

''Oh, come off it, man. Does she look like one of those females whose attics are to let?'' the marquess asked, as she raised one interrogative eyebrow at him. He beckoned again and she leaped lightly down to make her way purposefully toward them.

The balloonist's expression of dismay was dispelled somewhat as he saw the poise and aplomb with which she made her way through the crowd. She certainly did look like a young lady who knew what she was doing. He watched her as she sized up the ropes securing the basket and the apparatus on the ground—an observant young person, to be sure, but he was not entirely certain he wanted to take her up in the basket. Females could be unpredictable and were inclined to scream at the oddest moments. Why only yesterday his Effie, who had born him seven children without seeming to pause from her heavy household chores for a moment, nursed them all through fevers and broken limbs, and was death on spiders and other unpleasant crawly things, had shrieked and nearly fainted at the sight of a curious mouse who had invited itself into the kitchen. However, this lady, smiling in a amicable fashion all the while she was summing him up with clear gray eyes did not seem like the sort to be unnerved by much of anything. But, well, you never knew about people. Her friend seemed to be a alright sort of fellow, top of the trees with those horses, and accustomed to command, the balloonist felt sure, but there was something else about him that made him different from most of the Quality. Perhaps it was his calm assurance, a directness in his gaze that made you know he recognized you as a person in your own right. For some obscure reason, the balloonist felt he could trust him.

''Here is the lady to whom I was referring,'' the marquess held out his hand to help Caro over some coiled ropes. "Caro, this is Mr.—Mr. . . . I do not apologize. I completely forgot to introduce myself. I'm Nicholas Daventry."

And if he's plain old Mr. Daventry, I'll eat my hat, the balloonist thought to himself, though he liked Nicholas the better for it. "It's Timmins, sir, Richard Timmins."

"Pleased to make your acquaintance, Mr. Timmins. Let me introduce you to Lady Caroline Waverly who, if I'm not much mistaken, is well on her way to becoming a ballooning enthusiast." Nicholas smiled quizzically at Caro.

"Oh, yes. It looks perfectly thrilling. It must be blissful to be up there among the birds looking down on everything below." Caro smiled so shyly at Mr. Timmins that he instantly became her devoted slave.

"I have been trying to persuade Mr. Timmins to allow you up in the basket so you can take a peek at those very sights. I have assured him that you haven't a single disastrous female trait, not being a clinger, squeaker, or a fainter."

If Mr. Timmins harbored any reservations over the marquess's proposal, they disappeared the instant he saw Caro's face light up with anticipation.

"Oh, how very kind of you, but I should not wish to discommode the balloonists in any way." She smiled gratefully at Nicholas, trying not to appear too eager lest she make Mr. Timmins feel obliged to acquiesce.

He, however, having decided from the lady's reaction that she was as much a right one as her companion, was already hailing his fellow balloonists and requesting them to descend.

Inclined at first to be as skeptical as their confrere, they too were soon won over by the genuine curiosity and interest of Nicholas and Caro. This initial impression only improved as the couple, mindful of staying out of their way, did not impede their procedures in the least, merely climbing into the basket quietly and unobtrusively and watching carefully as they prepared to ascend again.

Caro held her breath as they floated gently skyward and watched in delight as the world expanded below her feet and the press of spectators became a multicolored patch on a swath of green surrounded by houses interspersed with church spires. So this is how birds must feel, she thought to herself as she, ever mindful of causing concern to the balloon's other occupants, peered carefully over the side.

Nicholas leaned back, his eyes fixed more on Caro than on the scene below. What an intrepid little soul she was, so immersed in the whole experience that she never stopped to consider the thousand little objections that any other woman would have raised if she even had the temerity to become involved in such an escapade in the first place—what would people think, would her coiffure or her costume become disarranged, what of the danger? Why, the marquess hardly knew any men who would have relished the challenge as much as Caro did and he took great pleasure in her palpable enjoyment.

Nicholas had not experienced such a sense of shared adventure since he had left the army and it was not until now that he realized how much he had missed this or how very lonely he had felt amongst the rest of the fashionable world. While it was true that he was welcomed as never before by the *ton,* even hailed as one of its leaders, he had never felt much kinship with any of them—not even those members of it that he had known for years.

In his youth he had chosen the army because he genuinely wished to help his country and because the prospect of spending his time drifting from Brooks's to Manton's to Tattersalls and back again, engaging in inane conversations with all of those who were doing precisely the same thing, bored him beyond all bearing. In the army at least, he had had the opportunity to test his skills and intelligence and he had discovered that he enjoyed a life where the success he gained and the respect he commanded were earned by his own personal skill and daring.

Though he had been closer to his brother officers who shared his preference for an active and adventurous life than he had been to those bent on the empty life of amusement in the *ton,* Nicholas had found them to be almost totally uninterested in the larger issues behind the battles they were fighting. Unlike them, he had always been intensely curious about the social and economic forces being brought into play as well as the political ones and he had found no one, with the possible exception of a serious gray-eyed eleven-year-old perched on the stairs at Mandeville Hall, who had wondered the same things and asked the same questions he did. Upon his return to London, the new Marquess of Everleigh had sought out men of affairs for intellectual stimulation, but he had found them sadly timid and unadventurous as far as the rest of their lives were concerned and it had begun to appear that he would never find anyone that combined the same thirst for both physical and intellectual challenges that he had.

Now, observing Caro as she hung over the edge of the basket looking back from time to time to ask a question—how long could they stay aloft, how high could they go, how far could they travel, and how much control did they have over their direction—Nicholas realized that, at last, he had found just such a person. He was completely taken aback by such a discovery. It had never occurred to him, whenever he had wished for a true companion who would look for the same things in life as he did that such a person might be a woman, and it required a certain amount of consideration to adjust to the idea.

Such an adjustment was not accomplished without a deal of reflection and the marquess, his mind totally occupied with this novel concept, was strangely silent as they descended. He merely nodded as Caro thanked the balloonists profusely for their generosity. Nor did he respond to the general hubbub of interest when they returned to the carriage.

"Cousin Caro, Cousin Caro," Ceddie, unable to contain himself, burst out, "did you have the most bang-up time? Could you see very, very far? Did everything look very, very small? Oh, I wish I could have gone."

Caro smiled at his enthusiasm. "Whoa, Ceddie. One question at a time. Yes, it was wonderful and I should like very much to have taken you along, but as it was, they were exceedingly reluctant to allow a woman, a grown-up woman to be sure, but still a woman on their craft. It was only because a very important personage spoke on my behalf that I was given such a rare concession. But perhaps I behaved well enough that they will consider taking passengers in the future. I should dearly love to fly somewhere."

"So should I," Ceddie chimed in. Then, lowering his voice confidentially which, for Cedric, meant merely confining it to the hearing of all of those in the barouche, "Is Lord Daventry a 'very important personage'?"

"Very," Caro responded firmly, her eyes twinkling up at Nicholas who, upon hearing his name, had turned around.

"He has a great deal of influence and can advance all sorts of one's pet projects. One must be very careful to behave around him so as to give him a favorable impression. I certainly try to do so," she concluded piously.

"Humbug!" Nicholas grinned. "I should venture to say that the majority of times I have encountered you, you have been in a compromising situation or on the brink of one."

"What a bouncer!" Caro gasped. "And quite untrue! Why I behaved perfectly unexceptionably at the opera and the theater."

"Both rare occurrences." The marquess nodded in mock solemnity, and added, "At which I felt privileged to be an observer."

"Dreadful creature. You talk as though I were always in a scrape."

"Well, aren't you?"

"Not in the least. Why, most of the time I lead a perfectly blameless existence." Seeing the amusement in his eyes, she faltered. "Well, it *is* a blameless existence, just not a conventional one," she defended herself.

"Precisely. And most of the *ton* would consider that to be one long scrape. I know, for I have led a similar one."

"Well, at least I am not asking anyone to rescue me from it," she rejoined hotly.

He laughed. "No, I should say you are resisting some very concerted efforts to do so." Then, seeing the look of doubt in her eyes, he continued, "And I commend you highly for it. How else is society to improve if we don't have some members who refuse to follow its dictates blindly? But, come, we should be going. It has clouded over and I don't want Clary to become chilled, nor do I want to keep you and the boys out so long that Lavvy will forbid our next outing."

"Where is that to be?" Ceddie was agog.

The marquess smiled mysteriously. "Why, if I told you that, it wouldn't be a surprise now, would it?"

"I hope you stay with us forever, Cousin Caro," Ceddie sighed ecstatically. "If you're there when Lord Daventry visits, he takes us on expeditions. If Mama is there, he just sits there while she makes smiley faces at him."

Caro was hard put to choke back a spurt of laughter at the thought of Lavinia's expression were she to know how her youngest described her carefully contrived flirtations.

She stole a glance at Nicholas who, she was gratified to see, was also having difficulty containing his mirth. He quirked one mobile brow and nearly overset her, but she quickly turned it into a cough and was able to reply with only the slightest quiver in her voice, "Why thank you, Ceddie. That is most kind of you, but I suspect it is just as much your company and Clarence's as mine that is responsible for this delightful outing."

Both boys looked hugely pleased. Then Clarence, remembering his manners, turned to the marquess. "We are exceedingly grateful, sir. Thank you ever so much."

Not to be outdone, his brother piped up, "Yes, thank you, thank you, thank you."

His exuberance almost drowned out Caro's own whispered "thank you," but sensing rather than hearing it, the marquess looked down into the deep gray eyes which, serious now, were clouded with the effort to convey her gratitude, not only for the outing, but for his recognition of the type of person she was and his appreciation and encouragement of that person. "Thank you. I can't tell you what it means. I . . ." Caro fell silent as she groped for words.

Nicholas grasped one slim gloved hand in both of his. "No thanks are necessary, Waif. It is *I* who should thank *you,* for I have never enjoyed London half so much before you arrived. Why I . . ."

He was cut short by Ceddie who shouted, "Look! Look! They're off!" And they all turned to look as, cut loose from its moorings, the balloon sailed gracefully into the distance.

The ride back was relatively quiet. Even Ceddie was silent, tired by the excitement of the ascension and occupied with all the new sights and sounds around him.

Clary, delighted at being able to join them, was busy with her own thoughts. In truth, witnessing the last interchange between her brother and Caro, had been more highly gratifying to her than any balloon ascension. Reflecting quietly to herself, she decided that she could not remember when she had seen Nicholas so relaxed and happy. Though she really knew very little of Caro, she suspected that the same was true for her. Watching them together, Clary sensed a communication and rapport between them that was almost tangible and while she was delighted for them, it did make her feel the tiniest bit lonely. After all, Nicholas had been her closest friend and ally for as long as she could remem-

ber and, though he did not know it yet, he had now found
someone who could be even closer than she.

Then Caro, as if sensing her thoughts, turned. ''I hope
you enjoyed yourself, Clary. If balloon ascensions are not
one's passion, I could see how they could be very dull indeed, especially when everyone else is too involved to carry
on any worthwhile conversation.''

Somehow, without Clary's knowing precisely how, Caro
moved nimbly from ballooning to music and to Clary's most
recently acquired pieces. Soon they were chatting gaily
about Signor Clementi, the opera, and a whole host of intriguing topics and Clary realized gratefully that, rather than
losing her closest companion, she was gaining another. By
the time they reached Grosvenor Square, she was as well
pleased with the entire day and the company as everyone
else. Indeed, for each and every member of the party it had
been the high point of the Season—a Season each one of
them had expected to be boring in the extreme.

24

THE PROMISED VOUCHER had arrived from Lady Jersey and now neither Caro nor Lavvy had any excuse to put off joining the select throng Wednesday evening. Lavvy, who had avoided anything that smacked of an official introduction of her cousin to the *ton*, for once protested almost as loudly as Caro. "I vow, it is too fatiguing of Sally to do this. Now there is no help for it but to go and I can think of nothing more dull than an evening at Almack's. You are like to be bored to tears for I know I shall be."

Which must be the first time you have ever considered what my feelings in the matter might be, Caro, instantly suspicious, thought to herself. Resolving to foil any possible scheme of Lavvy's, she smiled resignedly, "I suppose we must go since Lady Jersey has been so kind, but we needn't stay very long."

"No." Having been forced into bringing Caro to the temple at which the Upper Ten Thousand worshipped, Lavvy was not about to forego a moment of the opportunity to dazzle everyone. "Having made up our minds to attend, we shall do it justice. I have not been this age and I know I shan't be able to see everyone who wishes to see me if we only go for a short time. It is too fatiguing, but one does have a duty to one's fellow creatures, you know."

One's fellow admirers, more like, Caro remarked cynically to herself, but she managed to keep her expression cheerful as she replied, "You are right. We must put forth our best efforts."

Later, in conversation with Helena, she was able to give vent to her true emotions. "It is most unfortunate. I had planned a quiet evening at home reading *The Practical Gardener*. Now I shall be obliged to smirk and make empty conversation while Lavvy holds court and complains to me that Lord So-and-So is so importunate or vows that do what she will, the Duke of This-or-That remains absolutely besotted with her.''

"That's as may be, but you will just have to cast her in the shade," Helena declared, warming to the theme introduced by Sir Evelyn at the theater.

"How can I possibly do that? And besides, why should I wish to? I do not care to excell at those arts she has made herself mistress of," Caro declared defiantly.

"No, of course you do not," her companion soothed. "But anyone who spends a moment in conversation with you will find hers empty by comparison. She may appear very well, but the minute she commences speech, she loses a good deal of her charm, while you, by contrast, increase it. Now, unless you show the *ton* what the alternative to spoiled beauty can be, it will continue to be enamored of women such as she.''

"Yes, Helena," Caro responded meekly, but there was a twinkle in her eyes.

"You could be surprised. If you approach it all in the right frame of mind you could find yourself tolerably amused.''

And, realizing the justice of her friend's remark, Caro resolved to do just that.

It was wonderful, she reflected to herself as she mounted the stairs to the assembly rooms that evening, what a difference one's perspective could make. Now that she had made up her mind that the best way to advance the cause of women was to excell in the fashionable world rather than avoid it, she did not feel the usual paralyzing sense of boredom and distaste creeping over her as she surveyed the brilliant assemblage before her. It helped when she caught sight of Tony Mandeville's large form making its way self-consciously through the crowd, and the expression of astonishment on Lavvy's face at the sight of her sporting-mad brother in Almack's hallowed halls was worth whatever ordeal Caro would be forced to face the rest of the evening. Tony's face lit up when he caught sight of her. "Caro!"

"Tony, whatever are *you* doing *here?*" Lavvy's tone was a mixture of curiosity and suspicion.

An aggrieved frown clouded the viscount's ordinarily sunny countenance. "Now Lavvy, I thought you would be pleased as punch to see me here. Why you've been after me for years to come, and now that I have, you don't seem the least bit glad to see me. Why I was even about to offer to stand up with you.''

"I am delighted to see you here," the countess began acidly, "but you might have seen fit to tell me . . .''

Whatever animadversions she wished to make on her brother's character were drowned out by a cheerful voice at her shoulder, "Tony, there you are, old man. Lord, what a crush. I had a devil of a time following you. Hello, Lady Caroline. Happy to see you. Tony thought we might find you here, eh what Tony?'' Captain Allen, beaming happily at Caro as he bowed over her hand only served to exacerbate Lavvy's annoyance. It was infuriating in the extreme that Tony, who never set foot in Almack's and who, moreover, had spent a great deal of his life loudly protesting that he would not be caught dead inside that rigidly proper establishment should appear of his own free will now that Caro was here, when his sister had been in dire need of his escort for some time.

Lavvy was so exasperated she didn't know which way to look and her ill humor was not improved by the eagerness with which Tony's friends, who also had never been known to darken Almack's doors, clustered around Caro. It was outside of enough! Why the chit didn't even make the least push to appear presentable, much less take the trouble to ingratiate herself with the *ton*. If it hadn't been for Lavvy's introduction, no one would have paid the least mind to Lady Caroline Waverly, and now, all of a sudden, she was the center of attention. Why even her own brother, if Lavvy could trust her ears, was asking her to join him in the next country dance. What was this world coming to?

"Why, whatever is the world coming to?'' a gay voice echoed in her ear as Sally Jersey, dripping with diamonds, hurried over to greet them. "Why, Tony, you incorrigible boy, I had never thought we could lure you here. We have done well indeed, or perhaps it is the company.'' With a significant look at Caro, the lady smiled dazzlingly up at him. "And to show you just how charmed I am by your presence, I shall allow you to partner me in the quadrille.''

Tony, completely out of his depth, blushed like a schoolboy. "Thank you, most honored,'' he mumbled.

The lady laughed and tapped him with her fan. "Don't be afraid, I shan't eat you. We shall enjoy ourselves, you

will see,'' she declared gaily as they headed toward the
floor leaving the others to gaze with varying degrees of
amusement after them.

''Oh lord, he's in the basket now. Tony don't like to dance
above half.'' Lieutenant Forbush was so relieved that it had
not happened to him that he was thoroughly enjoying his
friend's discomfiture.

Even Lavvy found it somewhat diverting to think of her
dance-shy brother partnering the patroness of an institution
whose very name, until now, had inspired the utmost horror
in him.

They might have stood thus, staring at the picture of the
uncomfortable Tony fighting his way through the figures of
the dance, a heavy frown of concentration wrinkling his
brow while his lovely partner laughed and flirted, had not
a coolly elegant voice broken in on them. ''Lavinia, my
dear, and Lady Caroline. I had hardly dared hope for the
pleasure of your company. I must say you are both looking
charming.'' And Sir Evelyn materialized beside them.

Lavinia turned to him and held out her hand as though
she were drowning. ''Why thank you dear Sir Evelyn. You
are too kind. One does one's poor best, you know. You are
quite correct in thinking that we had not planned to attend,
but Sally Jersey was so insistent that I show Caro all the
important haunts of the *ton*. After all, what could I do? The
poor girl has been buried in the country this age. Of course
I have not come to dance. I shall join the rest of the dowa-
gers arranged along the wall.'' Lavvy looked hopefully at
the immaculately attired peer.

''Not dance! What? And deprive us all of the sight of the
beauteous Countess of Welham gracing the floor? Why, I
have never heard such a dreadful thing and I take it upon
myself to dispel such a ridiculous notion. You will excuse
us?'' He extended a graceful hand to the triumphant Lavinia
and, smiling at the rest of them, led her toward the floor as
the musicians struck up the first strains of the next dance.

A few seconds later, a heavily perspiring Tony appeared,
to slump gratefully against a pillar. ''Whew! Glad that's
over. Where she got the idea that I'm a damned caper merchant, I'll never know. Glad you're not the sort of woman
who wants a man to do the pretty with her all the time,
Caro. You and Clary are the only restful females I've ever
had the pleasure of meeting and you're a sight for sore eyes

I can tell you." Tony smiled gratefully at Caro as he caught his breath. "What women see in all this, I should like to know. Why Lavvy just ain't happy unless she has some poor fellow dancing attendance on her and making pretty speeches all the time."

"Thank you, Tony," Caro replied absently, her mind occupied with the disturbing discovery that there was some small part of her—an infinitesimal one to be sure but there, nevertheless—that envied her cousin as she whirled around the floor laughing and smiling, assured that she was drawing admiring glances from one and all. For a moment, Caro wondered wistfully what it would be like to be so supremely confident of one's power to attract. For the most part, Caro never gave her appearance a second thought, but observing her exquisite cousin, the light gleaming on her golden curls, diamonds glittering on her flawless skin and her graceful figure shimmering in a satin dress covered with silver threaded net, Caro felt like a great overgrown schoolgirl, gawky and dowdy in her plain white muslin, rather like a carthorse next to a thoroughbred. But before she could become too overwhelmed by such dismal thoughts, Captain Allen broke into them.

"You're in the right of it, Tony, and that's all very well if a woman wants some Bartholomew baby who don't know anything beyond what his tailor tells him. Why your sister Lavinia ain't flesh and blood, she's a doll. You won't notice anyone but someone like Sir Evelyn wasting his time on her. She's like some beautiful painting that one is only supposed to admire from afar, but she's a cold fish, even if she is your sister. A man wants a bit of a real woman—someone who can enjoy life with him, someone who's warm and . . ." suddenly aware that he was coming dangerously close to being indelicate in the presence of a lady, the captain came to an awkward halt. "Begging your pardon Lady Caroline, not the sort of thing to discuss in front of a lady. Ahem, would you care to stand up with me? It seems a dashed shame to be here next to a beautiful woman and not take advantage of the chance to ask her to dance."

Unsure of herself, and not liking to attract the least amount of attention, Caro would have demurred, but the captain seemed so genuinely unaffected and friendly that she wavered. She was still wavering when Lavinia, who had arrived just in time to hear the captain's proposal responded in accents of horror, "But you must not! It's the waltz—most improper. And besides, buried in the country as she has been, Caro hasn't the least idea how to do it."

But once again, emerging from nowhere, Lady Jersey chimed in gaily, "But I am certain she must know how to waltz. Anyone who sits a horse as gracefully as Lady Caroline must be an excellent dancer. Captain Allen, I recommend Lady Caroline Waverly as a partner. Ah, excuse me, there is Mrs. Drummond Burrell waving at me—some crisis, no doubt. I must be off." And smiling maliciously at the chagrined Lavinia, she flitted away as quickly as she had appeared.

Caro and the captain proceeded to the dance floor in silence where Caro began doubtfully, "I don't know. Lavvy is right. Though of course I understand it in principle, I have never actually done the waltz before."

"Never fear, it ain't that difficult," the captain reassured her. "Just follow me. Sally's right. Any woman who can handle a horse like Xerxes can waltz."

Caro remained unconvinced, and her first few steps felt tense and awkward, but her partner, confident of her ability to pick it up, chatted gaily about the finer points of a hunter he had seen at Tattersall's the day before and in no time Caro was able to relax and give herself up to the music. In fact, she quite liked the smoothness and the motion and was somewhat disappointed when it was over.

Not so Lavinia who had been forced to listen to her brother's approval. "Knew Caro could do it. Got a lot of bottom, that girl, quick on her feet too. Can do anything she puts her mind to." It was galling enough to hear this from the ordinarily unforthcoming Tony, but to do so in Sir Evelyn's presence—Lavinia's patience was sorely tried by the time the dancers returned.

Nor did Sir Evelyn refrain from repeating this praise once Caro's partner had restored her safely to their little group. Several of the captain's cronies had appeared, ostensibly to talk to their friend, but their attention was all for his companion. "There, Lady Caroline, what did I tell you? I knew that it would not be long before your natural grace and your own particular brand of charm would be recognized," Sir Evelyn remarked smugly, stealing a glance at Lavinia. "No need to look so blank, dear girl. You may lack the classic features of our acknowledged incomparables, but there is a certain special allure about you—call it magnetism—that makes the rest of them appear frivolous in comparison. And when the *ton* discovers that you possess wit as well as beauty, you shall make the rest of the accredited diamonds seem like the merest of schoolgirls. For who would wish for a Venus with all her petty vanity when one could have a Diana instead," he concluded smiling enigmatically.

"Why, thank you. You are too kind." Caro was somewhat taken aback. Unused to the ways of the *ton* she might be, but there was no mistaking the distinct undercurrent to the comments of this middle-aged exquisite. Try though she might, Caro could not quite fathom its meaning.

Her cousin, however, was in no such confusion, and thoroughly annoyed, she resolved to put an end to such a miserable evening as quickly as possible. Sighing gently, she lifted one delicate white hand to her brow. "The heat, the crowd . . ." She wrinkled her brow prettily. "You will think me a poor frail creature, I know, but I have lived such a quiet existence for the past year that now the least excitement brings on the headache. Caro, as you are also unused to all this, I know you will not object if we leave before the appointed time. You have been seen and that is enough." She turned as Sir Evelyn placed a chair behind her and tenderly helped her into it. "Thank you." she put her hand to her brow and sighed again as he sent Tony off to order their carriage.

25

SILENCE REIGNED during the ride home, each of the carriage's occupants preoccupied with her own thoughts, all of which were unsettling. For the first time in her life, Lavinia had felt her absolute assurance in the supremacy of her beauty and charm slip the tiniest bit. And for the first time in her life, Caro was confronted with the vision of herself as a woman whom others found attractive. Even more surprising was that Lavvy seemed to sense this. Though Caro herself was no dissembler, Lavvy was, and Caro knew that prior to Sir Evelyn's remarks, nothing could have been farther from her cousin's mind than a fit of the megrims.

Caro would never have considered herself any sort of competition to the beautiful Countess of Welham, but she did derive a certain amount of satisfaction at having put Lavinia's nose out of joint, even for a moment. It was true that to an incomparable such as Lavinia, Captain Allen and Sir Evelyn were not the sort of quarry worthy of serious attention, but their obvious admiration of another woman, and a woman whom Lavvy had written off as unworthy of consideration, and was not the sort of situation to put the countess in a very favorable mood.

In fact, Lavinia's ill humor was such that other members of the household were inclined to remark on it. Accustomed as she was to her mistress's demanding ways, Miss Crimmins had finally withdrawn in hurt silence when, during the nightly ritual of brushing the countess's golden curls, she was sharply adjured not to pull so.

"I am sorry, my lady. I am applying the same pressure as customary," Crimmins had responded stiffly.

"Well then, stop," Lavvy snapped. "It's giving me the most frightful headache." Her minion's offer of lavender water gently applied to the temples only exacerbated her the more until, suffering in earnest from a truly pounding headache, she ordered shrilly, "Just go! Leave me in peace and quiet."

Never one to gossip about her idol, Crimmins would have borne it all in uncomplaining silence had not the majestic Wigmore so much forgotten himself as to observe to her that Almack's must have been very thin of company, the ladies having returned so early and the mistress being so out of sorts. "But I know you will have restored her spirits as you always do, Miss Crimmins," he remarked, unbending enough to lavish a wintry smile of approval on that grateful lady.

"Oh, I certainly hope, that is, I am persuaded her ladyship will feel much more the thing once she has had a good night's rest," the abigail fluttered, her face unbecomingly flushed at the signal honor of being noticed by Mr. Wigmore himself.

But the night brought no rest nor any counsel, and the countess awoke in as wretched a condition as she had gone to bed. The uncertain state of her nerves was attested to the next evening when, entirely forgetting the interested presence of both Susan and Crimmins, she rounded on Caro as her unsuspecting cousin was descending on the way to the Countess of Nayland's rout.

Reputed to be the event of the Season, it was an entertainment not to be missed even by those most secure in their favorable standing among the Upper Ten Thousand, and no one with the least pretensions to fashion would have missed it for the world. Accordingly Caro, much to Susan's delight, had decided to honor the occasion by appearing in the ball gowns recently delivered from Henrietta Street.

"Oh, my lady, you look just like a goddess," Susan had breathed as the shimmering satin settled over Caro's slender figure.

Caro laughed. "Your loyalty makes you foolish, Susan, but I thank you kindly all the same." And in truth, Caro could not refrain from admiring herself in the looking glass. The gown of blush-colored satin was cut low all around the bust while the short waist revealed beautifully sculpted shoulders and a long graceful neck. The lines were extremely simple with only the plainest of trimmings at the bottom, a flounce of blond lace whose weight made the material swing enticingly around her while the scalloped hem occasionally allowed a tantalizing glimpse of delicate ankles and elegant feet encased in satin slippers. Susan had tamed the unruly dark curls into a smooth, shining braid letting a few loose ringlets fall to caress the slender neck. A strand of pearls threaded through the thick braid emphasized its glossy blackness.

None of the effect was lost on Lavinia who, having selected a toque which she had considered to be in the first stare of fashion, suddenly felt matronly and uneasily recalled a phrase from that month's Ackermann's *Repository* in which the author declared toques to have declined in popularity. Nor was this improved by Tony, there under threat of instant death to escort his sister and cousin, who exclaimed ingenuously, "By Jove, Coz, you look as fine as fivepence!"

Where had the chit come by that gown? Lavvy wondered furiously. No ordinary seamstress had fashioned that elegant concoction and Lavvy felt reasonably confident of her ability to recognize the creations of Bond Street's most fashionable modistes. Her eyes narrowed for a moment as she surveyed her young relative. Then, recovering quickly, she adopted an expression of cousinly concern. "My dear, that neckline," she began doubtfully.

"What is wrong with my neckline?" Caro's voice was low and calm with only a hint of defiance in it.

"I realize that, country-bred as you are, you can have no notion of these things, but, well, it is a trifle low. Do allow me to lend you something to make it more discreet. I have some net that will answer to the purpose. Here, girl," she beckoned to Susan. "Go fetch the blond tulle I just purchased. Crimmins will know where to find it."

"No, stay please, Susan. Cousin Lavinia is too solicitous. With her as my example my mind is perfectly at ease now that I see her decolletage is a good deal lower than mine. But I thank you for your concern, Lavvy," Caro continued serenely as, allowing Tony to help her into her wrap, she proceeded toward the waiting carriage leaving a dumbfounded Lavinia in her wake and bringing a quickly concealed smile of triumph to Susan's face.

Crimmins, also a witness to the entire scene, and not deigning to acknowledge the existence of the rustic cousin's maid, stalked off in high dudgeon. Small wonder her poor mistress was in a state of nervous exhaustion with such goings on. A fine thing it was for that young miss to give herself airs when, but for her mistress's kindness, she would still be buried in the country.

However, Crimmins was alone in her position. Over the weeks, Caro's never-failing kindness and her concern for the two lonely little boys had won the hearts of the rest of the staff, with the exception of Mr. Wigmore. Having listened to the account of Daisy, one of the upstairs maids, who had overheard the entire scene while putting things to rights in the drawing room, the household rejoiced in Caro's success.

"She looked like a queen, she did," Daisy reported as they sat around the kitchen table. "It made her ladyship as mad as fire to see Lady Caroline in such finery." Daisy smiled reminiscently. Relatively new to the countess's establishment, and in awe of Miss Crimmins and the stately butler, she had been a silent admirer of the enterprising Susan who refused to acknowledge the absolute sway those two personages exerted over the rest of the servants.

It was not that Susan was in the least bit disrespectful. On the contrary, she was always quiet and courteous. Nevertheless, her self-possessed demeanor made it abundantly clear that, while she might accord them the respect due to their positions, she in no way considered herself to be inferior. Nor did she consider her mistress to be any less important than the countess—for all her beauty and reputation in as an incomparable.

It was quite the opposite, in fact. And while Susan was ready to concede that the Countess of Welham was a diamond of the first water, she was by no means willing to admit that this gave that lady superiority to someone who was not only beautiful in her own unique way, but intelligent and kind as well. More than once, Susan had cut Crimmins short in mid-tirade of "My lady does this" or "My lady would never consider doing that" or "My lady only mingles with the likes of Duchess So-and-So" with her quiet response that undoubtedly these were all very well and good for those who wished to shine in such a limited sphere, but the mind of Lady Caroline Waverly was on higher things, and she devoted her abundant talents and energies to nothing less than the improvement of mankind.

Lady Caroline Waverly was striking rather than beautiful, but she was certain to turn heads tonight. Susan felt privileged to have witnessed the skill that had called forth this distinctive beauty. And if the little maid were not mistaken, the countess too had appreciated the subtle but distinct transformation wrought by Violette Winwood's artistry.

Susan could have hugged herself with glee at the look on the faces of the countess and the high and mighty Crimmins as Caro had swept regally down the stairs, but she would not for the world have betrayed her feelings by so much as a flicker of an eyelid to those two, and a precious pair they were too. She only hoped that the Marquess of Everleigh would be there tonight and would himself see that the Countess of Welham, for all her little airs and graces, could not hold a candle to Lady Caroline Waverly.

Sitting uncomfortably in the carriage across from a rigidly silent Lavinia, Caro was, to her disgust and dismay, wishing much the same thing as her devoted maid. The evening, thus far, had been quite a revelation to one who considered herself to be different from the rest of the *ton* and quite enjoyed being labeled a bluestocking. Now, riding along, feeling the delicate touch of a curl as it nestled against her bare neck and relishing the rich sheen of her gown picked up by the light of the torchères, rubbing an appreciative hand over the silky material, she reflected on the pleasure to be derived from knowing that one was looking one's best.

A mocking smile tugged the corners of Caro's mouth as she admitted ruefully to herself that an elegant, becoming, and extremely fashionable gown could do a great deal for one's sense of confidence and well-being. Much as she despised herself for it, Caro was forced to acknowledge that she felt a certain degree of triumph over Lavvy who, though elegantly attired as usual, lacked a certain amount of *éclat*, and who had not been quite quick enough to hide the chagrin she felt when she realized that Caro's costume was far more original than the tasteful but boring white-lace dress over white satin slip that she wore. The corsage of rose satin was, as Caro had put it, cut lower than Caro's own, but despite its daring decolletage and the best adornments the Bond Street modistes could dream up—full-blown roses and seed pearls on the sleeves, heavy rouleaux of satin on the skirt—it looked obvious and overdone in comparison with the simple revealing lines sculpted by Violette Winwood.

If Lavinia could be made uncomfortable by her cousin's appearance, then, Caro reasoned, she must be in her best looks and for some inexplicable reason, she wanted Nicholas to see her that way. Even now, she remembered the oddly intent expression in his dark-blue eyes as he had accepted her stammered thanks for the trip to the balloon ascension. There had been a look there that had made her feel very special as though she meant something to him. Caro suddenly found herself wishing that she was important to him, that he would think her as beautiful and charming as he apparently thought her intelligent. Caro sighed. She might as well wish for the moon. What chance did she have to stand out among the beauties of the *ton?* None. And besides, was that what she really wanted? It was all very strange and confusing and, as their carriage drew up in to the Countess of Nayland's magnificent portico, she resolved to put such treacherous thoughts out of her mind.

The enormous entrance hall was awash with light and crowded with the cream of the *ton* making its way slowly to the head of the marble staircase where the countess, ablaze with the famous Nayland emeralds, greeted her guests effusively. "Lavinia, my dear. How delightful to have you amongst us again. You look lovely as always," she cried, extending a beringed hand and brushing a heavily painted cheek against Lavvy's smooth white one.

Her ill humor, somewhat mollified by this signal mark of favor from one of London's premier hostesses, Lavvy presented her cousin with creditable good grace. However the countess's exclamation of "Charming! Completely charming! A credit to you, my dear. I can see she will soon be acknowledged an incomparable," did little to improve her temper. Lavinia, who was not the least inclined to relinquish the title herself, especially to a chit like Caro, bit her lip in annoyance, but before things could deteriorate further, the ubiquitous Sir Evelyn came to the rescue.

Knowing that an event of such splendor and magnitude would induce Caro to wear one of Violette's creations, he had arrived unfashionably early so as to help orchestrate her appearance as best he could. Though he might wish resounding success for Caro, he did not wish to infuriate Lavinia to the point of destroying any chances her cousin might have. Thus the meddling exquisite had made it a point to be on hand to pour soothing oil on troubled waters and distract Lavinia long enough for Lady Caroline to win the recognition she deserved. Consequently, he had placed himself strategically so he would be able to see them the moment they arrived and he hurried towards them as best he could as soon as they were free of the countess. "Ah, Lavinia! Now the ball has truly begun and the countess's entertainment is complete," he exclaimed, bowing low over her hand.

"Flatterer." Lavinia tapped him playfully with her fan. "I am willing to wager that there is hardly a woman in this room to whom you have not addressed the very same words," she scolded. Nevertheless, she looked pleased. The frown that had begun to wrinkle her brow smoothed out and the lips which had been compressed curved into a satisfied smile.

Sir Evelyn clasped a hand to his heart in mock horror. "Countess, you cut me to the quick. Why you know I worship at your feet alone. And to prove that to you, I am going to remove your cousin and introduce her elsewhere, so that I may have you all to myself and I shall settle for nothing less than the first waltz with the most beautiful woman in the room." With another flourish, he bowed again over her hand before taking Caro's arm and whispering, "Come. There is someone I wish for you to meet."

Having thus adroitly separated Caro and Lavinia, he was free to bring his protegée to the attention of some of the more notable members of the gathering. Sir Evelyn was no fool. He had caught the twinkle in Caro's gray eyes as she observed his manipulation of her cousin and he could feel her clear-eyed gaze on him as he led her through the crowd. Turning to her, he shrugged in a deprecatory way. "Well, what would you have me do, leave you to die of ennui while Lavinia held court?" He grimaced so comically that Caro could not help laughing. "There, that's better. You must look as though you are enjoying yourself. Then people around you will relax enough so that you actually do so. But come, I wished to provide you with companionship worthy of you and so I shall. I spoke to Castlereagh about you. He remembers your father most kindly and naturally asked to be made known to you. When I last left him he was over by that pillar . . . ah, yes. There. He is nodding at me. Come. You shall see. This evening will not be as dull as you expected." Gliding behind an enormous dowager in purple satin, Sir Evelyn gained the pillars where the distinguished statesman was deep in conversation with a

young man whose worshipful gaze made him appear more
like a religious supplicant than a young man about town.

Without Caro's understanding precisely how he did it, Sir
Evelyn succeeded in making both men look up as they approached. "Pray continue as you were, gentlemen," he
waved a delicate white hand. "I have not brought this delightful lady over here in hopes of finding her a partner, but
on the premise that this is perhaps the only place in the
room where she will find the conversation to her liking. I
know, my lord, that her distinguished father is known to
you. However, despite Therese Esterhazy's assertion that
Lord Waverly was accompanied everywhere by his lovely
daughter, I should be quite surprised if you were to recognize her in my beautiful companion."

A singularly charming smile banished the Foreign Secretary's preoccupied expression, "I am most happy to
renew our acquaintance for indeed I do remember you as a
little girl with a mop of tangled curls who was far more
interested in her new pony than in her father's friends even
though one of them was Talleyrand himself. I lost a great
ally in your father, for I had truly counted on him to help
me restrain Alexander and his greedy Russians. Your father
was one of the few men I knew who truly had some insight
into their character. But enough of that. I collect that far
from charming European potentates as you once did, you
have come to take the *ton* by storm." He raised one delicate
interrogative brow, flashing again the smile that had en-
slaved more than one woman.

Caro was momentarily at a loss, but again the ever-helpful
Sir Evelyn came to her rescue. "Oh, come now, my lord,
you would not expect Hugo Waverly's daughter to concern
herself with such paltry matters. Leave those to lesser
women. Lady Caroline is far more interested in the affairs
that bring you sleepless nights than she is in the recent al-
teration in shape of Leghorn bonnets or the latest *on-dit*,
which is why I introduce her to you. But you must excuse
me as the only reason I was able to wrest her from her
cousin's side was to promise Lavinia that I would partner
her in the waltz." And with an airy wave of the hand, he
was off across the room, making his way gracefully between
couples, bowing here, smiling there, until, in no time at all,
he was back at the beauty's side.

"It is quite obvious, since I have not been aware of such

a charming presence as yours in diplomatic circles, that you are not following directly in your father's footsteps, but are turning your attentions to other matters, Lady Caroline. And pray, what might these be? I am sure that young Wallace, here''—the Secretary gestured toward the earnest young man who now seemed to be almost as taken with Caro as he was by his idol—''is as eager to know how you busy yourself as I.''

'Young Wallace', apparently bereft of speech, confirmed his lordship's speculation by bobbing his head enthusiastically.

Having previously met, if not with outright scorn, at least with polite incredulity, Caro hesitated to elaborate, but the Foreign Secretary seemed so genuinely interested and listened so carefully to her tentative answer that she soon found herself relaxing, and in no time at all was deeper into a discussion of the problems besetting the administration of the Poor Laws than she ever had been with Helena or even the marquess.

26

AND IT WAS THUS that the marquess, leading his mother into the crowded ballroom first saw her. Indeed, the moment they crossed the threshold, his eyes sought her out and in no time found her. Caro was half a head taller than many of the women in the room, and with her masses of dark hair, queenly carriage, and the distinctive gown that clung to her slender form, she was an arresting figure. For a moment Nicholas could hardly believe it was she, so sophisticated and almost exotic she appeared, and then he saw her ready smile and could almost hear her throaty laughter as she enjoyed one of her companion's witticisms and he knew that this alluring woman—for that was what she had most definitely become—was in fact his Christmas Waif.

Nicholas felt as though the breath had been knocked out of him. Where had the large-eyed innocence gone? And how had she transformed herself into such a seductive creature? It did the marquess's uncertain temper no good to observe that most of the male opinion in the room agreed with him, as more than one pair of masculine eyes were surveying this exquisite new addition to the *ton*. Damn it! She had no idea what she was doing. She was a child playing with fire. Why, Castlereagh, even Castlereagh, imperturbable statesman that he was, and old enough to be her father besides, was gazing at her like someone besotted. Nicholas stood stock-still, overwhelmed by the most intense, most confusing emotions he had experienced in his life.

On the one hand he wanted to strangle Castlereagh and tear Caro away from all the ogling eyes. On the other, he wanted to shout to everyone in the room, "Look at her! Isn't she beautiful? Isn't she clever and charming? I know. I discovered all those things long ago." Nicholas caught himself up short. In some strange way, he felt personally responsible for what was Caro's obvious triumph. But why should he feel that way? After all, she was only Lavvy's younger cousin.

Suddenly he realized that it had been a very long time since Caro had been nothing more than Lavvy's cousin to him. Very early on, she had established herself as a person in her own right. Then, ever so slowly, bit by bit, she had won his respect, his support, and eventually his admiration, until before he knew it, the marquess had become as concerned for Caro's welfare as he was for his mother's or his sister's.

Good God, Mama! Fortunately for his peace of mind, the Marchioness of Everleigh, so long absent from such scenes of revelry was feasting her eyes on the glittering assemblage before her, but not before she had noticed her son's absorption in a certain fascinating woman across the room from them. That in itself was not usual. Nicholas, much sought after since he first had appeared on the social scene, had an eye for beautiful women, but the countess had never yet seen such a mixture of admiration, tenderness, and longing on his face as she now saw. Even the incomparable Lavinia Mandeville had never inspired such a look. Hurriedly concealing a sly smile, the marchioness quickly looked away so as not to give the least indication that she was aware of the unusual drama being enacted in her son's mind.

"May I procure you a chair, Mama?" Even to his own ears, the marquess's voice sounded odd. Laughing to cover up any hint of strangeness in his tone, he continued, "I had best find you a place near a pillar lest you be crushed to death by the devotees of fashion." And he went off ostensibly in search of a chair, but his eyes kept straying to a certain spot of the ballroom where a particular person was engaged in what appeared to be a delightful conversation. Really, for one who supposedly detested such affairs, Caro seemed to be remarkably at ease. In fact, one could be pardoned for thinking that she was quite enjoying herself. Nicholas ground his teeth and began to hunt in earnest for a chair which he found at length—a rickety affair, more gilt paint than wood, but it would have to do.

By the time he had struggled with it back through the crowd, and bowed politely to all the town tabbies who had quickly converged on his mother, and ensconced her safely, Caro was nowhere to be seen. Nicholas blinked and looked again only to realize that she had been obscured from view by the broad back of her partner, who was none other than Tony Mandeville. Nicholas blinked again. The only time he had ever seen the viscount on the dance floor, it had been under extreme and obvious duress with either his sister or someone as determined as Lady Jersey as his partner. As Caro was neither of these, it appeared that Tony was actually there of his own volition.

Had it been any other time or any other woman, the marquess would have been highly diverted. As it was, he was only further enraged. Not content with enslaving Castlereagh and capturing the attention of every man in the room, Caro was now working her charms to quite miraculous effect. Tony had the same appreciative smile on his face that he had hitherto reserved for Tattersall's most prime bits of blood. The puppy! What right did he have to look so entranced? Why Caro could run rings around him. She would be bored with him in a fortnight, though, at the moment, she looked far from bored. Even as the marquess glowered in their direction she burst into delighted laughter. "Since when did Mandeville know how to approach the fair sex," he growled under his breath.

Had the marquess but known the cause of Caro's mirth, he might have been somewhat mollified, for having tried her utmost to follow the steps of the dance as they should be done, Caro finally gave up and allowed herself to be led to Tony's own peculiar version of it. Practically able to hear his labored counting under his breath, she laughed, "Tony, you would not handle the reins so cowhandedly. If you simply adjust to the music as you would to the gait of any horse, believe me, it will go much better and I shall follow you whatever you do."

He grinned. "Dashed sporting of you, Caro. I never really could do this stuff, and with m'mother always watching and the girl always expecting me to be a blasted caper merchant, well . . ."

"I know. I feel most fortunate that Papa was such an excellent dancer and used to help me. He always said that a woman who could converse intelligently was a treasure, but one who could do so while dancing was one who could rule the world. And as ruling the world rather appealed to me when I was six, I heeded his advice." From these reminiscences, Caro moved deftly to even safer topics, and in no time at all, her partner was moving easily and naturally—

so easily and naturally that he was surprised when the music ended. Caro nodded sagely. "There. You see, that wasn't half bad, was it?"

"Well, if that don't beat the Dutch!" Her partner was genuinely mystified. "You're an amazing woman, Caro, a . . ." but the rest of his remarks were cut short as the marquess materialized next to him. "Why hello, Nicholas. Wherever did you come from?"

"Come to take your partner from you, lad. Know you aren't much in that sort of line so I thought I would relieve you from such discomfort."

"Who says I was uncomfortable?" The viscount looked aggrieved. "As a matter of fact, I was just beginning to enjoy myself. I tell you, Caro is an amazing woman," he remarked to the marquess's retreating back as Nicholas led Caro to the floor. "Amazing woman." Tony shook his head and went off in search of the more congenial company of Captain Allen and Lieutenant Forbush.

"Well, that was certainly high-handed of you," Caro began impetuously. "Tony and I were just settling into a good discussion of Lieutenant Forbush's chances of making it to Brighton in his curricle in under three hours, given his swift but unpredictable cattle."

"How else was I to get you away? You're always immersed in conversation with one admirer or another." Even to the marquess, in the grip of unexpected emotions, this sounded churlish. "I mean that you are so constantly surrounded by gentlemen that it is impossible to be alone with you." Lord, that sounded no better.

"Alone?"

"But naturally, I wished . . ." But what precisely had he wished? Was it to tell her how lovely she was; how he ached to hold her? Worse and worse! Nicholas hadn't even known that himself until his treacherous impulses had betrayed him. Whatever was wrong with him? Caro wasn't the sort of woman to make his pulses race. Only one woman had done that and that had been when he was in his salad days. No, to him Caro was more of a companion, the sort of person you could count on to talk sensibly about serious topics, one that you could trust not to exert any feminine wiles. That's it. She was a comfortable sort of person. "Well, I . . ." He looked down into the big gray eyes, the soft lips half parted, and all thoughts of comfort were driven from his mind. Get a hold of yourself, man, Nicholas admonished himself severely. "I had meant to ask your opinion of Parliament's passing of the Seditious Meetings Bill."

It was no good. She wasn't making him feel the least bit comfortable now as she tilted her head quizzically at his obvious discomfiture. Where had she learned to smile like that with the provocative little quirk to lips which he longed to kiss. In fact, that was all he wanted to do—lead her off onto the balcony just outside and sweep her into his arms.

"The Seditious Meetings Bill? Why, of course I think it is an abomination. To be sure, there have been riots here and in other parts of the country, but in the main I believe that if such meetings were not threatened with forced dispersal they would end peacefully of their own accord." There was no response. Caro looked up. Though the marquess was gazing intently down at her, somehow she had the feeling that he did not see her at all. "My lord?" She raised one dark brow questioningly.

"Where did you learn to dress like that?" he blurted.

"What?" Truly, the conversation was becoming odder and odder.

"I had thought that your mind was above such things, that you scorned to cast out lures the way other women do," he hissed.

Caro straightened indignantly. "It is, I mean, I do. And I don't see what cause or what right you have to criticize me."

It was an unanswerable reply, but Nicholas, goaded by forces beyond his control retorted, "You are no different from the rest. Once you have caught people's attention, you are as eager as any of the rest of your sex to court admiring glances."

"I am not!" she gasped, pale with fury. "I dress to please myself and if I wish to appear as beautiful as I can for myself, then I do *not* see what affair it is of yours!"

"Not to mention Tony Mandeville's. You have cozened him nicely, and . . ."

"If I were a man, I would hit you," Caro seethed. She was so angry now that her breath was coming in gasps. "As it is, I think it is grossly unfair of you to provoke me in such a public setting where you know I can't."

"Very well then," he retorted pulling her through the French doors onto the balcony. Nicholas had only meant to find a private place where they could continue the argument, as it was now apparent that that was what the conversation was rapidly degenerating into. But when he found himself alone with Caro in the cool darkness with the light from the ballroom creating a warm glow behind her, washing over her bare shoulders, revealing the tantalizing curves, and casting a shadow in the soft hollow at the base of her throat, he could think of nothing else but how intoxicating it was to be near her and how desperately he wanted her.

Caro too felt some of the fury drain away as she stepped out into the fresh air. The music was faint, the breeze billowing the curtains was gentle, creating an aura of unreality. A queer lassitude stole over her as the marquess turned to look at her, the white of his shirt front catching the light and emphasizing the angles of his face, the square jaw, high cheekbones, the deep-set blue eyes whose expression remained unfathomable. Puzzled, she stepped closer trying to read him, her gaze steady, her lips parted in an unspoken question.

It was too much. With a groan, Nicholas pulled her toward him and brought his mouth down on the soft full lips, moving gently against them, then more insistently as he felt them part beneath his and the rush of breath as she sighed softly.

For a moment Caro was too astonished to react. A strange languor swept over her immobilizing her in the marquess's arms. As his lips came down on hers and she felt their warmth and inhaled the scent of his clean linen and spicy soap, all she wanted to do was melt against him and revel in the strength and security of his embrace. It felt so safe and so comforting to be held so close. She hadn't been held since she was a little girl and she had forgotten how wonderful it felt.

His hands slid slowly down her shoulders to her waist. Caro felt their caress through the thin material of her gown and her breath caught in her throat. Suddenly she wanted him to go on kissing her more and more, holding her closer and closer, their bodies meeting all the way down to their toes.

So this was what it was like. And with a clarity that she would not have thought possible, given the heightened rate of her pulse and the irregularity of her breathing, Caro envisioned a certain look she had seen in the eyes of women like Sally Jersey as they had drifted slowly over the marquess. No! A warning voice sounded in her head. I will *not* be like those others. And with a supreme effort, Caro tore her lips away and gasped for air, "I told you I was dressing to please myself and not others, but if this is the result of my rash decision, I quite appreciate your concern. Good evening, my lord." With a swirl of skirts, she turned and was gone, leaving her bemused partner staring after her.

27

REENTERING THE BALLROOM, Caro would gladly have given all she possessed to leave it without having to endure, at best, polite conversation, at worst, curious stares for the rest of the evening. Fortunately for her peace of mind, she was not so well-known in the *ton* that her absence had been remarked. Though the Marquess of Everleigh was an object of much more interest, she and Nicholas had hardly begun to dance before their contretemps and thus no one had had much opportunity to realize that she had been the Marquess of Everleigh's partner. There was one, however, who did notice. "And where is Nicky?" Lavinia questioned her sharply upon her return. The countess's eagle eye had discerned the marquess the moment he had entered the room—not that it was at all difficult to pick out his tall athletic form and self-possessed air among the multitude of beaux who owed their distinction to their tailors rather than to their characters.

"Oh, he saw someone he wished to speak to and I assured him I was quite capable of making it back here on my own," Caro replied airily.

Lavvy frowned. "That is indeed odd. I know he was dreadfully put out to see me dancing the waltz with Sir Evelyn when he was so eager to lead me out, but one cannot sit in a man's pocket, after all, and surely he must have known the dance would be ending soon."

"No doubt," was the absentminded reply. Really, Caro wished her cousin would stop chattering for a moment at least so she could put her confused thoughts in order. But peace was not to be hers, as not very many minutes later, Captain Allen came to request the pleasure of a dance. He was closely succeeded by Lieutenant Forbush and so many others that Lavinia remarked waspishly, "Really, Caro. You must be less coming. All those dances, all those partners. You wouldn't want people to think you fast.''

It was all Caro could do to keep her jaw from dropping. But after all, Lavinia had always considered caprice to be her prerogative, and if she wished to berate her cousin for coming out of the unfashionable shell that had previously been so embarrassing to the countess, so be it. Caro shrugged and turned back to Tony who was wondering aloud if she had as yet seen Captain Allen's new hunter. ''Magnificent animal, most powerful shoulders I've seen—Irish, you know.''

''No, I had not. Where did he find the creature?'' she replied abstractedly, trying desperately, but unsuccessfully to keep her eyes from following a tall form on the other side of the room. Fortunately, Tony was entirely satisfied with remarks made at random, for Caro's mind was entirely preoccupied with the upsetting scene on the balcony. She would never have believed it possible that she, Caroline Waverly, bluest of bluestockings, could find herself in such a position—as though she were any flirt out to catch a rich prize in the parson's mousetrap. And the worst of it was, she had enjoyed it. While it was true that her mind had rebelled, it was long after her body had shown her that there were other things she had failed to take into account when considering the relationship of the sexes.

All of a sudden, she felt absurdly innocent and naive, foolish too, as she thought back to a time when she had been advising a young maid considering marriage to the ostler at the local inn. ''Tess, you must not be in such a rush to throw away your freedom. At the moment you are free to come and go and work wherever you choose. If you throw in your lot with Matt, you will be forever tied to his whims and his fortunes.'' At the time she had thought the girl's simple answer, ''But, miss, I love 'im and I wants to be with 'im.'' foolish in the extreme. Now, recalling the glowing look, the tender softness in the eyes, Caro could better understand Tess's just wanting to be near the lad. After all, if Caro had not had her much vaunted pride and independence to consider, would she not still be locked in the marquess's embrace—or worse—on the balcony?

It would have relieved Caro's mind considerably to know that directly on the other side of the room, Nicholas's thoughts were equally in a turmoil. But while Caro had tried to put them aside as she engaged in one dance after another, Nicholas completely ignored the festivity around him as he propped his broad shoulders against the convenient pillar and stared blankly at the dancers whirling around him.

Whatever had possessed him to do such a thing? As one who had had more lures thrown out to him than he cared to remember, the marquess was not one to force himself on an unwilling lady. And lord knows, no one in his right mind would have called a devotee of Mary Wollstonecraft willing. That is precisely the problem, old man, he took himself severely to task. You aren't in your right mind. While it was true that there had been distinct provocation, it had not been so much because she wished to attract admirers, but because she had wanted to prove as much to herself as to others that she could capture as much interest as the best of them. She was forcing the *ton* to pay attention to and accept what she was by beating them at their own game in spite of her intellectual eccentricities. He saw it all now. She truly had done it for herself, but the effect was no less staggering than if she had dressed deliberately to pique his interest. And it was precisely her unconsciousness that had made it all so irresistible.

With women like Lavinia, the marquess, after his initial disillusionment, had been so acutely conscious that he was being flirted with that he was not in the least danger of falling victim to their charms. But along came Caro, mindful of her new gown, to be sure, but still entirely unaware of its effect, and it was this innocence combined with unconscious sensuality that had been his undoing.

Nor had this feeling lessened as he had pulled her to him. At that point, so many other women, their goal accomplished, lost interest or, like Lavinia, became concerned that their coiffure would be disarranged or their gowns crushed. Not Caro. Without a thought for outward appearance, she had melted in his arms. For an instant, he had thought he felt the generous lips quiver in response to his. Though she had remained virtually motionless, he had sensed intuitively that she was alive with energy and passion underneath his caressing hands and for a moment, looking down into the half-closed gray eyes, he had wanted to wrap his hands in the luxuriant dark hair, bury his head in the curve of the soft neck and trail kisses the length of the enticing body molded to his.

But Caro would not have been Caro if her mind had not quickly reasserted itself and once more made her mistress of her body and the situation. Her words had made him feel like the veriest fool, an importunate coxcomb, but that did not stop him from wishing to do it all over again. Stealing a glance in her direction, the marquess was overwhelmed with longing as he caught sight of the slender form being waltzed around the floor by Captain Allen. That puppy! Ordinarily, the marquess would have dubbed the bluff and genial captain the best of good fellows, but at the moment, he wanted nothing more than to wring the young man's neck. An excellent soldier he might be, but he was no more fit to be a companion to the clever Caro than Tony was. Her intelligence, her grasp of affairs, were wasted on him.

The more he considered it, the more Nicholas realized that such a rare combination of talents would be wasted on most men. Come to think of it, he, Nicholas Daventry, was one of the few people who could truly appreciate Lady Caroline Waverly. But what was he to do about it? He had seen the fury in her eyes just before she had left him standing like a nodcock on the balcony. Where any other woman was concerned, Nicholas would not have wasted a moment worrying—a carefully selected bouquet, a few well-chosen words of apology, some flattering remarks concerning the intoxication of the moment, and the fair victim would have been mollified and ready for more. Not so with Caro, for it had not been her sense of propriety that had been so much offended as her sense of her own integrity. If propriety had been in question, it might have been simpler, for Nicholas had discovered that ladies who invoked that god of the *ton* did so more for convenience than because they truly subscribed to it. Once propriety came into conflict with the vanity of capturing an eligible prize, it was usually quickly dispensed with.

Caro, however, was another case. Her values, arrived at after years of reading and serious reflection, were immutable. That was what had attracted him to her in the first place. That was what had made her a trustworthy companion, someone he wished to share his life with, and that was what made it supremely difficult now, because he had trespassed on those values. Good God, could that be Nicholas Daventry speaking? The man who had joined the army precisely because life had been so dull and predictable, the man who had railed against the enviable fate of inheriting titles and vast estates because it threatened his freedom now wishing to spend the rest of his life with one woman, and a damned stiff-rumped bluestocking at that?

The implications of it all quite took his breath away. Even in his salad days when he had been top over tail in love with Lavinia, he had not truly wanted anything more than to kiss her and be acknowledged as the favored suitor, and he would have found himself at a standstill if she had actually accepted him. Now he had visions of Caro at Everleigh riding hell-for-leather across its fields, sharing conversations with Clarissa, romping with children and dogs, but most of all, smiling up at him with her wise sweet smile, questioning him, challenging him, encouraging him to educate the tenants and the villagers in the surrounding countryside, to reform the Poor Laws, and lastly, clinging to him and kissing him so he knew that she loved him as much as he did her.

Love! The marquess jerked himself upright. This couldn't be love! Why he hadn't even thought of Caro as a woman until this evening, and now he was envisioning her as his wife! No, that was not entirely correct. He still remembered how the sight of her slim figure clad in breeches had taken his breath away, or, sometimes, looking deep into the gray eyes, he had felt an unaccountable tenderness welling up within him. But was this love, and if so, how long had he been this way?

He supposed that in a way, it had begun so long ago when she had offered him her quaint wisdom and sympathy over Lavvy's rejection. He had warmed to that same loving concern that she had later towards Cedric and Clarence. Afterwards, he had come to appreciate the quick and inquiring mind and the indomitable spirit, a spirit that appeared to win the allegiance of everyone except possibly Lavinia. It had been such a comfortable feeling—more a sense of shared ideals and common goals—that it had quite crept up on Nicholas unnoticed until now when he very much feared he might have jeopardized the entire thing. Caro was nothing if not resolute, and once she had made up her mind, she was unlikely to change it. Judging from the way she had fled his presence, it was going to take all his address to get her to listen to him, much less forgive him for the insult to her character. And then, if by some miracle he accomplished that, then he could begin to try to persuade her to become his wife. That in itself seemed an impossible task, for what did he have to offer as inducement to a lady of independent means who treasured her autonomy and freedom above all else?

The marquess sighed. The objections seemed insurmountable. Again he looked across the room to see her gazing absently over the crowd while Tony chattered on. Then some remark of Tony's made her smile her generous open smile with a hint of mischief in it and Nicholas knew that whatever it took, nothing was going to stop him from convincing her of the rightness of it all. It was going to be difficult, perhaps the most difficult thing he had ever attempted. The marquess sighed.

At that sigh, the Marchioness of Everleigh looked up. In truth, her son had been behaving most strangely this evening. She had never seen him so impatient to attend one of these affairs, and from the moment he had arrived, he had appeared tense with anticipation, his eyes eagerly scanning the room. After procuring her chair, he had disappeared so quickly she had had no idea where he had gone. Then, in what seemed no time at all, he had materialized at her side, his face white and set, his eyes dark with some emotion she could not fathom.

Alerted to her son's perturbation, the marchioness watched him covertly as she chatted with friends and well-wishers eager to welcome her back after so many years of absence from London's fashionable haunts. Soon she noticed that the marquess's eyes, when not staring blankly into space seemed to focus in one direction. Following his gaze, she noted them fixing again on the woman who had first caught his interest when they entered the ballroom. Observing more closely, the marchioness was delighted to discover that the mysterious female was none other than Lady Caroline Waverly of whom her daughter had spoken so often and so warmly. A speculative gleam appeared in the marchioness's eye and a casual remark of Clary's came to mind. The marchioness had thought nothing of it at the time, but as Nicholas had driven off to escort the young lady now conversing with Tony Mandeville to Parliament, Clary had observed quietly, "Now there is a woman to match wits with our Nicholas in political and other matters." A secretive smile had hovered over her daughter's lips as she said it. Now, scrutinizing the gathering frown on her son's brow as the young lady shared a laugh with her companion, the marchioness began to appreciate the significance of Clary's expression. Her daughter had always been a sensitive and observant child, particularly where her favorite brother was concerned. Perhaps she had tumbled to something that neither her mother nor her brother, or even the young lady herself was aware of. The marchioness could have hugged herself in delight when, as Lady Caroline was again led to the floor, Nicholas turned abruptly to his mother remarking, "You are looking fagged to death, Mama. It is time I took you home."

"Very well, Nicholas," the marchioness agreed meekly though she wasn't feeling the least bit tired. In truth, she had not felt so well or so hopeful since her husband and eldest son had died. But she allowed him to escort her to the carriage without a murmur. Even after she had been tenderly helped into bed by her devoted Miss Trimble, the marchioness lay awake wondering, hoping that at last her son had found someone worthy of him.

28

THE MARCHIONESS OF EVERLEIGH was not the only one to lie awake far into the night after the Countess of Nayland's rout. Lavinia, thoroughly put out at the success her dowdy little cousin from the country seemed to be achieving, and losing interest in the entire thing once Nicholas had left, pleaded a headache in order to leave at the earliest possible moment. She was rewarded for this by the onset of the genuine article the minute the cousins set foot in the carriage, but her pettish complaints—the terrible crush, the boredom of the same old routine with the same dull beaux, the jolting of the carriage—went unnoticed by her companion who had far more serious concerns on her mind.

Caro could hardly wait to get to the safety and privacy of her own rooms. Barely bidding Lavinia goodnight, she hurried upstairs, tore off her clothes, and tumbled into bed, not even ringing for Susan.

However, she was not allowed to push aside her devoted servant this easily. No sooner had her head touched the pillow than the little maid came bustling in with a cup of hot milk for her mistress. Not having heard her bell when the ladies returned, Susan knew something was amiss. It was not unusual for Lady Caroline to dispense with her ministrations in the evening, for frequently Caro, unlike any other mistress she had ever heard of, remonstrated her as she left for a long affair, "Now no waiting up for me. I know we shall be out late and I am quite capable of putting myself to bed." But this particular night, she had yielded to Susan's protests and promised to ring for her whatever the hour in order to share what the maid was certain would be a triumph.

In truth, Caro was so upset that she had entirely forgotten this promise and was astounded to see Susan standing by her bed bearing a cup of steaming liquid. If Lady Caroline had forgotten or ignored her promise, the maid had reasoned, then something undoubtedly was most definitely wrong, and a cup of hot milk, while not a panacea for the ills of the world, could at least ensure one a better night's rest.

"Oh, thank you, Susan." Caro sat up wearily, a frown wrinkling her brow. She remained thus for some time sipping the comforting hot liquid in silence and staring into space.

Now Susan knew there was something disturbing her mistress. Though Caro occasionally forgot something, she never failed to apologize when she became aware of her oversight. Susan's appearance was mute testimony to their agreement to discuss the countess's rout, but still Caro said nothing, merely swinging her bare feet and frowning harder.

"Shall I brush your hair, ma'am? You might find it soothing. Was it a sad crush?"

Caro came to with a start. "What? Oh, I beg your pardon." At last she looked at the maid, smiling apologetically. "I am sorry, Susan. Yes, it was ever so crowded. I am told that everyone who is anyone was there." Seeing her maid's expression of eager anticipation, Caro hadn't the heart to dismiss her. "Yes," she smiled slowly with a touch of her old impish gleam in her eye, "I do believe you would have been proud of me. I danced any number of dances and I even spoke at length with Lord Castlereagh himself. I cannot say I was an overnight sensation, but I do believe you could say I conducted myself creditably."

"Oh, miss, I am that glad." Susan breathed, ready to hear more, but the look of unhappy abstraction had returned.

"I shall try to marshal my thoughts so I can relate them to you tomorrow, but right now I am rather tired," her mistress apologized.

Susan was forced to be content with this, but she departed convinced more than ever that something was troubling Caro. If it's the countess, I'll, why I'll . . . Susan gave up for lack of suitable punishment, but somehow she didn't think it was Lavinia who, according to Jim the footman, had come in looking a veritable thundercloud. From the start Caro had had her cousin's measure and now, having lived in the beauty's household, she was never particularly surprised or upset by her selfishness, merely ignored it as best she could and proceeded on her own way. Besides, Lady Caroline would have been irritated rather than upset at her cousin.

No, this was something far more serious. Susan had never seen Lady Caroline like this and she was resolved to get to the bottom of it. Mulling it over on her way to the kitchen and later in her room under the eaves, she finally concluded that Lady Caroline must be in love. Yes, that's it! Nothing else has ever discomposed her before, not when the river at Waverly flooded out the newly planted rye, not when the fox got into the chickens, not even when Cook broke her leg and the household was at sixes and sevens. It must be a sort of problem she has never encountered before, and since there's hardly a one she hasn't dealt with, it must be love.

Alone at last in her own room, tossing and turning until the bedclothes were a perfect tangle, Caro was thinking much the same thing. Don't be such a ninny, Caro. Why there isn't a situation or a person that you've let get the better of you, not Colonel Ffolliot-Smythe, not Lavinia. Why should you go all to pieces just because a man kisses you? After all, men do things like that all the time to women and they don't come apart. But that was just it. Deep down inside, Caro didn't want to think that the tide of emotion that had swept over her was in the common way of things. Surely the breathless giddy feeling that had threatened to overwhelm her was not just some physical response? Surely it was because Nicholas was someone with whom she had shared a particular understanding and companionship? And surely he must have felt a little of what she had felt, hadn't he?

Caro shook herself. It was all such a lowering experience. She didn't *want* to feel that way about anyone, to long to have them go on holding her and caressing her. She didn't want to wonder if they felt the same way. She particularly didn't want to listen to the little voice in her head that warned her that he must have been that way with scores of women. After all, the first time she had encountered Nicholas Daventry, he had been embroiled in a somewhat similar scene and, as she forced herself to review the evening and the way Sally Jersey and the other ladies of the *ton* had smiled at the marquess, Caro was compelled to accept the depressing conclusion that it was highly improbable that Nicholas was affected the way she was, if at all. Very likely he had forgotten all about it. And you would do well to do so yourself, silly goose, Caro admonished herself fiercely as she thumped the pillow for the twentieth time into what she hoped would be a shape more conducive to sleep.

Thus resolved, she at last fell into a fitful slumber from which she awoke feeling, if not refreshed, at least fixed in her determination to put the entire incident behind her. With this in mind, she arose as early as possible without discommoding anyone, fortified herself with a strong cup of tea, and buried herself in the morning paper with the grim intention of reading it cover to cover and jotting down her own thoughts and concerns before heading off for a vigorous ride in the park. With the fresh air and exercise to clear her head of treacherously intrusive memories of the previous evening, she could plunge into a day of vigorous activities, all selected to improve her mind, strengthen her character, and prove to herself that she was a woman of intelligence and decision who did not need to rely on the delicious feelings aroused by a pair of strong arms holding one close or by a pair of bright blue eyes gazing intently down at one as if reading and understanding one's very soul.

"Oh, bother," Caro sighed aloud as the print of the *Times* swam before her eyes. This was going to be a more difficult task than she had imagined. She frowned, gulped a restoring draft of tea, and applied herself more firmly to the "Introductory Article to a Series of Essays on the Changes in the National Affairs and Character and on the Measures Caused or Required by Them," but halfway through it, she again drifted back to the previous evening and the curious effect that Nicholas's kiss had had on her. It was as though somehow, despite her best efforts, something had been missing from her previous life. Until she had felt the warmth of his hands on her skin, she had not been aware of the lack of it. Now, having, if only for a moment, experienced that closeness, she only wanted more.

Somehow Caro managed to get through the day. She applied herself diligently to her reading, poring over Mr. James Sowerby's newly printed treatises on *Midland Flora* and, accompanied by Helena, attended a concert that evening held at Mansion House to benefit the Royal Institution for the education of poor children in North Street and to encourage the establishment of a female school. For a moment, given the illustriousness of the performers who had contributed their services gratis for this cause, Caro worried lest she encounter the marquess and his sister there, but her fears proved to be unfounded and she was able to enjoy the concertante for violin and violoncello and the flute concerto with a reasonable degree of equanimity.

However, the uncertainty of Caro's mental state had not escaped the sympathetic eye of her companion who, unaccustomed to such listless conversation from her normally vivacious friend, was curious as to precisely what had occurred at the Countess of Nayland's rout. Helena resolved to keep a closer watch on things. In truth, Caro had so much encouraged her dear Miss Gray to take advantage of all the intellectual and cultural delights the metropolis had to offer that Helena now wondered, somewhat guiltily, if she had been neglecting her duties.

To be sure, Caro had engaged her services more to satisfy society's dictates for respectability than because she actually needed the older woman, but now, sneaking a glance at Caro's somber expression, Helena worried over the cause of her friend's unusual silence and searched her mind for some way to help her. She vowed to pay more attention to Caro in the days to come.

This was not an easy task as Caro threw herself into an unceasing round of activity. The *ton* saw her at this exhibition and that musicale, at ridottos, balls, and riding in the park. In truth, it appeared she was never at home to accept the quantities of floral tributes that arrived from various partners won over by her friendly ways and engaging conversation. Nor was she ever around when the Marquess of Everleigh called, which he appeared to do with great regularity, never leaving a note or staying to speak with any other members of the household. In fact, Helena would not have known he called at all had she not been crossing in the upstairs hall one day when Wigmore's stately tones floated up the stairs. "No, my lord, Lady Caroline is not at home. You have just missed her again, sir. She drove off not five minutes ago. I shall tell her you called."

"No, thank you, Wigmore. I shall try again. One of these days I shall catch up with her," was the weary reply.

Something in the marquess's tone made Helena think that this was not the first time such a scene had occurred, but how was she to know? Certainly Wigmore was not one to gossip, nor was Helena, but she made it a point to be within earshot at the same time the next day, and the next, enough to convince her that the marquess had important business with her friend and that Caro had equally compelling reasons for being elsewhere.

She smiled to herself as Wigmore closed the door on the marquess. So, at last someone had recognized the woman that lurked within the serious bluestocking. Furthermore, judging by the transformation Caro had allowed Violette and Susan to work on her, Caro was not entirely oblivious to the marquess. And Helena was certain that it was the marquess for whose benefit it had all come about. Covertly observing Caro in gatherings as she chatted with Tony Mandeville or danced with Captain Allen, Helena remarked that no matter how charmingly she conversed or how often she smiled, the smile never quite reached her eyes. Upon entering a ballroom or a theater, Caro would look anxiously and hopefully over the crowd as though seeking someone in particular. Then, apparently not finding this person, she would sigh, the tension would go out of her, and she would move in among the crowd, but the vivacity was gone. The energy that had set her apart from the rest of the *ton* was no longer there and Helena was at a loss as to how it was ever to be recovered. It was significant that on all of these occasions, the Marquess of Everleigh had not been in attendance. Helena wished that somehow she could do something to throw these two together as they were so obviously missing the other's company.

29

BUT BEFORE THE SITUATION could deteriorate much further, the opportunity for which Helena had been praying presented itself. Though not an advocate of the radical nature of Mr. Cobbett's or Mr. Hunt's schemes for improving the condition of the less fortunate of the British populace, Caro, nevertheless, admired the reforms they were trying to bring about and the zeal and determination with which they went about their task. More than once she had lamented to Helena the constrained existence of the gently born woman which kept her from attending political meetings where these famous agitators might be heard, or from becoming a member of the Hampden Club. Mr. Hunt's famous speech at Spa Fields had only made her all the more eager to hear the famous orator and she was occasionally heard to mourn the fact that the repressive measures recently enacted by Parliament were likely to prevent her from doing so.

Knowing the intrepid and sometimes obstinate nature of her companion, Helena pricked up her ears one morning as Caro, casually perusing the paper remarked, "Oh, and here is notice that Mr. Hunt is again to address the crowds at Spa Fields." She made no further mention of the event, but Helena, having later made careful note of the day and time, was on the alert. Certain as she was that Caro meant to attend, she was not quite sure precisely how she planned to effect her escape and ensure her safety in such a mob. However, having often witnessed the resourcefulness of the mistress of Waverly Court, Helena was prepared for anything.

Thus on the morning of the proposed gathering, when the young maid sent in search of Caro returned with the answer that she was nowhere to be found, Helena was prompted to mutter under her breath, "Which is to say, we now know exactly where she is to be found."

That settled, Caro's companion lost no time in dashing

off a note of the Marquess of Everleigh requesting his presence immediately. Such an action was, perhaps, a trifle irregular, but Helena had seen enough of the marquess to know that he had little regard for the petty niceties considered necessary to proper conduct in the fashionable world. Then too, as someone immersed in the political events of the moment, he was the person best qualified to understand the gravity of the situation and to know how best to deal with it.

He came with gratifying speed, and there was such a look of concern in his eyes as he strode into the drawing room, having taken the stairs two at a time, that Helena knew she had not been mistaken either in invoking his aid or in his interest in Caro.

"Thank you for coming so quickly, my lord. I do beg your pardon for intruding, but I am . . ." she began.

"Your note hinted that Caro, I mean, Lady Caroline, was in some sort of danger," he interrupted without preamble, his dark brows drawn together in a worried frown.

Helena looked at him straightly. "Yes, I believe so. She is ordinarily as capable of getting herself out of a scrape as she is at tumbling into one, but this time I fear she may encounter more difficulties than she bargained for."

Helena repeated Caro's remark at the breakfast table which had aroused her suspicions. "So you see, I very much fear she has gone to hear him speak. It is not that I am anxious about her reputation, but the mood of the crowds has been so ugly of late, and that of the forces for law and order equally so. I worry there may be some sort of confrontation. I have no idea how she escaped from the house or how she disguised herself, for she would never be so rash as to embroil herself in something like this without precautions."

The marquess was listening intently, but at the mention of disguise there was an arrested expression on his face. "Tony's breeches," he breathed.

"What?" Despite her familiarity with Caro's eccentricities, her companion was taken aback.

"Never mind," he flung over his shoulder as he hurried out. "I shall recognize her." The marquess refrained from voicing the fear that other, less honorable men than he might also notice that the slim youth was not what she pretended to be and take it into their heads to. . . . He could not bear the thought, and resolutely putting that out of his mind, as well as all the other dreadful possibilities that presented themselves to an imagination that always seemed to be over-active where she was concerned, the marquess threw himself onto Caesar and headed in the direction of Spa Fields, stopping only to send a footman to Daventry House to alert Watkins that his master required him to follow him there in the carriage with all haste.

By the time Nicholas reached the vicinity, such a multitude had gathered that he despaired of ever singling Caro out among the crowd. Anxiously scanning back and forth, he edged Caesar cautiously into the midst of the throng. But they, none too well-disposed towards one possessed of enough wealth to be astride a horse, were singularly unyielding. Nicholas sighed. It did indeed appear to be a hopeless task and the crowd, which had been waiting impatiently for the promised speakers to show up, was growing restless; its mood beginning to turn ugly enough to be a cause of serious concern.

At last his eyes lighted upon her, and Nicholas almost laughed out loud with the sheer relief of it. He should have known that no matter what the gathering, be it the most select of the Upper Ten Thousand or the most lowly and discontented rabble, Caro would stand out. Somehow there seemed to be an aura of purity and self-possession that surrounded her and set her apart from the rest. Disguised as she was by Tony's breeches and a cap that must have been borrowed from one of the stable lads, she nevertheless could not hide the erect posture, the proud tilt of the chin, and the alert expression as she surveyed the scene. However, she was separated from him by a sea of rough-looking characters and Nicholas was at a loss as to how to proceed.

He had just resigned himself to making slow but steady progress using Caesar's broad shoulders to clear a passage to her when a whisper ran through the crowd, "Pssst, it's the guards!" Spectators twisted their necks looking nervously in either direction and glancing suspiciously at their neighbors while trying to locate possible avenues of escape.

The moment Caro had arrived at the meeting place, she regretted her rash decision. She should have known the crowd would more closely resemble the angry mob that now surrounded her than the gentlemanly audiences of the more enlightened liberal political lectures she had attended. But her thinking had been none too clear in the past two days and, driven by a need to prove to herself that despite a momentary weakness at the Countess of Nayland's rout, she was the same independent Caro Waverly as ever, she had thrown caution to the winds. Now, observing the grim-set faces on either side of her, she was not so sure. She cast about for some opening through which she could slip unnoticed, but there was none. Worse still, the crowd was growing restless and some of the people around her began to mutter, "It's a trap, lads. Hunt ain't going to come and we'll be trampled like sheep." True or not, Caro had read enough of the unpredictable and excitable nature of revolutionary mobs to know that she was in serious danger. She began to wriggle between burly bodies in a frantic effort to escape, when a beefy hand grabbed her shoulder. " 'Ere, lad, and just where do you think you're going?"

Caro had only a momentary glance at a ferocious grimy face peering down into hers when someone shouted, "The guards! Run for it!"

The hand let go of her so abruptly that she fell just as the mass of people exploded wildly in all directions and she found herself falling helplessly. Caro grabbed wildly for something, anything to stop her from pitching headlong underneath thousands of frenzied feet, but just as she reached out to grab the belt of a solid-looking fellow ahead of her, something struck her in the side of the head and the world went black.

Not five yards away, Nicholas saw her go down and, frantic with worry, he leapt off Caesar, pulling the struggling horse along with him. Using the animal as a shield against the worst of the onslaught, he bent over the crumpled form and gathered her up in his arms. There was no time to lose as the multitude, egged on by shouts of "Treachery! Soldiers!" was near to panic.

With a tremendous effort, the marquess tossed Caro's limp body across the saddle and swung himself up behind her, pulling her upright against him and urging Caesar away from the headlong rush and towards the carriage which he spied waiting patiently for him in Exmouth Street.

After what seemed like ages, they at last reached the carriage and a worried-looking Watkins, whose eyes had been anxiously scanning the crowd. His face broke into a smile of relief as he spied Nicholas. "I'm that glad to see you, sir. It's a right nasty mood they be in."

"Yes. And the less we linger here looking like gentry, the better off we shall be," the marquess replied grimly as he tossed the coachman the reins and slid down, still maintaining a firm grip on his unconscious companion. Once on the ground, he pulled her gently down into his arms, making straight for the carriage while the coachman secured Caesar to the back and leapt onto the box.

At any other time the marquess would have marveled at his servant's skill in convincing three nervous horses to ignore an unruly mob and thread their way through the crowded streets, but his mind was totally taken up by the pathetic bundle in his arms. Whenever Nicholas had envisioned Caro, as he had so often done in the past few days, he had pictured her as he had last seen her—slim, tall, and vibrant with passion. It seemed impossible that such a magnificent creature could be so frail and helpless as she now felt in his arms.

From the moment the crowd had started to panic, Nicholas had experienced a fear greater than he could ever remember having endured, even during the bloodiest battles in the Peninsula. There, death had been omnipresent, but though he was fond of his comrades-in-arms and would have rushed to their aid without a moment's hesitation, he had always known that everyone there with him had chosen to assume the same risks he had assumed and with the same sense that he had, of a job needing to be done that outweighed personal considerations. Now, it was entirely different. From some unfathomable reason, he felt responsible for Caro. True, she had never given the least indication that she needed help from anyone. In fact, he expected that had she been conscious, she would have resisted all offers of assistance. But seeing her so pure, so lovely, even concealed as she was by the ridiculous hat and dusty breeches, among the angry brutal mob, had made his throat constrict with fear for her. Agile as she was, she was no match for men who had spent their entire lives in hard physical labor and who, in their rush to protect themselves, would have killed a fellow spectator as soon as look at him. Nicholas had forced his way as quickly as possible towards her, but seeing the great ruffian who had knocked her down in his haste to get away, he was beside himself with rage and terror at the inevitable rush of the mob and his helplessness to stop it. At last he had reached her and he was so relieved to find her that he had wanted to fall to his knees, gather her close to him, and never let her go, but instead, in his concern over their escape, he'd had to put all that out of his mind until he had gotten them to safety.

Now, in the security of the carriage he could at last relax as the waves of relief washed over him. For the longest time all he could do was sit, gently stroking her hair, marveling at the softness of her skin, and the way the long dark lashes fanned out on her pale cheek. There was a slight smudge on her brow where the fellow's arm had knocked her, but it didn't appear to be serious. Nicholas had seen enough of war to know that she was only temporarily unconscious and, oddly enough, he welcomed the opportunity to be with her thus, caressing her cheek with his hand without worrying about how she would react upon waking in the arms of someone who seemingly had angered her enough that she had been avoiding all possibility of contact with him for the better part of a fortnight.

Caro sighed and stirred. She looked so childlike and defenseless that he could not help brushing her brow with his lips. She sighed again and he pressed his lips gently to hers. The kiss was much softer than that at the ball, but infinitely sweeter. Her lips were so soft and delicate, so innocent and so generous, as if made to share the passion he knew lay underneath the demure exterior. No, *demure* was not precisely the word, for Caro was a vibrant creature whose very being expressed an energy and enthusiasm for life, but it was a childlike enthusiasm and the marquess badly wanted to awaken the woman he felt certain lay beneath.

Caro stirred again, muttered, nestling more closely to him, and all such thoughts fled from Nicholas's mind, pushed aside by a wave of such tenderness that even he was taken by surprise. "Hush, my love," he whispered, gently pushing aside a strand of dark hair that had fallen across her face. "Hush. I have you safe. Rest, little one." He stroked the shining hair, tracing the firm curve of the cheek, smoothing the frown from her brow.

Nicholas would have been more than content to ride this way forever, but Watkins, no more taken in than his master by the lady's disguise, had pulled up before reaching the Countess of Welham's mansion.

''My lord,'' he leapt down and whispered urgently. ''Be you wanting me to stop out here or back in the stables?''

''In the stables. Thank you, Watkins. You're a good man.''

The carriage made its way around back and the marquess dispatched one of the grooms to fetch Susan, who appeared immediately, wide-eyed with surprise at the strange summons.

''Susan, your mistress has been slightly hurt.'' Seeing the maid's look of dismay, the marquess hastened to reassure her, ''Truly 'tis nothing. In fact, it would be far worse if the rest of the household were to hear of it than the injury is in itself. If I can carry her, can you ensure that we return her safely to her rooms without notice or comment?''

The maid nodded and led him to a side door that opened onto a narrow stairway. They climbed several flights of stairs until they reached a door which, putting a finger to her lips, his guide carefully opened before peering out. Then, beckoning to him, she led him to her mistress's room where she pulled back the coverlet. Reluctantly, Nicholas laid his burden down on the bed, covering her carefully before leaning down to kiss her brow. ''Rest, my love,'' he murmured, laying her hand on the coverlet.

The dark lashes fluttered and the gray eyes stared at him blankly for a moment, then Caro frowned in puzzlement. ''Nicholas?''

''Yes, love,'' he took her hand.

''What, what happened?''

''You were struck unconscious. I brought you home.'' Not wishing to distress her, he spoke calmly and matter-of-factly, as though this were an everyday occurrence, but his heart was pounding. More than ever he wanted to snatch her back up against his chest, holding her tight and safe until she had recovered. Then he wanted to smother her with kisses and tell her just how much he loved her.

The gray eyes regarded him gravely for a moment. ''Thank you for coming to my rescue. I don't deserve it. I have nothing but my own folly to thank for such a disaster.''

He kissed the hand in his before laying it back down. ''Think nothing of it, love. Now, go to sleep. There's a good girl.'' And without giving her a chance to reply, he crept out as silently and surreptitiously as he had entered, keeping an eye out for the other inhabitants of the countess's elegant establishment.

Echoing his words, Susan helped her mistress out of the incriminating clothes and then, pulling the curtains and assuring her that she would tell anyone who asked that Caro had gone to bed with a headache, she too departed leaving Caro to darkness and a host of unsettling thoughts.

30

THE REST THAT Nicholas and Susan had urged on Caro simply refused to come and she lay alone in the darkness staring at the ceiling for what seemed like hours. Hazy as the events of the afternoon were, one clear impression remained and that was the indescribable sensation of comfort and safety she had felt in the marquess's arms. Imperfect as the memory was, she did know that from the moment darkness had enveloped her, she had felt somehow that he was there watching over her, caring for her, protecting her, and she had relaxed. The only problem was that she had wanted it to last forever and that wish filled Caro with alarm.

It made her fear for her peace of mind and her hard-won independence. Were these the merest facade? Caro had striven all her life to learn how to take care of herself, to manage her life as well as anyone so she would never need to depend on anybody for sustenance of any sort. And she had been proud that she was so self-sufficient and self-contained. What a mockery it was! As soon as the faintness had assailed her and the strong arms had seized her and held her close, she had allowed them to support her, savoring the shelter they offered and gratefully abandoning the struggle to fight the crowd and her own weakness. Desperately trying to recall in clear detail every tender caress, every whispered endearment, she hoped fervently that she had remembered it all correctly. Could it really have been true that the marquess had stroked her hair, kissed her, and called her "my love," reassuring her that he had her safe? Even more surprising was how passionately she wished for this to be true. She wanted Nicholas to hold her tenderly and take care of her. She wanted him to love her and cherish her as much as she loved him.

And she did love him. That was the upsetting thing. If it had just been lust she had felt when he had first kissed her, that would have been bad enough, but at least it would only have been her body that had betrayed her. Now, she felt as though her mind and heart had somehow deserted her. Slowly, without being in the least aware of it, Caro had come to count on the marquess for so many things—stimulating conversation, amusement, and a shared perspective on people, politics, and life itself—that he had become very necessary to her happiness. This growing dependency made her wish to get away, to forget about him before it could grow any stronger.

Caro sighed and turned over, burying her head in the pillow. But feeling its softness and smelling the sweet lavender scent only reminded her of how infinitely comforting it had been to lean her aching head against a firm chest, inhale the marquess's reassuring masculine smell and let him take care of her for the moment.

No. I won't let myself, she told herself resolutely. He was just being kind, helping someone in need the way he would his mother or Clary or Ceddie or Clarence. I should be grateful for his kindness and that is that.

But something inside her longed for so much more, longed to feel loved and protected by him forever. You can't have that, she admonished herself severely. He doesn't love you. You're not the beautiful sophisticated sort of woman who appeals to him and, furthermore, you don't wish to be, nor do you wish to be looked after for the rest of your life. Oh, but how nice it would be at least to share one's life, its burdens, and its joys with someone like the marquess. It had made things like the excitement of a balloon ride, the endearing antics of Ceddie and Clarence, the intensity of parliamentary debate all that much more enjoyable when she could look over at Nicholas, catch his eye, and know that he was appreciating it all just as she was.

Caro gave a great sob and gulped for air. Get hold of yourself before it is too late, she counseled herself. Return to Waverly. Take up life where you left off. Immerse yourself in the works that make you feel truly happy and worthwhile. And, after talking severely to herself in this vein for some time, she resolved to do just that.

But she knew deep in her heart of hearts that she had never truly known happiness before—the contentment of being useful and productive, yes—but not the heady joy of life as she had lived it in the past few weeks. However, having chosen a course of action and settled upon a mode of existence, empty though it might appear by contrast, she was able to view the future with enough equanimity to fall into a fitful sleep, knowing that the next day she would be going somewhere she could at least find peace if not happiness.

The minute the smallest crack of daylight was able to creep under the curtains, Caro was up and about, dispatching Susan to ready a footman to alert Dimmock and Tim, and packing the few essentials while she wrote notes to Helena and Lavinia explaining that urgent business had recalled her to Waverly Court and that she hoped they would forgive her abrupt departure. It was the flimsiest of excuses, but she knew Helena would be too tactful and Lavinia too uninterested to tax her on it.

That accomplished, there was nothing left to do but climb into the carriage and stare unseeingly out the window at London coming to life as she enjoyed the peace that solitude brought. She had even left Susan behind on the pretext that she needed her to supervise the rest of the packing. At first, the maid had protested, wanting desperately to be with her mistress in order to minister to her in all the little things and ease some of the strain she saw in the pale drawn face, but she had allowed herself to be overruled when she saw how much Caro needed to be alone.

The staff at Waverly Court understood this too. Once over the initial surprise of their mistress's return, they went about their duties as normally and as inconspicuously as possible never once letting on that down to the lowliest scullery maid they were watching over Caro with all the concern and sympathy of a worried parent.

"Now, something's happened to upset her ladyship," William announced, gravely surveying the group assembled at the kitchen table. The moment he had opened the door, William had known that his mistress was more upset than he had ever seen her, more at a loss and alone than she had been even when her father had died, and his heart ached for her. She's fallen in love, he thought to himself. There's nothing else that would cause her to look as though the wind were knocked out of her, nothing else that she couldn't handle. Why if I ever find the fellow, I'll, I'll. . . . Caro's ordinarily phlegmatic henchman could barely contain his fury, but he knew it would only make matters worse if Caro sensed this, so he contented himself with calling together a general meeting of the household after their mistress, weary from the ride and loss of appetite, had crawled into bed.

"If any one of you does anything to upset the mistress, or lets on by so much as the blink of an eyelid that we know something is upsetting her, I'll have that person's hide." William frowned fiercely at them all. "And you know I'm a man of my word. Now be off with you, and let's do what we can to give her ladyship the peace and quiet she needs."

They all trooped silently out of the kitchen, each one resolved to fulfill the assigned tasks so well that whatever was ailing her ladyship would be helped somewhat by see-ing how smoothly her household and her estates were running.

However, it seemed to the staff that there was little like-lihood even of this happening, so dazed and distant as Lady Caroline was, not eating, not reading, only paying the most perfunctory attention to her surroundings and making what was obviously an effort to respond to anyone who came in contact with her.

"Poor lamb," Mrs. Crawford sighed gustily as she shared a cup of tea with William. "I always did wish for her to fall in love, but not this way. It's a wicked shame, that it is, and I'm sorry if I ever wanted her to go to London to be among those town beaux. It's a nasty selfish lot they are, just like that cousin of hers, if I've heard aright. Why there's not a man alive as is good enough for her ladyship, and certainly there isn't one worth this grief and that's as sure as eggs is eggs." She nodded vigorously, gulping down the last of the tea before going to discuss with Cook another delicacy to tempt her mistress, though she knew full well it would again be returned to the kitchen untouched.

If Caro was overwhelmed by an unhappy lassitude, the marquess was quite the opposite. Having spent an equally sleepless night contemplating far pleasanter thoughts than Caro's and spinning plans for the future, he leapt out of bed the next morning full of energy and eager to set these plans in motion.

Downing his coffee and barely touching his eggs and rasher of bacon, he waited impatiently until a reasonable hour for making calls chimed on the clock in the hall. Then he was off to Grosvenor Square in a fever of anticipation. All he had been able to think of since putting Caro to bed was of how sweet and defenseless she had looked lying there among all the pillows and of how he longed to lie next to her and hold her close, giving her some of his warmth and strength until she recovered. Then his mind would recall the night of the Countess of Nayland's rout and how he had caught his breath when he first saw her, how much he wanted her when he had looked down into her half-closed eyes and felt her body quiver in response to his kiss.

Wrapped in these enticing daydreams, he hardly noticed the ride to Grosvenor Square, and it was a minute before he recognized Ceddie and Clarence sitting disconsolately on the steps, their faces the very picture of gloom. Something must be very much amiss for two ordinarily irrepressible lads to look so woebegone and be sitting in such a way in front of the countess's elegant establishment.

"What ever is the matter? I can't think when I last saw such Friday-faces." Nicholas dismounted and handed the reins to a groom who had run forward eagerly to take a place on the step next to the boys.

"Cousin Caro is gone," Ceddie intoned in lugubrious accents.

"Gone?"

"We don't know why. Mama says it was something at Waverly, but surely she wouldn't leave without telling us good-bye." Though more in command of himself, Clarence was as visibly unhappy as his younger brother.

"Oh." The marquess felt as though the wind had gone out of his sails. She didn't wish to see him after all. He knew Caro well enough to be certain that her estates were carefully looked after by capable enough people that no emergency would be so dire as to require her immediate presence. So what could have sent her posthaste away from London? The only answer could be that his attentions were unwelcome. The day that had seemed so bright and full of promise was now dark and gloomy. All his energy drained out of him and he felt like a traveler in an impenetrable wood who suddenly realizes that he has no idea of the way out.

"You could help, sir, couldn't you?" Ceddie's anxious voice brought him back to reality.

"What? I'm sorry, I was not attending."

"I said you could bring her back," Ceddie maintained, confident that his hero could accomplish any task, no matter how difficult.

"I'm not at all sure, my boy. If she wished to leave London, doubtless she had her reasons, and once she's made up her mind, there's no stopping her. She's a lady of great decision."

"But she'll listen to you. She likes you best of anyone. You could tell her how much we miss her and she would come back."

Nicholas was so bemused by this reply that he was silent for some time. He wanted to ask Ceddie where he had come by this opinion. The lad was intelligent and perceptive. Often children were more clear-eyed in opining the true state of affairs than their elders. Perhaps there was hope after all. Perhaps she did care for him just a little bit?

"I don't know, lad. I am not altogether certain that I have any weight where her opinion is concerned."

"Oh, but you do, sir," Clarence broke in. "She is always telling us what you said about this or that. And when she reads the paper, she is forever saying 'I must ask his lordship what he thinks of this.' "

"Besides, whenever she's with you, she is much more smiley than she is with Mama, Miss Gray, or Tony," Ceddie piped up.

This was news indeed! The marquess digested the information slowly, wondering what to do next while Caesar stamped impatiently and the boys regarded him anxiously. He might have deliberated thus forever had not Helena appeared at the door to warn the boys that their mother was asking for them. They leapt up quickly and headed indoors, but not before Ceddie turned to appeal one more time, "You will help, won't you, sir?"

"I'll do my best," Nicholas promised, smiling faintly.

Helena raised a quizzical eyebrow. "They think for some absurd reason that I can convince Lady Caroline to return to London," he explained.

"Well, you can," was the blunt reply.

Nicholas stared.

"I hope you will forgive me if I am being indelicate, my lord," Helena began. Ordinarily Caro's companion was not one to put herself forward. She never hesitated to state her opinions forthrightly when questioned, but she shied away from volunteering them. This time, however, it was different. When two people were so obviously miserable and so obviously trying not to impose on the other, it was time that someone else take them in hand. She had thought no one could have looked as wretched as Caro had when she had left early that morning, but that was before she had seen the marquess. He, too, wore the same pale, set expression, that same lost and bewildered look in his eyes. Helena would have felt sorry for anyone who appeared thus, but somehow it was doubly poignant in two people who customarily seemed so self-possessed, so energetic, and so purposeful.

"I quite agree with Ceddie and Clarence. In fact, I would venture to say that you are the only person who could bring her back."

Nicholas continued to gape at her stupidly.

"She cares a great deal for you, my lord."

The marquess shook his head dismissively.

"Yes, she does," Helena averred. "It's just that she is a very proud and independent person and the idea of having one person mean that much to her, particularly a person of whose regard she is entirely unsure, who hitherto has always admired her cousin, is unsettling in the extreme. What else could she do but seek out peace and quiet to overcome this weakness of hers?" Helena paused to consider the effect of her words. Seeing the marquess brighten, she was encouraged enough to continue, "Of course I have not spoken to Caro of this, but it appears to me that you are not indifferent. If I am correct and that is the case, I should urge you to go to Waverly Court at once before she has talked herself out of the entire thing."

For a moment, Helena thought her words had not sunk in. Then Nicholas grabbed her hand and pressed it to his lips. "Thank you," he murmured fervently. "You are a kind and courageous person. Caro is indeed fortunate in counting you her friend. Tell Ceddie and Clarence I shall not rest until I have her word she will return." And with a crooked smile and a wave, he leapt on Caesar and clattered out of the square.

And a rare to-do it will be when you bring her back as your affianced bride, Helena thought to herself. She could hardly bite back the smile as she pictured the countess's reaction to the news.

Nicholas rode like a madman, not even stopping at Daventry House to inform them of his whereabouts. All he could think of at the moment was Caro and how he longed for her. Ceddie and Helena had given him new hope and he was determined not to return to London until he had convinced Caro that he wanted and needed her, of the rightness of it all. Nicholas had never been so sure of anything in his life and he wanted her to share that feeling.

However, by the time he had reached Waverly Court, some of the doubts had come creeping back. She had been angry at him at the ball. Had he been like every other coxcomb in thinking that she wanted him simply because he wanted her so very badly? It had seemed that she had been glad to see him after her accident, and surely she would not have nestled close to him if she had despised him? Still, she had been semiconscious at the time.

When William opened the door at last, Nicholas had worked himself up again into a torment of worry. William's first reaction when he saw Lady Caroline's visitor was one of anger. *He's the one, miserable scoundrel. I'll show him a thing or two.* And he was on the verge of denying his mistress was in when, taking a closer look, he saw the strain and uncertainty reflected in the marquess's face. In fact, his expression so closely resembled the one his mistress had been wearing, that her would-be protector thought better of himself and decided to usher the visitor in without giving Caro the benefit of a warning. *Far better that these two deal with each other immediately than giving them time to master their emotions and let their pride reassert itself.*

So, with a "Do come in, sir," William led the marquess directly to the library where Caro was half-heartedly trying to go over the accounts.

It was practically the same scene as when the marquess had first accosted her over selling her land. She was even wearing the same simple morning dress. But how pale and tired she looked. There were dark circles under her eyes and the corners of her mouth drooped. In his anxiety for her, Nicholas forgot all his apprehensions and hurried across the room to clasp her hands in his. "Caro, my girl what ever is wrong?"

Taken completely by surprise, Caro rose and stood transfixed, gazing mutely up at him. *Oh, she was glad to see him! She couldn't help it.* Seeing the broad shoulders, the dark-blue eyes so full of concern, she just wanted to throw herself on his chest and sob out her confusion and unhappiness. Then, with a tremendous effort, she regained control of herself. *After all, she had no idea why he was here.*

She mustn't betray how glad she was to see him. If he were just stopping en route somewhere, such a response was bound to render him acutely uncomfortable.

"I'm . . . I'm quite well, my lord," she replied gravely, withdrawing her hands. "I thank you for your interest. It is merely that I had business at Waverly."

"Nonsense." He tilted her chin up so she was forced to look at him. "Don't gammon me, my girl. I wasn't born yesterday and I know your affairs are perfectly in order. Now, out with it. What's troubling you?"

The gray eyes suddenly swam with tears and she shook her head, unable to speak.

"Caro, my love, I thought we were friends, you and I. I though you trusted me enough to know you could confide even your darkest secrets. Surely, nothing could be worse than attending a radical meeting dressed in breeches?" He smiled tenderly down at her.

Caro was so overwhelmed by it all she couldn't have replied even if she would have. 'My love' he had called her. She had never thought to hear anyone, especially Nicholas, speak to her so. Until now, she had never wanted anyone to, and now she wanted it so desperately that she felt like a weak woman, the type of woman she despised for being so dependent on a man for happiness. She was no better than all the rest.

Seeing her agony of hesitation, Nicholas reached out and led her gently to the couch where he sat her down and then, still retaining her hand, placed himself next to her. "Come. I don't wish to upset you. I would do anything in the world to spare you pain, but, Caro, I love you so, I want you so, that I must know."

A tear spilled over and rolled down one soft cheek.

He wiped it away. "Please. I don't mean to distress you. I just want to tell you I love you. If you don't love me, just tell me and I shall go away and never bother you again."

At last, Caro found her voice. "I do, I do love you, only . . . only I don't want to," she wailed. He remained quiet, regarding her gravely. "It's just that I don't want to be like all the other women. I don't need anyone, I do very well by myself, I . . ."

A finger on her lips, he stopped the torrent of words. "My love, don't you think I feel the same way? I was such a weak fool in my calf-love for Lavinia. I never wanted to feel that way again, but this is different. You make me strong. You see all that I am, all that I try to do, and your understanding makes me stronger. I only want to do the same for you. I want more than a wife, I want a friend, a companion, someone I can admire and respect as I admire and respect you. And,'' he played his trump card, "if you marry me, you will command all that I have to give you encouragement—my vote, my wealth, all that I have. Besides . . .''

Caro looked up questioningly.

"I want you in the most desperate way." He kissed her gently. "With my heart." His lips touched her forehead. "My mind." They traveled to her cheek. "My soul." They caressed her jaw. "And my body." His lips covered hers tenderly, then insistently as he gathered her to him, reveling in the softness of her body in his arms, molded to his, and the quickening of her breath as her arms went up around his neck and she responded shyly at first and then with increasing passion. "Ah Caro, Caro," he sighed, burying his head in the sweet scented warmth of her neck.

Caro felt the characteristic languor creep deliciously over her as she gave herself up to his embrace. Then, once again, her mind reasserted itself and she struggled upright. "But, Nicholas, are you quite sure?"

"Sure?" He stared at her. "Of course, I am sure. So you think I do this sort of thing with everyone I meet?"

The irrepressible dimple appeared at the corner of her mouth. "No, only with unapproachable bluestockings."

He gave a shout of laughter.

"No, seriously. When I first met you, you were madly in love with Lavvy. I'm not Lavvy."

"Thank God," he muttered fervently, his lips seeking hers once again.

Once again hers parted breathlessly beneath his before she continued, "No, truly, Nicholas, Lavvy is so very beautiful and . . .''

He put a finger to her lips. "And you are a woman, sweetheart, and as such, evoke a passion in me and a longing to be with you that she never inspired. Besides''—he raised a quizzical eyebrow—"she never liked kissing. It mussed her hair. And, you, my little one''—he looked down at the generous mouth and the gray eyes full of promises—"you enjoy it very much, I think."

"Yes, Nicholas," she sighed.

"Then we must be married right away in case you take it into your head to enjoy it with other fellows such as Tony."

"Tony!" She was thunderstruck.

"Yes, Tony. I saw you at the Countess of Nayland's ball and you looked so lovely my heart ached. Then you would talk with Castlereagh and dance with Captain Allen and laugh with Tony until I was quite mad with jealousy."

"You were?" She looked pleased with herself.

"Yes, you minx, but you are mine. You always were mine from the moment I saw you wrapped up in that ridiculous shawl watching us all so scornfully as we made fools of ourselves. But you were so kind and sympathetic, I couldn't help but love you. In truth, I think I have loved you since then. You were so interested and eager."

"And you were so kind," she broke in, "sharing all your adventures and your stories with me."

"As I wish to share everything with you," he concluded gravely, looking deep into her eyes. "Please say you will share it with me forever?"

"Forever."